Jenny's Revenge

Center Point
Large Print

Also by James D. Best and available from
Center Point Large Print:

The Steve Dancy Tales
The Return

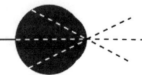

**This Large Print Book carries the
Seal of Approval of N.A.V.H.**

Jenny's Revenge

A Steve Dancy Tale

James D. Best

CENTER POINT LARGE PRINT
THORNDIKE, MAINE

This Center Point Large Print edition is published in the year 2016 by arrangement with the author.

The text of this Large Print edition is unabridged. In other aspects, this book may vary from the original edition. Printed in the United States of America on permanent paper. Set in 16-point Times New Roman type.

ISBN: 978-1-62899-907-5

Library of Congress Cataloging-in-Publication Data

Names: Best, James D., 1945– author.
Title: Jenny's revenge : a Steve Dancy tale / James D. Best.
Description: Center Point Large Print edition. | Thorndike, Maine : Center Point Large Print, 2016. | ©2015
Identifiers: LCCN 2015047197 | ISBN 9781628999075 (hardcover : alk. paper)
Subjects: LCSH: Large type books.
Classification: LCC PS3602.E785 J46 2016 | DDC 813/.6—dc23
LC record available at http://lccn.loc.gov/2015047197

33.95 (20.37)

3/16 Center Point

For Joe

Jenny's Revenge

Chapter 1

Six.

I assumed the clock in the tower of the new Denver Union Station was accurate. I reached into my pocket and glanced at my watch. It also showed six o'clock. I wound the stem a couple of times and tucked it back in my pocket.

"Are we walkin' or takin' a cab?" Sharp asked.

"Cab," I answered automatically.

The Inter-Ocean Hotel was only two blocks away, but we had just arrived from New York City with piles of luggage. My fiancée hung on my arm, but she seemed more interested in the new train station. We had left Denver only a few months previously and Union Station had looked like a battlefield as we dodged and weaved our way to our eastbound train. Somehow they had cleaned up all the construction equipment and debris to expose a stately Victorian building that was so wide it straddled three of the main arteries of this thriving town.

"Hell, let's walk and get a porter to bring our bags along later," Sharp said. "Do us good to stretch our legs. Been sittin' for nearly a week."

I thought a second about the value of our

belongings, but I abandoned my reservations when Virginia spoke.

"I prefer to walk too. I want to see what else is new."

A man denies his fiancée little, so I pointed out our bags to a porter, tipped heavily, and the three of us traipsed down the boulevard as if we didn't have any worries. In fact, we didn't. Life seemed perfect at the moment.

Denver had indeed changed in a few short months. Buildings had been finished and others started. No vacant lots remained in the two blocks to the Inter-Ocean Hotel. Huge fortunes pulled from the dirt made townsfolk keen on accumulating the accoutrements of a major metropolis. Less than twenty years old, Denver had boomed after gold and silver were accidentally discovered by prospectors on their way to the California Gold Rush. Denver's new train station let arrivals know that this was a city to be reckoned with. In fact, the city's official name was Denver City, just in case a newcomer questioned its bona fides.

The Inter-Ocean Hotel was located on the corner of 16th Street and Blake. The Second Empire architecture with mansard roof made the hotel appear grand. We had stayed here previously and the four-story hotel could compete with finer establishments in San Francisco or New York. The decorations included brass chandeliers, satin trimmed velvet drapes, brocaded upholstery, and lace curtains.

A hotel clerk stood behind a polished black walnut semi-circular desk. I gave him my name and told him we had a reservation.

"Of course, sir," he said, with a smile meant to imply that he remembered me.

After studying a register, he slid a card in my direction before saying, "Welcome back, Mr. Dancy."

I picked up a pen to sign the registration card, but stopped midair when I saw the rate.

"Eight dollars per night?"

"Yes, sir."

"May I see the suite?"

Virginia squeezed my arm. "It will be perfectly fine."

I never took my eyes from the clerk. "I'm sure, but I'd like to see it just the same."

The hotel clerk nodded. Behind him on the wall was an annunciator with speaking tubes to every room. He picked up the speaking tube and plugged a wire into a socket to call for a bellboy, then reached behind him and took down a key from the highest row on the walnut rack. He held it in his hand as he patiently waited for the bellboy to arrive.

"I'll take a standard room," Sharp said from behind me.

"There are no standard rooms at the Inter-Ocean

Hotel," the clerk said grandly. "All the rooms have—"

"Quit the speechin' an' give me the room," Sharp demanded. "I have a reservation for the third floor."

Jeff Sharp, my closest friend, could be gruff on occasion, especially when he was tired and eager to get to his room. He was probably irritated at me for holding up his registration.

Sharp and I had sold all of our business interests to explore the American frontier of 1881. Neither of us owned anything that would weight us down. I had made my fortune in New York City with an exclusive gun shop and some astute railroad investments. Sharp had built his fortune owning and operating mines, but he looked more like the trail boss he had once been. In fact, he had tried his hand at numerous things at one time or another, even owning part of an import business which had allowed him to travel the world and get into predicaments in different languages. Sharp either enjoyed trouble or had experienced a nasty streak of bad luck. At times, it seemed as if he had reached his mid-fifties by the skin of his teeth.

"Is there a problem?"

The neatly dressed black man who asked the question was Barney Ford, owner of the Inter-Ocean Hotel. I knew him slightly from a prior visit.

"No problem, Mr. Ford. I just want to see my

12

suite before agreeing to the rate. Your prices have gone up since my last visit."

Ford extended his hand. "Mr. Steve Dancy, correct?"

We shook hands. "Yes, I'm surprised you remember. It's been months since we stayed here."

Ford laughed. "I try to not forget a guest, but you were memorable . . . as was your beautiful lady friend. Besides, I recently finished reading your book. Quite a yarn. I enjoyed it."

On our way to New York, we had stopped in Denver to catch our breath after a harrowing street fight in Leadville. Virginia and I had used the visit to buy wardrobes that would be acceptable in Eastern society. Our lavish shopping spree was the talk of the hotel and merchant class. Or perhaps it was our undisguised amour. We certainly paid little attention to anyone other than each other.

We had gone east to secure a license for Thomas Edison's electric lighting, but I had also wanted to bask in the glory of having my first book published. My novel about the Wild West sold respectably, but did not put my name on the tip of everyone's tongue. I did have the thrill of catching a young lady reading my novel on the train. I told her I wrote it and asked what she thought of the book. She barely looked up from the pages to give me a *go away* glance that conveyed disbelief and offense. The look was so withering that I vowed never again to say a word to strangers reading my book.

Ford turned his attention to the clerk. "Mr. Mills, please put the Dancy couple in the Presidential Suite. The rate will be eight dollars per day." He turned to face me. "Will that be acceptable?"

"Of course. That's very generous."

"Not at all." He smiled. "I'll make it up on liquor and dining. You have expensive habits."

I laughed. "That's a fair deal."

"I eat lavish as well," Sharp interjected from behind me. "And I promise to consume vast quantities of yer best Irish whiskey."

Ford shook Sharp's hand. "I remember you well, Mr. Sharp. You tried to seduce every maid in my employ."

"Succeeded, on occasion," Sharp responded jovially. "Does that disqualify me for a concession on a suite?"

"Mr. Mills, please put Mr. Sharp in the suite next to the Dancys. Charge him the same rate."

"Do I gotta leave the maids unruffled?" Sharp asked.

"Yes . . . at least during working hours." He slapped Sharp on the back. "Now, sirs, I am running a business here and I have affairs to attend to." He interrupted his departure. "Mr. Sharp, I have a large supply of Jameson's. I expect my stock to be depleted upon your departure."

Sharp rubbed his chin and pretended to mull

it over. "The Jameson's no problem . . . but damn . . . not during working hours?"

Ford chuckled, but iterated, "Not during working hours." He turned to me. "We have your trunks in storage. Would you like them delivered to your suite?"

"Yes, thank you, but no rush."

We had left our trail clothes and other garments in storage until our return. We had also boarded our horses at a nearby ranch, but would not be in a hurry to bring them into town either. They were better cared for at the ranch until we left for Durango, our next destination.

"Anything else?"

"Do you know Joseph McAllen?"

"Yes, he heads the local Pinkerton office. I believe he's a friend of yours."

"We planned to meet him in an hour for supper. Could you please tell him we'll be late? Make him comfortable and charge his bill to our room."

"Of course."

"No need," Sharp said. He hooked a thumb at us. "My friends' dalliance will not interfere with me meetin' the good captain. We'll be makin' our first withdrawal from your whiskey stores."

Captain Joseph McAllen was another friend who had traveled with us from New York. I had engaged his services several times, but now I was as close a friend to him as the bad-tempered McAllen would allow. Sharp had a long-term relationship with McAllen that was far stronger than mine. The two men respected one another. In the beginning both had been leery of me, but after we had survived a few dangerous situations, the three of us learned that we could depend on each other.

Barney Ford brought me back to the situation at hand. "Mr. Dancy, we'll delay delivering your trunks until you come down for supper."

All I said was thank you. I didn't need to draw further attention as to why I intended to be late for supper.

Two bellboys accompanied us up the stairs to our suites on the fourth floor. On the second floor landing, one of them asked, "Either of you two gentlemen gamblers? The Cattlemen's Room at the Windsor hosts the fairest games in Denver."

Sharp stopped climbing. "Son, does Mr. Ford know yer pitchin' a competin' establishment?"

"No, sir, no pitch. Lots of folks want to know where there's an honest game." He set our luggage on the floor. "Figured you looked the type."

"The Inter-Ocean tables ain't honest?" Sharp asked innocently.

"Of course, sir. I didn't . . . it's just we got no high-stakes tables."

"How much do they pay ya if we happen to wander over to the Windsor for a few hands?"

"Sir, taking a gratuity from another establishment would be disloyal to Mr. Ford."

"It would," Sharp said with an edge. "How much?"

The bellboy picked up our luggage and started to climb to the next floor. "I apologize for my comment. I was only making conversation."

Neither Virginia nor I had moved during the exchange. The pitch hadn't surprised me. Hotel employees often hustled well-heeled guests. I was ready to resume my climb when Virginia grabbed my elbow.

She faced the bellboy who had remained silent. "Do you also encourage guests to visit the Windsor?"

"That was not our intent, ma'am."

"Of course it was. Take our bags to our suite." She tugged on my elbow. "We need to return to the lobby for a moment."

I could guess what she wanted to do in the lobby. I thought about dissuading her from tattling, but decided she was right. Ford had treated us well, and he deserved to know that these boys were picking up extra cash by steering gamblers to another establishment.

Speaking fast, the first bellboy said, "Ma'am, we didn't mean anything. How 'bout we just forget it."

"I'm afraid it's too late for that, young man," Virginia said. "I don't know what Mr. Ford will do, but I've run a business before and I never put up with employees working behind my back."

"Mister, can't you control your wife?" the bellboy pleaded to me. "You'll get my best service the whole time you're here."

I held my thumb and finger very close together. "I had this much sympathy for you until you said that." I closed the space between my thumb and finger. "Now I have none. Get our bags to our suite and then go downstairs to see Mr. Ford. He'll want to talk to you."

He threw our bags to the floor. "Go to hell. Take your own bags up these stairs. For your information, I have another job waiting for me where the guests aren't a bunch of prissy swells."

The boys turned and raced down the stairs.

Sharp chuckled before saying, "Go on up. I'll go to the lobby and meet you in a few minutes."

"What for?" Virginia asked. "The boys quit."

I knew why Sharp was heading downstairs. I picked up two bags and smiled. "Virginia, those scamps ran off with the room keys."

We laughed as we resumed our climb. On the next landing, we encountered a man bounding down the stairs two at a time. He was dressed in black with his suit coattail tucked suggestively behind a nickel-plated Peacemaker with a walnut grip. He brandished a hardness that was all too common in the male dominated frontier. As he came onto the landing, he tipped his hat to Virginia, and then while still ogling Virginia, rudely backed into me so I almost fell down.

He gave me the slightest glance before bowing and apologizing to Virginia.

"I think I'm the one you hit," I said.

He made a show of looking me over from head to foot. "You need to toughen up cowboy. There are all kinds of bumps out here in the West."

I realized I looked citified in my New York suit with a clean-shaven face and neatly trimmed hair. I also appeared unarmed because I wore my .38 in a holster under my armpit. I almost laughed when I visualized Sharp throwing the rascal down the stairwell before he could have finished that sentence. I, on the other hand, wanted to avoid violence, so I swallowed my anger and started to step around the stranger.

"Your lady friend is watching," he taunted.

"Yes she is. She wants to know if I've learned to control my temper. I don't want to disappoint her."

"Maybe she's trying to determine which of us is the real man."

"I already know it's not you," Virginia said. "Go on down to the lobby. There's no more fun here."

He regarded her suggestively and appeared ready to make a lewd remark. Instead, he said, "Your skirt's pretty big, ma'am, but not big enough to hide this scaredy-cat."

Virginia gave him a long, hard look before she

shrugged indifferently and said, "Go ahead, Steve. You have my permission. Kill him."

The man laughed uproariously, and then waved dismissively at us as he continued down the stairs, laughing all the way.

Chapter 2

T he expansive view overwhelmed the grandeur of the Presidential Suite. The parlor spanned the entire width of the building, providing an unobstructed view east and west. On one side, the Rocky Mountains looked majestic and fortress-like, while in the other direction, no obstacles or points of interest interfered with the vista of a limitless prairie stretching out to the horizon. I knew the Great Plains only gave the impression of being flat. In truth, the land gradually sloped away from this five thousand foot high city, making the horizon seem further away than would be the case in a level landscape.

The roominess and pleasures of the suite helped me get over the rude behavior of the man in the stairwell. Virginia's exhortation to kill him surprised me, but her teasing tone made it clear she was joking. At least it was clear to me. Since the man went away laughing, he must have recognized her humor. I told myself that bellicose men inhabited every corner of the frontier and if I was going to avoid violence, I would need to ignore quarrelsome slights. Besides, I had other things in mind. The suite possessed another welcome luxury—real privacy. On the train, our Pullman compartment provided concealment, but not privacy.

I had met my fiancée, Mrs. Virginia Baker, in Leadville, Colorado, where her husband had worked as a mining engineer before a fatal accident. She was two years younger than my thirty-one years, and we were in love, looking for a time and place to get married. Recently, we had experienced some dangerous situations, but now the future looked adventuresome, safe, and fancy-free. We were both inflicted with wanderlust and eager to travel around the western states. I especially wanted to visit California to investigate the regions around San Diego and Los Angeles. Sharp and I had made an agreement with Thomas Edison to distribute his lighting inventions west of Denver, excluding San Francisco, so I wanted to scout electrification opportunities. Also, San Diego supposedly had one of the world's great harbors and having made a fortune in railroads, I appreciated the profit to be made by transporting people and wares.

After we took advantage of our newfound seclusion, I suggested ordering supper delivered to the room, but Virginia squashed the idea. She enjoyed her meals hot, which would not be the case if a tray had to be carried up three flights to the fourth floor. We freshened up and arrived at the dining room only a quarter hour past our agreed upon rendezvous. I spotted Sharp and McAllen sitting at a corner table with their heads bent close together.

"You two look as if you're conspiring," I said as we approached. "Are you plotting a bidding strategy for thoroughbreds?"

McAllen looked annoyed, which puzzled me. He had returned to Denver to quit the Pinkerton National Detective Agency so he could start a horse ranch outside of Durango. His daughter lived near the town with his ex-wife and her new husband, who happened to be the town minister. Starting his ranch should have put him in an agreeable mood. He loved nothing more than his daughter and horses. Instead, he looked his normal dour self.

"Good evenin', Steve, Virginia. Could you give Jeff and me a few more minutes?"

"Why?" Sharp asked. "Don't ya trust 'em?"

"Trust has nothin' to do with it. My instructions are to keep this confidential."

"What instructions?" I asked. "I thought you went to the office to resign."

"One last assignment." McAllen took a big gulp of whiskey and snapped his glass onto the table.

"Why?" This came from Virginia. "You were determined, Joseph. What happened?"

"A thousand dollars happened. It's the cushion I need to start my ranch."

"Don't do it," Virginia said. "There will always be *one* more job, and an extra thousand will always looks tempting."

McAllen angrily waved over the steward to refill his glass. After the steward acknowledged his signal, he turned to us. "Sit. I'm not goin' to shout up at you and include the whole damn room in our conversation."

"Sorry to intrude," I said testily. We sat and scratched our chairs up to the table. "I thought we had been invited."

"For supper, not to butt into my business."

"Seems you don't have a business . . . other than corralling bad men," Virginia said.

"Bad women on occasion, too." McAllen pointedly glared at Virginia.

I thought an argument might ensue, but instead, Virginia smile broadly.

"Tell us what's wrong, Joseph?"

The steward finally came over, so we ordered drinks before McAllen answered. "The extra money will help, but I was given another incentive to do this job. A horse ranch doesn't start payin' for a couple years. A guaranteed buyer makes everythin' a hell of a lot easier."

"Let me guess," I said. "The Pinkertons will

give you a purchase contract only if you do this one last job."

"Yep. How'd you know?"

"It's how I'd do it," I answered.

"Damn you, Steve! That's not how someone treats a friend."

"The Pinkerton Agency is not your friend, they're your employer. When I said I would do it that way, I meant if I needed the service of one specific employee intent on skedaddling, I'd use whatever leverage I had. But I wouldn't do it to anyone at this table."

Virginia tried to lighten the moment. "So, if I wanted to skedaddle, you wouldn't use everything in your power to stop me?"

I feigned a forlorn expression. "If you decided to skedaddle, it would mean all of my power had been spent."

"Poor man." She patted my hand. "I guess I'll hang around then." She turned to McAllen. "Now Joseph, how do we help you get this job done so *you* can skedaddle?"

"I don't need your help." He looked uneasy. "I need Jeff's help. That's what we're talkin' about. You lovebirds go plan your weddin'."

"Oh, I think that'll take only moments," Virginia said. "With the exception of Maggie, our guests are sitting around this table."

Maggie was McAllen's daughter. We wanted a small wedding in an open meadow officiated by a minister, so Maggie's stepfather seemed a good choice. Although I intended to invite friends from my days in Pickhandle Gulch, I doubted if any of them would make the journey from Nevada. Likewise, I suspected that Virginia would invite Michael, her protector when she ran a general store we owned together in Leadville, but he would probably be busy as the new owner of the shop.

"Joseph, I think Virginia can help," Sharp said.

"How?" McAllen demanded.

"She can be a distraction, somethin' pretty on my arm. Help me act the old fool."

"Hell no," I blurted. "I don't know what this is about, but Virginia's not involved."

"It's not dangerous, Steve," Sharp said defensively.

"I don't care. Virginia has been in enough trouble. Leave her out of your plans."

"I want to know," Virginia said.

Damn. She sounded excited.

She almost bounced in her seat, as she said, "What's this about? And will it get us to Durango sooner?" Turning toward me, she gave me a glancing kiss on the cheek and a sweet smile. "Don't you want to hurry our wedding along?"

"No!" I swiped at my cheek as if to erase her coquettish ploy. Then a stammered, "I mean no to you getting involved. Virginia, you were shot for god sake. Your leg may have healed, but my guilt at putting you in danger has not. I don't want you involved in Pinkerton matters. They can hire a woman, if they need one."

"A prostitute ain't appropriate for this brand of work," Sharp said.

"Why a prostitute?" I asked. "If I recall, Pinkerton employs women." I looked at McAllen. "In fact, I believe I've encountered a couple of very capable women agents."

"The Denver office has no women," McAllen said. "If you object, we'll go with our initial plan."

"I object."

"Well, we're not married yet . . . and may never be if you think you're making all my decisions."

"Don't tell me you want to do this?"

"Because of your rudeness, I don't even know what this is. I want to hear and make up my own mind."

This wasn't going to get better for me, so I simply said, "Okay, tell us."

"A rich gent got suckered in a private poker game at the Windsor, and wants it set right," Sharp said offhandedly.

"He lost a lot of money and he's convinced the game was rigged," McAllen explained. "He can afford the money, but won't abide the loss of pride. He hired us to catch them cheatin'."

"I'm confused," I said, actually peeved instead of confused. "You quit, and they won't give you a horse contract unless you solve this horrendous crime. To solve this awful offense, the Pinkerton National Detective Agency needs the *great* Captain Joseph McAllen to soothe the ego of some rich fool. In fact, it's so important for you to be personally involved that you intend to hand the task over to Jeffery and my fiancée? What the he—"

McAllen's hand slapped the table. "Do not ridicule me!"

"I wasn't. I—"

"I'm no fool, Steve. Callin' me the *great* Captain Joseph McAllen was meant to belittle . . . and you know damn well not to call Sharp Jeffery."

We all stared angrily at each other. Then I realized my thought was inaccurate. The three of them were staring angrily at me. I had been in a contented, even blissful mood before walking into this room. Somehow, I had instantly angered everyone I cared about.

"I apologize . . . to everyone. Can we start again?"

There was only a short silence before McAllen said, "Forget it. I was out of sorts because I wanted to get out of here." He swallowed a shallow sip of his whiskey and exhaled slowly. "The client's name is Harold Whitlock and he's a big cog in Denver business and politics. He's our biggest client and has even bought services in Chicago, where he's made friends with some of the boys who haven't worked outside of an office in years. I've done work for him in the past. Good work. Perhaps too good. Now, he insists I work this assignment or he will cut off all business with the Pinkertons."

I thought a second. "This is ludicrous. How are you supposed to entrap these men? Everyone knows you're a Pinkerton."

McAllen threw up his hands. "Whitlock thinks I can just tell them I quit. He wants me to let it be known that I need a bigger grubstake to start my ranch. So, I plan on winnin' my stake by playin' poker."

"They'll never buy that," I said.

"That's why I'm askin' Sharp to be the mark." Nobody said anything, so McAllen continued his explanation. "The men runnin' the game are scoundrels. They played Whitlock like a fiddle. Let him win small every Friday night for weeks. Then they took him for thousands in a single night. I suspect everyone at the table was in on it." McAllen shook his head. "Damn it, this'll take weeks."

I waggled my finger between Virginia and me. "You realize we'll need to pretend we're not together? It's a bit late for that."

Sharp winked at Virginia. "I was thinkin' she could pretend to be workin' two rich gents."

"Bad plan," I said without a moment's pause.

"How so?" McAllen asked. "These boys would

jump at a chance to fleece a rich miner with more money than sense. A role Jeff can play with ease."

Sharp laughed at what others might take as ridicule. He often played the rube to get a better deal in business or to avoid a conflict he'd rather ignore. He missed his calling as a thespian. He had the act down pat, but I saw a problem with McAllen's plan.

"Virginia and I have already been seen around town . . . now and before we went to New York. We haven't been shy about our engagement. It's too late for her to play the role of a paramour." Sharp nodded reluctant agreement, and then started to say something. I stopped him with a raised hand. "Besides, Sharp is a skilled poker player. He's played all over the world for big stakes and small. He'll never be accepted as an easy mark."

"They don't know that," McAllen said defensively.

"If they're smart, they'll see signs that he's playing down. What you need is a real rube. Someone rich and impulsive . . . and truly lousy at poker. Someone who has an attractive fiancée he's anxious to impress."

Everyone smiled.

Sharp asked, "An' who might that be?"

"Me, of course."

Chapter 3

Finely attired patrons wandered the lobby of the Windsor, which competed with the Inter-Ocean for opulence. Virginia and I had dressed appropriately for a lavish evening at one of the finest establishments in Denver. Virginia shined like one of Thomas Edison's incandescent light bulbs. She was stunning. I knew this as a fact because men in the lobby kept stealing glances at her. Although her fashionable New York dress extended to just under her chin, the fitting had been expertly tailored to flaunt her graceful figure. If her job was to distract, she performed her role perfectly.

It took only one stroll around the lobby to spot the quieter of the two bellboys who had summarily resigned to avoid *prissy swells*. He looked nervous as we approached.

"Good evening, young man. I believe we're here at your invitation."

"I thought you were offended."

"Not to poker, son, just to your disloyalty. Now that you work for the Windsor, there's no reason you shouldn't get your stipend for luring a rich gent and his fiancée to the Windsor's renowned poker parlor."

"In that case"—he made a sweeping wave of his arm—"may I show you to the Cattlemen's Room?"

I nodded and we followed him across the lobby. McAllen had explained that we would need to gamble in the public Cattlemen's Room before being invited to the private gambling parlor. This disappointed me because it meant weeks of playacting before dealers tagged us as dupes ready to be fleeced. Virginia came up with the idea of letting it slip that we were leaving Denver in three weeks to get married in Durango. If we didn't blunder, that should encourage the swindlers to hurry their invitation to the high stakes game. We'd start tonight by jauntily losing a couple hundred dollars and acting as if the loss was inconsequential.

"Does your fiancée always accompany you when you play?" asked the bellboy.

"I do," Virginia responded. "And if you want a tip, you will address me directly. I'm not an appendage."

"Excuse me, ma'am. No offense intended." A thought seemed to strike him. "Do you intend to play, ma'am."

"Would that be awkward?" she asked.

"Yes, ma'am. The last woman to play poker in the Cattlemen's Room was Calamity Jane . . . and some question her gender. Women are not forbidden, but they're not generally welcome."

We arrived at the entrance and looked over a boisterous room with six poker tables and a long bar lined with chattering men and women. Against the far wall were four faro tables. I preferred faro to poker because there was less skill involved. In poker, my face or mannerisms gave me up and everyone at the table knew my hand before I played it. I was competitive, so I avoided poker because the game made me look foolish.

Virginia looked at our escort. "I see plenty of women."

"Those are . . . let's say employees. None came with the men they're attached to."

I hoped Virginia didn't mention that she ran a general store in a tawdry neighborhood where whore houses and cheap saloons competed for the cash in a miner's pocket. We were supposed to be witless, wealthy city-slickers, not old hands in the ways of the West.

"You mean they're prostitutes?" Virginia exclaimed in a tone that made her sound titillated to be in proximity to such wickedness.

"We never refer to them in that manner. This is a respectable place and these are respectable women." He winked. "That is, until they venture upstairs."

She hugged my arm. "Now I know I'll accompany you to all of your poker games. I'll not have you *venturing* upstairs."

"Don't worry, you're my lucky charm. Stay close."

Virginia pursed her lips. "I hope I'm more than a charm."

"You are, indeed," I said, as I kissed her cheek. I turned to the bellboy. "I see no open seats. Can you arrange a game for me?"

"Step over to the bar and I'll take care of it. Five or ten dollars?"

He was talking about the ante. Most casual poker players went for a dollar table, but they evidently needed to find another parlor. We wanted to move things along, so I told him to get me a ten dollar table. At the bar, I ordered a Jameson's for me and a Manhattan cocktail for Virginia. As we waited for our drinks, I saw that I was the envy of most of the men in the room. The so-called *respectable* ladies were younger than Virginia, but they already looked worn and their gaiety affected. Virginia, on the other hand, looked natural and fresh, like a society gentle-woman . . . albeit with a strain of mischief in her veins which made her look all the more alluring.

The bellboy returned before we had taken more than a couple sips of our drinks. He had secured me a seat at the furthest table. As I approached, I saw five well-dressed men wearing countenances displaying not a speck of gaiety. These were serious gamblers. Two of the men had women standing behind them with a possessive palm on their shoulder. This meant Virginia would not be barred, but it also meant it would be difficult to read my cards without one of these women onlookers stealing a peek.

There were perfunctory handshakes all around and I was informed that conversation was discouraged. I bought three hundred dollars' worth of chips and received a stack smaller than the two obvious winners at the table. After a few hands, I realized this would be a short night, or I would be losing more than my initial buy of chips. At least one player aggressively raised each hand, forcing me to fold promising cards. I was just thinking I should have started at the five dollar table when I was dealt two pair which turned into a full house after the draw. My winnings from that one hand sustained me for another hour.

All during the play, two bosses wandered the floor. If someone said more than a sentence, one of them would tap the offender on the shoulder. The room was noisy, but all of the talk and laughter came from the bar and a few observers that leaned against the walls. The Cattlemen's Room was a gambling hall, not a social club. Once I accidentally showed my hand and spotted a slight squeeze of the next player's shoulder by his female companion. I surmised that after a venture upstairs, the women negotiated an arrangement that included services beyond bed. Most gamblers wouldn't consider this serious cheating because a poker player ought to know how to protect his cards.

In short order, I was done. I had lost every chip, plus another twenty dollars I spent to stay in the last hand. I didn't need to fake poor playing. I was bad and everyone at the table knew it. I stayed in too long with poor cards and I repeatedly drew too long shots. Worse, my face gave away my cards and my intentions. Now, I only needed to show I didn't care if I lost.

I stood up. "Gentlemen, it has been a pleasure. I've lost my limit, so I'll bid you good evening and wander over to the bar for a nightcap. One of these days, I'll get the hang of this game."

"Come back to play again. You're always welcome at this table."

The man who said this had a huge stack of chips in front of him, including most of mine.

"If you'll have me, I'll be back tomorrow evening."

"We'll save you a seat."

"Don't get too eager," I laughed. "I only wager three hundred a night. I figure that's a decent limit for a little fun."

"You can afford three hundred dollars a night?" one of the players asked incredulously.

"I view losses as a cost of learning the game. I *will* get better gentlemen, and when I do I'll raise my limit."

Virginia tugged my arm. "Come along, dear. You can have your fun for a few days, but we have a date to get married in three weeks."

"Sounds like you're about to get corralled," said the winning player. "Just make sure the gate's ajar so you can escape on occasion."

She smiled. "Oh, he can get out for a game of poker, but not for big money . . . not after we're married. We need to plan ahead . . . for a family."

"It's the planning part I like," I said to ribald laughter.

I kissed her lightly on the lips, and she led me away from the table.

Chapter 4

I played poker four of the next six nights. The other players at our table always greeted me like a long lost friend. The cost of their friendship was never in doubt, especially after I won about two hundred dollars and quit for the night. They beseeched me to remain for another hour. My new friends thought I not only owed them the two hundred, but also my nightly allowance of three hundred. Overall, I was down nearly a thousand dollars, and they acted like there was something unjust about me taking home my meager winnings.

Meanwhile, Virginia made friends with the women who worked the room. Her ladylike attire and demeanor distinguished her from the showy prostitutes, so men kept their distance from her. This made me somewhat less concerned about her sidling up to women for hire, but I still feared she was playing a dangerous game. When I cautioned her against spending too much time with the hostesses, she said she wasn't going to stand behind me the entire night, but if I preferred, she'd talk to men. She turned on her heels without waiting for me to express a preference.

No one questioned the roles we played. Mostly, I guess, because we told the truth. McAllen had explained that using our real history would make our stories hold up to scrutiny. We said we were from New York City and Philadelphia respectively, and we both came from wealthy families. We fell in love not only with each other, but with the West. Our friend Jeff Sharp was a rich mine owner, who preferred to gamble on mines instead of poker. We didn't deny our friendship with Captain McAllen, but let it be known that he was quitting the Pinkertons to start a horse ranch in Durango. His departure was being delayed because of a squabble over the bonus he had been promised when the company loaned him to the New York office on special assign-ment. It seemed New York thought the bonus ought to be covered by Chicago and vice versa. McAllen didn't care who paid him, but he refused to finalize his resignation until paid by someone. In the meantime, we killed time by shopping during the day and playing poker at night.

At the end of our fifth night of gambling, a gentleman approached and offered to buy us a drink. When we demurred, he insisted that he had an attractive proposition for us that he could only discuss in private. Virginia possessively hugged my arm and told him we had other plans for the remainder of the evening, but if he wanted, he could meet us for breakfast at the Inter-Ocean Hotel. She then proceeded to tug me out of the gaming room with a naughty glint in her eye.

"I think he was the boss of the high stakes parlor," I said.

"He was. The girls pointed him out to me last night."

"Then why decline his offer of a nightcap?"

"We can't appear eager. Besides, we'll be more in control if we're the hosts."

"Damn . . . so that seductive look wasn't real?"

"Steve, we have roles to play." She laughed at the look on my face. "Come on. It's late. Let's get you to bed."

The naughty glint was back and I quickened my pace.

Chapter 5

Breakfast felt like another card game. The sixtyish man from the Windsor Hotel introduced himself as Alastair Huntsman, and he affected airs commensurate with his pretentious name. Throughout the meal, Huntsman talked about everything except poker. He gently dug into our background to confirm our story, and then whispered Denver gossip like it would have some importance to us. He complained about the difficulty in managing a gaming room for Denver's rich and powerful, and tried to convince us that the men who played in his parlor were spoiled, overly demanding of personal comforts, and careless when it came to gambling. I pretended to be interested in his endless chit-chat, but silently became irritated.

"I'm curious, Mr. Huntsman," Virginia asked, "how does the Windsor make money from these games?"

"Your fiancé hasn't told you? When he cashes in his chips, we withhold five percent. We call it the house cut."

"I only won one night, so the house's cut was not foremost on my mind," I said.

"Surely, five percent doesn't bring in enough money for such a fine establishment," Virginia said.

"Right you are, young lady. We make far more money on refreshments. Our clientele demands the finest liquor and extravagant late evening food."

Virginia smiled. "And then, of course, you have private entertainment."

"Yes, of course." Huntsman seemed genuinely embarrassed. "I hesitate to bring this up, but it has been noticed that you've befriended our hostesses. This has become somewhat awkward for us."

"How is that?" Virginia asked, innocently.

Huntsman fidgeted with his silverware. "I think you know." When she refused to respond, he added, "You're a lady . . . and they're not."

"I'm aware of the difference. I was asking why it's awkward."

"One night a man might misinterpret your friendliness and cause a row. We would like to avoid that occurrence."

"I can handle drunken advances. Besides, Steve is close by. I may enjoy talking to these women, but I won't leave my fiancé alone with them."

"Then may I ask you to remain close to Mr. Dancy?"

Virginia laughed. "No . . . I don't think so. The hostesses are far more interesting than a frivolous card game."

"Then you present us with a problem, Mrs. Baker." He turned to me. "Mr. Dancy, sooner or later, one of the men will make an untoward advance. Trouble could ensue. I have a—"

"I'm fully capable of handling one of your patrons," Virginia interrupted. "As you say, Mr. Huntsman, I'm a lady, but I've been in some tense situations that took a steadiness of nerve, so I'm confident I can handle your dandies. If you want my fiancé to continue patronizing your establishment, I'll be with him."

"I see." He again fumbled around with the silverware. "I was about to offer a solution, but it may not meet your approval." He hesitated once again, pretending to make a decision. "We have a room upstairs where our finer gentlemen play. It's private. Very private . . . and exclusive. By invitation only. If you were to restrict your play to that room, the potential for a problem would disappear."

"Are hostesses present?" Virginia asked.

"Yes, ma'am. Our very best artisans," Huntsman answered.

Virginia seemed amused at the term artisan, but ignored it. "How would this change anything?"

"You will not be subject to rudeness from riffraff."

"Aw, I see," Virginia said. "Gentlemen make tasteful illicit proposals."

Huntsman looked momentarily taken aback,

41

but merely added, "The relevant point is that they are far more seldom."

I leaned forward. "I don't understand. Why might this not meet with our approval? What's wrong with this solution?"

"The stakes are higher. Your three hundred dollar limit may make a short night of it."

I laughed. "Is that all? My limit is due to my poor play, not my purse. I want to learn the game without looking the fool. How much would it take?"

Huntsman did a good job of looking embarrassed. "Sir, it may require as much as a thousand dollars a night."

"Would I meet the elite businessmen of Denver?"

"Indubitably."

"Then it would be a worthwhile investment. I can leverage those relationships to earn back my losses many times over. If you're extending an invitation, I accept."

He stood. "Excellent. I'm sure you will find the games invigorating and the Larimer Room will be honored with your presence. Can we expect you this evening?"

"I'm afraid not," I said. "We have tickets for the Minstrel Festival at the Tabor Grand Opera House. Perhaps, tomorrow night."

"At your pleasure. Just ask for me by name."

After Huntsman left, Virginia turned to me

and asked, "Do we have tickets for tonight's performance?"

"I'll get them after breakfast. I want a break from poker. Besides, you said we shouldn't appear eager."

"I'm not eager. Now that we have our invitation, let's take a night off. I'm tired of those whores anyway."

"Whores? I've never heard you use that word, even to describe State Street women."

Virginia had run a general store on the edge of a tawdry neighborhood in Leadville and had gotten along well with the madams and working girls. They were welcome customers and she treated them decently. In fact, I had never heard Virginia say anything disrespectful about how they made their living.

"Those were honest women, or honest prostitutes, if you will. They never put on airs or pretended to be anything other than what they were. Their forthright view of sex as commerce was reasonable given their circumstances. These girls are greedy, deceitful, and as haughty as any of the society women I grew up around. Just because they charge a high tariff, they think they're above other women in their line of work. Worse, they think men are fools to be duped and their wives stupid strumpets who sell their bodies at far too low a price. They giggle and tell me that wives not only have to service their

43

husbands sexually, but they must cook, clean, and care for the children. All this while their men squander family money for a few minutes with them. They laugh about how fast they can complete the task, and tell each other tricks to use. They think it's funny that some men ask them to lay around awhile so other men won't know they couldn't last. They demand extra cash to pretend a man is virile. They think it's hilarious that a man's pride is worth more than his satisfaction. Those women are conniving and thoroughly unpleasant . . . and they gloat over cheating their customers."

I sat silent for so long Virginia began to look uncomfortable. Finally, she asked, "What's the matter? Did I say something you disapprove of?"

"No, I'm trying to figure this swindle. We've been assuming the men are in cahoots, but what if they have help from these hostesses?"

"How? Signals?"

"Perhaps. You said they were conniving and deceitful. I'll bet nothing gets by them, and if nothing gets by them, they've found a way to weasel into the scam."

Now it was her turn to sit silent. When she spoke, she said, "They won't talk . . . not to me."

"I know."

"What'll we do?"

"I don't know, but I sense this helps." I made

sure Virginia was looking right at me before I added, "I only have one more question for you."

"What?"

"Can these women be violent?"

Her eyes never wavered. "Yes."

Chapter 6

A few minutes after Huntsman left, Barney Ford sauntered over to our table and asked if he could join us for a few minutes. He made me nervous when he said he wanted to discuss business. As the owner of the Inter-Ocean, he probably objected to us taking our gambling elsewhere. I didn't want to be rude, but I couldn't tell him the truth about why we spent our evenings at the Windsor.

"I trust everything has been to your satisfaction," he said, scooting in his chair.

Without any visible signal, a steward brought Ford coffee service. I groaned inwardly because this meant he did not intend to be quick. Darn. I couldn't think of a good excuse, so I hoped Virginia would be cleverer than me.

He glanced at Virginia, who only smiled demurely. Evidently he decided to speak in front of her. "Mr. Dancy, I apologize for interrupting your breakfast. If you choose, I can set up an appointment."

"No, that's not necessary. We have no firm plans for the day. What can we do for you?"

"Mr. Dancy, Mrs. Baker, if I may ask, on your arrival, what did you think of Union Station?"

"Beautiful," Virginia answered immediately. "When we left Denver a few months ago, the mess hid the grandeur of the architecture. It's a fine entrance to your city."

Ford smiled in an obviously pleased reaction to Virginia's response. "I'm glad you like it. The town leaders worked hard to make it impressive."

"Well, you succeeded," I said, wondering how long the small talk would continue. "It's a fine gateway to your fair city."

"Funny you should use that term because we intend to build an actual gateway," he said. "To make a truly grand entrance, we intend to build an arch that will span the entirety of 17th Street to greet guests and returning residents alike. It will be a huge endeavor. I'm enlisting all the major businessmen in town to support the project."

I wasn't sure where this was going, but if he was soliciting a contribution, I would happily throw a few hundred into the coffer.

"May I?" he asked, holding up a portfolio he had carried to our table.

"Of course," I answered, wishing he would bypass the sales pitch and just make the solicitation.

Ford displayed a sketch of a triple arch. A wide center arch allowed carriages to pass and two small archways to either side accommodated pedestrians. Filigree wrought iron accented a stone Victorian design, and the word *Welcome* was carved across the top of the arch.

"Nice design," I said, noncommittally.

"Nice, but not dramatic," Ford said. "We want something spectacular. Something that knocks people off their horse."

"And how do you intend to do that?" I asked, ready for the solicitation.

"We want the Welcome Arch lit by over a thousand Thomas Edison light bulbs."

That took me aback. Did Ford know that Sharp and I held rights for Edison's inventions?

"Why do you bring this to us?" I asked.

"You know why. You control distribution for his bulbs, wiring, and connectors."

He did know. How? How many others in the West knew? Sharp and I had wanted a license to illuminate mines, but instead, Edison had awarded us full distribution rights for Denver and points west, excluding San Francisco. Edison chose a distribution franchise because he wanted control over his inventions and wide application. He insisted that we illuminate the cities of the West in order to use his inventions for mining.

"May I inquire how you came by this information?" I asked.

"A telegraph to Mr. Edison. He instructed me to see you."

A thought struck me. "You upgraded our suite to facilitate a deal."

He smiled. "The thought never entered my mind."

He said this in a tone that meant it had been uppermost in his mind. This meant that Ford didn't want a donation; he wanted to buy products I controlled. And what better way to advertise our wares than a blazing architectural wonder in the fastest growing city in the West. Every train passenger would see it, even if they only stopped here on their way further west. Sharp and I had already decided Denver would be our center for distribution. Beyond representing a large market, it possessed a train hub that would make large shipments relatively inexpensive.

"Did Mr. Edison tell you that I would be looking for a warehouse?" I asked.

"He did."

"I bet you have a property in mind?"

"I do." The conversation had come to the exact point he had wanted when he took his seat. "I can make you a good deal on a warehouse, buy your product once you have it shipped from New Jersey, and contract with you to electrify the Inter-Ocean." He gave me a steady look. "I want my hotel electrified before the Windsor."

"A warehouse lease," I mused. "And a thousand

light bulbs needing periodic replacement. You're proposing a long-term business relationship."

"*If* we can strike a proper arrangement." I looked quizzical, so he elaborated. "Beyond a reasonable price, a proper arrangement would include annual contributions for the education of black men in Colorado. We finance classes in reading, writing, arithmetic, and the workings of a democratic society." He hesitated a moment. "All of my business partners participate."

"In that case, I think another coffee service is in order. It appears we'll be here awhile hammering out the details."

Chapter 7

Huntsman had been gone for no more than five minutes before McAllen plopped into the chair he had just vacated. It seemed the morning was going to be one get-together after another.

"Hendersen's here," McAllen said without preamble. "Arrived on last night's train."

When we agreed to help McAllen, he had sent a telegram to St. Louis to recruit the best cardsharp on the Mississippi. If this assignment was to be completed successfully, we not only needed to be cheated, but we needed to catch them red handed, which meant learning the cheating ways of poker. I inwardly groaned. The prospect of playing cards day and night seemed tedious and dull.

"How do we do this?" I asked.

"After breakfast, you two should take a walk and shop for about an hour. Go from store to store and occasionally buy somethin'. One of my men will follow, and if he approaches to tell you your carriage is waitin', it means you're not followed. Get in the carriage and it'll take you to a house on Champa Street. Don't get out until it drives around back. Hendersen and Sharp will be waitin' inside. If my man doesn't approach you, return to the hotel and take the day off."

"I almost hope we're followed," I said. "Sitting on my butt all day is tiresome."

"Take a brisk walk." McAllen seemed indifferent to my plight.

"Where will we tell people we go?" Virginia asked. "We can't shop all day, every day."

"Don't you have arrangements to make for Edison? People to interview, property to survey?"

"We just completed most of our arrangement just before you came in. Ford is going to be our Denver partner."

"Good man, but tell him you want to check out alternatives before signing papers. Visit available properties, get an attorney, send daily telegrams, and talk to prospective superintendents. Move around the city. It will help with your story and be close to the truth so you'll look natural. The main thing is to get you quietly into the house so you can learn poker. We should have at least a week or so to get you grounded before they invite you to the Larimer Room."

"We've already been invited," I said. "We ate breakfast this morning with Alastair Huntsman."

"Damn. That's not good. It'll take weeks to teach you what you need to know." He paused. "Are they expectin' you tonight?"

"No," I said. "We told them we were going to the Tabor this evening."

"Good. That gives us two days. More. They'll let you win for a while before springin' the trap." He shook his head. "Short, but we should be able to get you ready."

"You don't sound sure," Virginia said warily.

"We can do it," McAllen said with more assurance. "Let's go. No time to waste."

"You want us to shop first?" Virginia asked.

"Not today. We're goin' to have to take some risk. I'll call one of our carriages and get you over to the house for your first lesson from Happy Hendersen."

I laughed. "Happy? Do all gamblers have nicknames?"

"Yes," McAllen said matter-of-factly. He stood, preparing to leave.

"Joseph, sit a moment. I have a question."

His expression expressed impatience, but he sat back down and waited wordlessly.

"Did Whitlock figure out how he was cheated?"

McAllen's expression turned from impatient to curious. "Are you lookin' for a short cut?"

"I am."

"Good thinkin'. Whitlock believes they switched decks just before the deal. He's probably right. It's clean and simple and gives each player a preset hand." McAllen stood to leave again. "Tell Hendersen to concentrate on a deck swap. This helps because he could never train you as a cardsharp in a few days."

"Virginia says the hostesses are a greedy lot. They might be part of the swindle."

McAllen gave me one of his looks meant to make me feel ignorant. "Of course they are." He whirled on a boot heel and walked out, but not before throwing a command over his shoulder, "Be ready in ten minutes."

Chapter 8

Virginia and I met Sharp and Hendersen at a small, but neat house on Champa Street. Other than a coffee pot on the stove, a card table and four chairs made up the only furnishing in the living quarters. Happy Hendersen looked nothing like I expected. He wore beat-up denim trousers, an open-collar shirt that was far from new and worn fabric slippers. His hair was mussed and he needed a shave. He even made the roughhewn Sharp look like a gentleman. This did not fit my image of a riverboat gambler.

He walked forward, hand extended. "Mr. Dancy, Jeff has sung your praises." He laughed. "Except for poker, of course."

We shook. "Can you fix that? We only have a few days."

"Damn, I thought we had longer. What the hell happened?" Sharp asked.

I explained our early invitation.

Hendersen shook his head. "It would take a month to make a decent player of you. I'm not sure what can be done in this short of time."

"We believe the swindle was done by switching decks," I said. "Can we just work on that?"

A smile slowly grew on his stubbly face and then he laughed heartily. "Of course, how stupid of me. You don't need to learn poker. Everything will be done for you. They'll let you win until they decide to take your money. Just keep playing the way you have. Any change would look suspicious, anyway. You only need to spot a deck swap. We'll work on it, but first, let's talk setup."

"What do you mean?"

He waved us over to the card table in the

middle of the room. After the four of us had taken seats, Hendersen explained. "You'll need to catch the dealer switching decks. After the deal, the original deck will be stowed somewhere out of sight, so the deck will only be vulnerable at the time of the swap, which means you have to anticipate the play. Understand?"

"Yep," Sharp answered for me. "Steve ain't gonna demand a search. It'll be five or six against one. 'Sides, a deck in a pocket can be explained away. Steve, ya gotta see this one comin'. If they're any good, that'll be the hard part."

I thought a minute about what Sharp had said. "Is this going to be dangerous for Virginia?"

"I'll be fine," Virginia interjected.

I stared at her, then at Sharp, then at Hendersen.

"I doubt there will be danger for either of you," Hendersen said. "Swindlers don't rob at gunpoint. They're tricksters. They earn a living by fooling people. The best ones do it without the mark ever knowing what happened. When caught, they blabber excuses instead of going for a weapon." Hendersen unemotionally returned my stare. "Virginia will be safe."

"Okay," I said. "But what if they do something besides a deck swap?"

Hendersen shook his head. "Unlikely. For this kind of swindle to work, they need one huge pot. That means everybody stays in and bets like hell. Your hand has got to look like a sure winner, but so do the others. The only way to pull it off is with a stacked deck."

"How much skill does a dealer need to swap decks?" Virginia asked.

"By himself, very skillful. Months and months of practice. But with the whole room in on it . . . easy. In a swindle with several players, only the mark needs to be distracted. Lots of ways to do it, but we're getting ahead of ourselves. Let's get back to the setup."

Hendersen effortlessly shuffled a deck of cards while he spoke. "It'll be late. They'll find excuses to buy you drinks. On the big night, they'll help you win small hands, so you'll think it's your lucky night. On prior evenings, they'll have played a few large stake hands. This will be theater meant to put you at ease with heavy betting. When—"

"On these prior big hands, do I fold or bet?" I asked, interrupting.

"Play your hand as you normally would. Stay predictable. On these early hands, they won't cheat because it doesn't matter who wins, only that you witness wild betting so occasional big pots seem normal. Back to the setup, the dealer will be to your immediate left. They'll want you to be the last to bet after a series of raises, but you can't wait until the cards are dealt because the switch will have already happened. This means you need to see it coming. One signal will be that they'll get you to bring more money before springing the trap."

"How?"

"Taunting and threats. They'll complain about you quitting after winning. They'll call you a hustler. They'll threaten to send you downstairs unless you give them a chance to get even.They'll insist you need to buy more chips, or at least bring more cash to the games. That kind of thing. You'll be surprised how convincing they'll be."

"What if after a few winning nights, I buy more chips without prompting? Pretend to be over-confident."

"Good idea. Play the fool, but don't overdo it. These men can tell what you're thinking before you do. Now let me show you a few different ways to do a swap."

Hendersen opened another deck of cards, this one with blue backs instead of red backs like the one he had been endlessly shuffling. He casually tucked one in his armpit as he began to shuffle the other deck with two hands. The move was so natural and unhurried it took me a second to realize he had just concealed the first deck. He suddenly glanced over my shoulder and smiled. I started to look behind me, expecting to see McAllen approaching, but realized it was a diversion. I snapped my eyes back around, but it was too late. Hendersen held up the deck so I could see the color had changed.

"Fast," I said.

He nodded. "Now I want to show you different ways to hide a deck."

Hendersen got up and disappeared into the bedroom. He reemerged in seconds wearing a dapper coat over his tattered work shirt. He sat down and demonstrated a series of swaps. He hid a deck in his shirtsleeves, coat pocket, waistband, between his thighs, under the table, and in plain view to the side of the deck in play. Each time, he switched decks as we watched. It was hard to believe he could look so unhurried, yet so fast.

"It's all in being smooth," he said. "Speed gets you shot, smooth gets you the pot. Add a diversion and I can swap decks in front of the best poker players."

I turned to Sharp. "Jeff, have you ever caught anyone swapping a deck on you?"

"Yep."

"Is the culprit alive?" I asked, joking.

"Yep . . . but he ain't got no front teeth."

I turned back to Hendersen. "What do I do if I catch them in the act? I can't punch them all."

"You'll need help," Hendersen said. "A loud signal to bring Jeff and others to your side, but first, you need to expose that second deck."

"How?"

"You need to know where it's concealed. If the armpit, jerk the elbow so it falls to the floor. If a shirtsleeve, grab the forearm and slide your hand down to the wrist. If the waistband, get behind the dealer and jerk him to his feet by the scruff of the neck. If he puts the deck in a pocket, you need to see which pocket and go straight for it. To hide it under the table requires an apparatus. Turn the table over. Don't worry about finesse. Once you expose the switched deck, all hell will break loose, anyway."

"What if the deck is in plain view on the table?"

"Most rooms don't allow an extra deck on the table with a broken seal, but in this case, the room and all of the other players are part of the swindle, so they may try it because they see you as an easy mark. If they position an open deck on the table, insist on examining it just before the switch."

"Won't they take offense?"

"Of course. At least they'll pretend offense, so make sure you do it only when you're certain. Claim to see a bent card and ask to show it to them."

"If they refuse?"

He sighed. "They'll refuse. Remember, *that* deck is stacked. They won't want you to get your hands on it."

"So?"

He shrugged. "Do it at gunpoint."

I didn't say anything, but I knew I had to figure out a better answer.

The remainder of the day was spent spotting a switch and exposing the concealed deck. I gradually improved, but my mind kept going back to the option where the deck was in plain view.

"How would a stacked deck get on the table?" I suddenly asked.

Hendersen rubbed his stubbly chin before answering. "It would have been slipped there several hands before. Probably by the person on the dealer's left. You can do this when most of the players are in on the con. If done right, the mark never notices."

Virginia asked a good question. "Who gets the winning hand?"

"It varies, but someone other than the dealer. Otherwise the mark might suspect a crooked deal."

"What do you think, Jeff?"

"Agreed, anyone other than the dealer or the mark. Maybe a previous big loser. Then if ya griped, they could claim ya begrudged the poor man a winnin' hand."

I thought about what they said, and then asked Hendersen, "Of all the options we've been practicing, how would you do it?"

Hendersen hesitated only a moment before answering that he would switch decks with one already on the table. He said it was simple and clean. I looked at Sharp and he nodded agreement. Damn. This was going to be more difficult than I thought. Then I had an idea. I decided to keep it to myself for the time being. I needed to think it through all the way.

The next order of business included various forms of distraction. Hendersen explained that a common ruse was for a hostess to expose cleavage while serving a drink, but it wasn't uncommon to drop a glass or stage a sharp argument in another part of the room. A man might swat Virginia's bottom to elicit a return slap. Another subtle technique would be for a player to burn his fingers lighting a cigar. The yelp would draw attention away from the dealer. Hendersen used Sharp to show us how these distractions worked. When it came to fondling Virginia's behind, Sharp's hand came close, but he never touched her. Virginia dutifully whacked him anyway, putting more energy than necessary into the slap. A mischievous smile told us she had enjoyed surprising Sharp.

We practiced the elements together. Hendersen would shuffle a deck, Sharp would cause a distraction, and then I would expose the concealed deck. Hendersen was deft and Sharp clever, but I became more adept with each round. A couple of times I even grabbed Hendersen's hand in the middle of a switch.

When McAllen showed up, we brewed coffee and took a break from cards. I needed it because I found the level of concentration exhausting.

Sipping hot coffee, I asked McAllen, "What happens after I expose the cheating?"

"I'll be downstairs," McAllen said. "Give a shout and I'll run up."

"A lot can happen in the time it takes a man to run up a set of stairs," I said.

"They'll get curious if I wait on the landing."

Hendersen gave me an appraising look. "You look like a pleasant sort, but Jeff says you know how to handle tough situations. He says you're a skilled gunman."

"You think this will come to gunplay?"

"No . . . as I said, these men talk their way out of trouble. But in truth, I don't know how this will end. I was only hired to teach you poker."

I turned to McAllen. "Well?"

He shrugged. "It could get dicey."

"With Virginia in the room?" I shook my head. "Joseph, I'll let them go before drawing my weapon. Pinkertons be damned."

"Virginia, as soon as Steve yells, you get out," McAllen said immediately. "Don't block the door because I'll come barrelin' in. Steve, you're right: do not draw a weapon. That could start a hellacious gunfight. Act dumb. Say somethin' like, 'What the hell is goin' on here?' Anything to delay action until I get into the room. I'll come in gun drawn, that's when you pull your gun. After we have them subdued, we march 'em off to jail to await trial."

"Oh hell," I exclaimed, dejected.

"What's wrong?" Sharp asked.

"The damn trial. That'll take at least a month." I gave McAllen a hard stare. "You'll want Virginia and me as witnesses, won't you?"

"Of course."

"Joseph, this little favor for you has already cost us a couple of weeks. Now you want us to hang around Denver for another month or so. In case you're unaware, we want to get married . . . and you're supposed to be starting a horse ranch."

"Steve, what the hell did you think? We'd just get Whitlock's money back and let these men continue to cheat. There was always gonna be a trial. My office can get it started in a week, not a month."

"Unless they get a good attorney, and it's not like they don't have enough money to buy the best. A smart lawyer can tie this up for months, maybe even get them off. Hell, all you got is me and Virginia as witnesses. The stacked deck could have been planted by us." I stomped around and spilled scalding coffee on my hand. After shaking my hand in pain and anger, I asked, "Joseph, do you believe they'd be convicted?"

He looked uncomfortable, a rarity. "Probably. But Whitlock wants more. He wants his money back, and he wants to embarrass the Windsor. Remember, this is about Whitlock regaining his dignity." He turned to refill his coffee cup, then slowly swung around to face us. "Steve, don't take any risks with this. It's a small job for a powerful, but *small* man. Just expose them and we'll do the rest. It will be over in days."

"I want to meet Whitlock."

"Steve, don't make trouble."

"Don't worry, I just want to talk. I won't make trouble for him, you, or the Pinkertons. I have a proposition for him that might make this go better. Trust me."

"Trust you? Steve, have you forgotten how many times I've seen you go off half-cocked? No, I can't let you see Whitlock."

"Joseph, the four of us can have supper together . . . or I'll get an introduction from someone else. Then we'll talk without you. Your decision." I waited a beat before adding, "You know I can always get close to an important person in this or any other city."

"I'll be present the whole time you talk?"

"Yes."

"Virginia will be there?"

"Of course, she's part of this."

McAllen put down his coffee and took his hat off of a peg. "I'll arrange it." He turned to Virginia. "I'm glad you'll be joining us. I expect it will take both of us to keep Steve from doing something stupid."

He left with a heavy footfall.

"Are we done for the day?" Hendersen asked after a quiet moment.

"No," I answered. I sat back down at the card table.

"Teach me how to switch the decks myself."

Chapter 9

Virginia and I wandered over to the Windsor the next evening for my first high stakes game, and Alastair Huntsman graciously led us up to the Larimer Room. The only furnishings were a card table, a few extra chairs for spectators, and a short mahogany bar. The bar was festooned with two pretty women who had not yet reached twenty years of age. They were dressed less flashy than their counterparts downstairs, but they still wore their profession with all of the clarity of an Anglican minister.

Expensive liquor bottles lined the shelf behind the bar, and a silver tray displayed tiny crystal bowls filled with shelled nuts. A sign over the bar offered steaks, oysters, and trout. In the corner, a beautifully gowned woman sat on a chair playing a lyrical tune on a violin. All of this opulence signaled that this was the height of Denver gambling.

I was in a good mood until Huntsman introduced me to the five other players. One was the lout who had ridiculed me on the stairs at the Inter-Ocean Hotel. I saw a flash of surprise on his face, but he quickly regained his composure and shook my hand as if we had never met. Huntsman introduced him as George Carson. Suddenly, a favor for McAllen took on additional meaning. I would be pleased to teach Mr. Carson a lesson in lawful behavior.

I immediately guessed that Carson was going to be the eventual big winner. The other men were dandies or grossly overweight. Only Carson had the rough and ready bearing that would deter an angry mark. I was pleased to see that he would sit across from me so I could easily keep an eye on him.

Virginia stood behind me for the first few hands, pretended to get bored, and moved over to the bar to make friends with the hostesses. Soon they were talking and laughing loud enough that the barkeep whispered a reprimand. One of hostesses immediately used the tray to place a dish of nuts beside each player. She leaned low, providing a gander at bountiful breasts barely restrained by a tight bodice. I noticed that each time a hostess served a drink or snack, she leaned over provoca-tively. Hendersen had predicted that they would immediately start this exhibi-tionist ritual to make it seem normal. He told me to enjoy the display, so I purposely appeared disposed to this type of distraction.

Carson couldn't seem to help himself. His bullying personality got the better of him on occasion, and he goaded me, despite the need for me to remain a pliable mark. I sloughed off his taunts as male jocularity, and everyone let me get away with it because they wanted to get beyond the moment without me taking offense. I may have acted indifferent, but I added each instance to a mental list for later settlement.

That first night I won over four hundred dollars. The amount surprised me because if this continued for every game, the stakes for the final hand would have to be very high for them to make up their losses and earn a suitable profit.

Later, when we returned to our hotel suite, we found Sharp and Hendersen waiting for us.

"How did it go?" Hendersen asked.

"Exactly as you predicted . . . except I won over four hundred dollars."

Sharp whistled. "That's gotta change. You probably did better than they expected, so they'll level things out tomorrow night. They ain't in a big rush."

"Virginia?" Hendersen asked.

"I got along with the girls and the barkeep," she said. "I don't think anyone suspects a thing."

"What's this?" I asked, picking up a folded telegram from a foyer table. It was addressed to me. I unfolded it and read it three times before swinging around on Sharp.

"Jeff, we need to go. Now!"

"What? Where?"

"Carson City. Richard's been killed . . . by Jenny for god sake. Jerimiah may be next."

"We can't go now," Sharp said. "Let's—"

"Damn it, we're going now. Jenny's killing my friends."

"I meant we can't go *right* now. We need to wait until tomorrow . . . for a train. What does the telegram say?"

I read, *"Jenny killed Rich. Revenge. Me next. Help."*

Sharp started pacing. I impatiently slapped the telegram against my palm. Hendersen and Virginia looked confused, so I explained that Richard and Jerimiah were friends from my early days exploring the West. I had wandered into Pickhandle Gulch in Nevada and started playing whist with the only educated men in town. In fact, in a small way, we were still business partners. I bought the sole hotel in town and gave each of our foursome an equal share. At that time Richard was the town printer and newspaperman, and Jerimiah owned the general store. Doc Dooley, our fourth, moved to Glenwood Springs, Colorado. Richard had won a seat in the Nevada Senate, which meant he spent a good part of the year in Carson City.

Last year, in an attempt to take over commerce in Pickhandle Gulch, Jenny's surrogates had badly beaten Jerimiah. After straightening out that mess, I had run away from a further encounter with her. In fact, I had run all the way to New Jersey.

"What does Jerimiah mean *me next?*" Sharp asked. "Why should he be next? He's not an important figure in town. I'll bet he's overly frightened because of that Pickhandle beatin'? 'Sides, Jenny wouldn't just kill outright."

"I *saw* her kill a man," I yelled. "Shot him twice from less than a foot away."

"She saved yer life," Sharp yelled back.

"McAllen has her right. That woman's conniving and ruthless."

"You must be talkin' about Jenny," McAllen said as he came through the door.

I turned to him. "Captain, I apologize, but I need to go to Carson City on tomorrow's train."

"Bad idea," he said, as he shrugged off a coat. "That woman is nothin' but trouble. You can't just run to her every time she beckons."

"She hasn't beckoned. Jerimiah has wired for help. He says she killed Richard."

McAllen turned his back to me to hang his coat. "Sounds to me like she twitched her index finger at you. Jerimiah may have sent the telegram, but Jenny composed the message. Let me read the telegram."

I handed it over.

"Who is this Jenny?" Virginia demanded.

I ignored her question. Despite being under twenty years of age, Jenny Bolton had grown powerful in Nevada business and politics. She had built an empire based on an inheritance from her murdered husband, but I feared she had also adopted his unethical methods.

"Richard probably used his senate seat to rein her in politically, so she killed him," I said almost to myself.

Sharp pointed to the telegram in McAllen's hand. "You got that from those few words?"

I was about to explain when Virginia loudly demanded, "Steve . . . damn it, who is Jenny?"

"A woman . . . no, a girl. I was infatuated with her. First, she rejected me, and then I rejected her. Her husband—"

"Her husband?" she exclaimed.

"Yes, her husband. She was sixteen and he was in his forties and the second most powerful politician in the state. He had been on a march to run just about everything in Nevada. He was assassinated because I convinced him to run for governor. His mother—"

"Tell me about Jenny." Virginia demanded.

"Why? Are you jealous? That doesn't seem like you."

"I'm not jealous. That telegram says she killed someone. You said you saw her shoot a man."

She gave me one of her no nonsense looks. "Is she after you?"

I hesitated. "I don't think so." I hesitated again. "She's disturbed. She suffered some terrible things . . . things that could drive any woman insane: sold by her father, multiple rapes, her husband murdered right before her eyes, and then she killed the assassin herself. She witnessed major political corruption, and she learned how to get her way in a man's world from a truly villainous mother-in-law. She masks her emotional wounds with a girlish effervescence." I could tell from Virginia's expression that I should have omitted that last sentence. I ignored her ire and answered her question. "Perhaps. Perhaps she murdered Richard to draw me back to Nevada . . . but that seems too much, even for her."

"Captain?" she asked.

"That woman would do anything. I think I better wire our Carson City agent and get a better description of what is going on."

"That will take too much time," I objected.

"A day," McAllen said in the tone he used when an argument was over.

"Okay, I'll wait one day . . . but I can't catch your card cheats in a single evening."

"I know. I also know this is more important, but I always get as many facts as possible before chargin' into trouble. I know that's not your style, Steve, but bear with me on this."

I nodded, and then I had a thought. "I have an idea that might move the card game fast. It probably won't work, but you get me a Pinkerton report on the goings on in Carson City and I'll try it."

"What idea?" McAllen asked. "You explain it to me first."

I did.

Chapter 10

The next night, Alastair Huntsman again escorted us upstairs. When I saw the players, I pretended to be perturbed and asked Huntsman to speak privately in the hall. He looked concerned, but led me out to the railed walkway that overlooked the main gambling parlor.

Without preamble, I said, "You told me the top businessmen in Denver would be in this room."

"These are very important citizens of our city," Huntsman protested.

"No they're not. As far as I can tell, none of them even own a business."

"They invest behind the scene, others do the work."

"Mr. Huntsman, I know the major businessmen in Denver, and these are not those men. I'm not a gambler. I play cards for recreation. If you're under the impression that these men run commerce in your city, I'm disappointed in your judgment."

"Mr. Dancy, I don't know who you expected, but these are substantial investors in numerous businesses. They can get you introductions. Please. I've promised these men that you would play tonight." He leaned to speak in my ear. "They want to win back their losses from last night, but I'm sure you've seen they're poor players. They'll be reckless tonight. You should buy more chips this evening because this is an opportunity to recoup your previous losses."

I pretended to think it over. "Very well, one more night, but my fiancée and I will be departing tomorrow for a short trip. When I return, I'll play downstairs . . . or if you prefer, at the Inter-Ocean."

"You are obviously free to do what you want. You'll always be welcome upstairs or downstairs." As if a new thought just struck him, he added, "These players are ripe for picking. Do you have enough cash? I could advance you a marker."

I showed him a fat wallet and said I was fine. I pivoted to return to the parlor and then hesitated.

"I think I'll visit the privy before starting play. Tell the gentlemen I'll be in shortly."

After my return, I wandered over to the bar for

a whiskey. I looked pointedly at Virginia and she gave me a slight nod. That meant Huntsman had conversed with the other players in my absence, which had been our intent all along. Now, hopefully, the gambit to separate me from my money would be accelerated to tonight.

Virginia insisted in carrying something very special this evening; a lead-weighted purse. In New York, a perilous situation had put Virginia in danger. McAllen had a woman Pinkerton agent teach Virginia how to wield this beaded purse as a weapon. She liked it so much, she asked to keep it. Since her dress ruled out a gun, she carried the purse tonight in case she needed more protection than either McAllen or I could provide.

The first hour of play confirmed that they didn't want to let a promising mark get away. George Carson kept losing badly, and crudely exposed his hand through expression or word. The rather badly acted show was supposed to make me feel overconfident when they dealt the big hand.

As the player to my right gathered in the chips, Carson got into a squabble with him. Carson acted upset because he had won. Everyone became engrossed in the argument. Carson first threatened to pummel the winner, and then said he might shoot him. The two gave a great performance and the room grew tense.

I had just dealt, so the player to my left had

been shuffling during the entire drama. He calmly laid the deck to his right and folded his hands in front of him.

In a calm voice, he said, "Come on, are we gonna play or argue? Relax, George. No reason to spend a week in jail like you did the last time you lost. Poker's poker. Sometimes you win and sometimes you lose."

"That was different. That bastard accused me of cheating. I don't abide insults."

"He was an idiot . . . and a bad poker player. You should have let it go. You're lucky he didn't die or they would've strung you up."

"Damn you, Karl, it was self-defense."

"You taunted him. Control your anger or something bad's gonna happen. Now, are we gonna play, or what?"

Carson swallowed the last of his whiskey. "Fresh drinks, then we play." He signaled the hostess over.

Karl picked up the cards and shuffled the already shuffled deck. When the hostess leaned low to serve our drinks, Karl presented the deck to me to cut. I waved a decline as I anticipated the hostess leaning in close to me. Without looking, I knew Karl had used the diversion to switch decks.

Just before he dealt, I said, "On second thought, I will cut."

"Too late, you already declined," Karl said.

"No, it's not. You haven't dealt a card yet." When he looked adamant, I added, "Otherwise, deal me out this hand. I need a break anyway."

He shrugged. "Sure, go ahead and cut."

I cut the cards, but left it to Karl to combine the two stacks as I sipped whiskey. As expected, he did some sleight of hand and restacked the cards as they were before. Just as he was about to deal, I sneezed and whiskey flew all over his face. I apologized as he quickly set the deck down and swiped at his face with his hand. Just then, one of the hostesses slapped Virginia, who returned the favor. As everyone looked over, I swapped the deck yet again. At the bar there were some harsh words whispered, an apology by Virginia, and then she returned to the table with her best smile and told us it had all been a misunderstanding. Her timing was perfect. We had agreed beforehand that she would insult a hostess to create a diversion.

We resumed play. My late cut was meant to unnerve the table and make them worry about the distribution of the cards. I presume they saw Karl negate the cut, but I wanted a tinge of doubt in their minds because my stacked deck might not have been a good replication of theirs. I had spent hours with Happy Hendersen stacking a deck that approximated the hands dealt to each player on the night that Harold Whitlock had been swindled. We could only hope that they would use the same or similar hands this evening. Hendersen suggested we place an element of uncertainty into the head, but not enough that they would discard the scam entirely.

Betting started aggressively. Everyone had a good hand, or one that could be filled in with a little luck. By the draw, there was already a couple of thousand dollars in the pot. Carson acted peeved again. He did such a good job acting that I would have believed him if I hadn't known he was holding four queens. Karl held a straight, the next man a flush, then Carson with his queens, and finally the player to my right held a full house, tens over eights. I held the fifth hand close to my vest.

"Huntsman says you're leaving Denver," Carson said.

"I have business in Omaha. We'll be gone a week or so," I answered.

"Then this may be our last chance to get even with you," Carson said.

I acted indifferent. "I'll be returning."

"Just the same, let's see if you got enough guts to stay in a real pot. I'm raising three hundred."

The bet was already two hundred, so Carson shoved five hundred dollars' worth of chips to center-table. The next player raised another two hundred. I was supposed to have a full house, aces over jacks, so I did what was expected, I raised another five hundred. After some appreciative whistles, the betting continued until I had over three thousand dollars of my money in the pot.

I examined every player and there was something obviously missing—tension. This pot was several times bigger than any previous pot, yet every player looked unruffled. This confirmed that they were all in it together. Every player except me knew how the cards would play out. A further raise would be meaningless to my purpose, so I met the last bet and called.

On Carson's turn to show his cards, he displayed four queens. The players to either side of him cursed and threw little tantrums. It was all great drama, but it came to an abrupt halt when they noticed I was unperturbed. Carson leaned forward and demanded to see my cards. With a flourish I fanned out four kings and a three. There was an audible gasp.

"What . . . how?" Carson stammered.

"That's impossible," Karl said, and then quickly added a feeble explanation of his remark. "I've never seen four hands like this before."

Carson flew to his feet. "You cheated!" he spat.

I stayed seated but was prepared to go for my gun if Carson even looked like he was thinking about drawing his. I stood when he charged around the table. Carson stopped short of arm's length.

"You damn cheater!" Carson screamed. "Don't

even think about leavin' this room with that money."

I decided I had had enough and my gun was in my hand before I consciously thought about drawing. It pointed at Carson's heart. I raised it slowly until it became level with his eyes, and then I pulled the hammer back with a loud click.

"Did that hand not go the way you expected?" I asked, evenly.

I heard a thud behind me. I instantly grabbed Carson by the collar and spun him around so I could see behind me without taking my eyes off of him. A hostess held a derringer, but she was no longer a danger. Virginia had slapped her across the temple with her purse. The supposed *artisan* dragged glasses noisily to the floor as she slid unconscious along the bar and eventually fell to join the broken glass.

Just then, five men surged into the room. Two of them looked dangerous: McAllen and Sharp. They entered hard and fast to startle any trouble-makers to inaction. Huntsman, another of the party, appeared nervous, while Whitlock looked elated. The fifth man, I didn't recognize. I assumed he managed the hotel. He wore an expensively tailored suit with a diamond-studded cravat, but instead of appearing in command of the situation, he looked highly uncomfortable.

"You cheated," Carson repeated, hardly giving the newcomers a glance.

I pulled a deck out of my pocket and dramatically laid it on the table.

"Why don't we have Karl deal this hand and see how it plays out?"

Carson looked at the deck, then at me, then at the group of men who had burst through the door. I could see him mentally weigh the odds.

"Go to hell," he said, as he moved to exit the parlor.

I used the barrel of my gun to stop his forward progress.

"You don't leave until my chips are cashed."

"That's Huntsman's problem, not mine," Carson said.

I threw McAllen a glance. "Captain?"

"If cash is not behind those chips, you all go to jail until we sort this out," McAllen answered.

"Ah hell, this weren't my idea." Carson pointed at Huntsman. "See him." Then he shoved his finger at me. "I'll deal with you later . . . you and your pretty little—"

He didn't finish because I wacked him across the mouth with my pistol barrel. I was being kind. If he finished the sentence, I might have shot him. I hadn't hit him hard, but blood seeped from his lip nonetheless.

No one uttered a word until the well-dressed man said, "Carson, you're fired. The rest of you are barred from these premises forever. You've sullied the good name of the Windsor."

Carson again leaned forward as if to leave, but I again added pressure to my gun barrel to halt his progress.

"Is there any money behind those chips?" I asked.

"Who the hell knows?" Carson said.

"You know. Did you buy your chips or did they give them to you?"

Carson sneered. "This weren't my game. I like direct action . . . if I want somethin', I just take it. They needed someone who could handle himself, so they promised me good booze, young women, and money to put you down if you got unruly. I didn't know particulars. I'm a victim here."

"What?" Virginia said aghast.

Carson gave Virginia a nasty look as he wiped his blooded mouth with the back of his sleeve. "Listen . . . dear, this is my job. Now it's gone. I don't care about these people. Throw them in jail for all I care, but I'm an innocent bystander who got cheated more than your boyfriend. Thanks to you two, I'm outta a job."

McAllen said, "You're an accessory to fraud."

"Accessory? Ain't that some kinda jewelry or ribbon . . . some worthless bobble?" He waved at the other men. "These here are yer criminal types. I'm just someone who knows how to handle himself."

I decided to deal with Carson later. My personal

feelings were not as important as getting Whitlock what we had agreed upon.

I repeated my question to Huntsman how much cash stood behind the chips.

"A few hundred. Maybe a thousand," Huntsman said. "We needed a small bankroll in case you had a winning night."

"Mr. Whitlock, how much did you lose?" I asked.

"Thirty three hundred," he answered.

I turned to the fifth man. "Who are you?"

"I'm Mr. Marker, general manager, and I apologize for this misdeed. I can assure you it will never happen again."

The use of the word misdeed infuriated me. "Do you know Mr. Whitlock?"

"We've met. He complained about being cheated, but I thought he was just a poor loser."

I already knew the answer to my question because of our conversation at supper with Whitlock. He had told me he complained bitterly to the general manager. At that meal, he also agreed to avoid a trial in exchange for another course of action.

"His complaint didn't raise concern?" I said. "You didn't see fit to keep a closer eye on what was happening inside your hotel?"

"I already apologized."

"We need more than an apology. I'll accept the short cash for my winnings, but you owe Mr. Whitlock thirty three hundred dollars."

"I do not!"

"In that case, I believe the Windsor scandal ought to be good for many, many newspaper stories." I pretended to think. "There's the fraud itself, the culprits, oh, and the complicity of a hotel employee, probably an article about your dereliction of duty, and then a few stories about the victims as they come forward. Yep, the *Journal* and *Post* will love this, especially after they get hold of some prurient details that will get the whole town buzzing with gossip."

"You wouldn't dare," Marker said.

"I would," I said flatly.

"As would I," McAllen added. "Since being engaged by Mr. Whitlock, we've discovered a number of unsavory practices at the Windsor. Perhaps enough to appeal to newspapers as far away as Omaha and Chicago."

Marker's jaw could not have been set firmer as he looked between me and McAllen. Finally, he said, "Very well, but only if this incident remains confidential." He looked at Whitlock. "Do you agree to keep it secret?"

Whitlock did not hesitate. "No."

"No? What do you mean?"

"I mean, no. I rather like the idea of newspaper stories. After a few others come forward, we'll engage an attorney and sue. I won't relent until you're fired." Whitlock looked smug. "You shouldn't have ignored me."

"You bastard," Marker said.

"Likely, but beside the point," Whitlock said. He couldn't conceal his glee at getting retribution. "When we're done with you, the only hotel you'll manage will come with fleas and lumpy mattresses."

Marker stormed out of the parlor. The players and barkeep tried to follow, but McAllen and Sharp blocked the door. McAllen told them to put the bank on the bar and then empty all of the money in their pockets into the cashbox. The enlarged pile of bills and coins would still not total my chips, but I appreciated McAllen's gesture since I hadn't thought of this particular coup de grâce. I had thought of another, however.

As the room emptied, I holstered my pistol. Carson gave me an insolent look as he moved to step around me one more time. I erased his smug expression with a blow across his jaw. He staggered back, so I hit him again with a left and finally another right. He crumbled.

Virginia came over and hooked her hand through my arm and smiled, but Sharp was shaking his head in abject disapproval.

"When we get a chance, I'll teach you how to do that with one blow."

Chapter 11

Jerimiah's sick," Sharp said.

Virginia and I were sitting across from Sharp on the train to Carson City. In a way, Sharp was returning home, except that he had sold all of his Nevada holdings.

"Sick? You mean ill . . . or something else?" I asked.

"Sick in the head. He hides in his room. Don't talk to no one. Afraid people are tryin' to kill him. He insists that Richard was murdered, and rants endlessly about Jenny Bolton takin' over the whole state."

We had caught a train to the Nevada capital the next morning, leaving McAllen to provide gist for the newspapers' stories. Unless we needed him in Carson City, we planned to meet up in Durango in a couple weeks.

The Carson City Pinkerton agent had cabled that Richard had been shot in his print office while setting type. A seat in the Nevada Senate was not a full time job, so Richard continued to make money as a newspaper publisher. He also made enemies. Evidently, he had run a series of stories exposing business and political corruption in the state. Despite these stories, the marshal ruled the killing a tragic accident. Several shots had been fired, most of which hit walls or signs, and so the bullet that hit Richard was easily dismissed as a random shot fired by a reckless drunk. Jerimiah told everyone who would listen that despite appearances, Richard's death was murder, plain and simple.

"The beating?" I asked.

"Could be the beatin' drove him over the edge, but I'd guess bein' alone hurt him more. Cut a man off from humanity and ya can break his mind. 'Sides, Jerimiah never was a brave soul."

Jerimiah had been severely beaten and then forced to live with limited food and water in a rock hovel. They took his money and denied him any way to get money, so he became trapped in lonely isolation. It didn't help that the beating cost him sight in one eye. I suspect he carried other scars I had never seen. After we rescued him, he seemed to revive, but he was more distant than when he chatted with anybody who wandered into his general store.

We knew the assault on Jerimiah had been orchestrated by underlings of Jenny Bolton. There was no denying her intentions; she wanted power and she used dastardly methods to get it. She had been trained by her husband, an ambitious rancher and politician who treated her like a prized possession. Her ruthless streak came from a truly reprehensible mother-in-law. When both the husband and his mother were killed violently, Jenny inherited the largest ranch in Nevada and a host of powerful political connections. She was smart as a whip, strikingly pretty, and cunning as hell. Despite being under twenty years of age, she was already worldly and rich, but also deeply scarred by violence, rape, and the people bent on controlling her. The world had treated her badly, and I supposed she wanted to get even. Heaven help us.

After rescuing Jerimiah, I didn't return to Carson City to punish Jenny for what she had done to him. Her threats and actions weren't aimed at me, and I just wanted to be done with Carson City, Nevada, Jenny Bolton, and trouble for that matter. Instead, I had convinced Sharp to accompany me to Prescott, Arizona, where he got into a pile of trouble—the hanging kind of trouble. Now I found myself gently swaying on a train heading straight back to the place I least wanted to go.

"You look unhappy," Virginia said.

"Not unhappy, apprehensive. I've got a bad feeling about this."

Sharp nodded agreement, which didn't help me feel better.

"Virginia, I wish you had waited in Denver," I said. "Would you go back after a day or two?"

"No."

She offered no further explanation.

"Why not? No matter the situation, it shouldn't take long. I'll be back before you know it."

"If you were gone ten minutes, I'd know it. We do things together now." She gave me a direct stare. "And quit trying to protect me. I want a husband, not a keeper." More glaring. "Do you understand?"

"Yes, but I'm afraid you don't understand what we might be heading toward."

"I haven't heard anything scary so far. A cryptic telegram, a random shot that killed a friend, and another friend who *might* have gone crazy."

"There's more," Sharp said.

"What?" she asked.

Sharp appeared as troubled as me.

"Damned if I know . . . but there's gonna be more."

Chapter 12

The St. Charles was not in the same class as the Inter-Ocean Hotel, but with the capitol across the street, it housed a fine restaurant that catered to politicians and their petitioners.

Sharp and I had a history with the St. Charles. Several months previously, I had published a novel about my experiences out West. For the most part, the book had been written at the St. Charles, and one of my misadventures occurred right in front of the hotel. I had engaged Captain McAllen and a team of Pinkertons to protect me from a notorious killer, and gunfire erupted while I stood on the porch of the hotel. A Pinkerton I had befriended was shot in the stomach and suffered a long, painful death. For this reason, the St. Charles felt melancholy, but I continued to stay there because I didn't want to avoid the memory of a friend.

After checking in, Sharp and I immediately walked to Jerimiah's boarding house. He wasn't in his room and the landlady said she had no idea where he could be, so we returned to the St. Charles. As we reentered the hotel, I heard a *psst* noise from the hallway leading to the kitchen. It was Jerimiah.

I walked over. "Howdy. Come on, we'll buy you supper," I said.

"No! Can we go to your room?"

"Jerimiah, quit this horseshit," Sharp snapped from behind my shoulder. "I'm hungry and no one's gonna bother you with us around."

"You don't know that," he protested.

I was startled by Jerimiah's appearance. Instead of looking his thirty-some years, he looked to be in his fifties. He had always been pudgy, with thinning hair, but now his clothes fit too tight and he only had a ring of hair around the base of his head that he had allowed to hang below his shoulders. Why did balding men let what little hair they still possessed grow to such unusual lengths? Did they believe that overly long hair on one part of their head disguised baldness elsewhere? At least Jerimiah looked well-fed. The last time I saw him, he had withered to skin and bones.

"We came all this way because you telegraphed," I said. "Eat with us in the dining room or we leave in the morning."

Jerimiah flinched like I had slapped him. He turned and fled.

"What do you make of that?" I asked.

"Not sure. The man's frightened. Is it real or in his head?" Sharp shrugged. "Do we go after him?"

"No . . . it's better we get another perspective before we talk to him anyway."

When we entered the dining room, something odd happened. Everyone pretended not to know us. For years this had been Sharp's hometown and he easily made friends with both sexes. He must have been bosom buddies with most of the men in the room and probably a few of the women. For my part, I had lived through the prior winter in this hotel, and although I spent most of my time in my room writing, I recognized several men I had dined with on occasion. Why did they all shun us?

Sharp and I came to the same conclusion at the same moment. We were in danger. We didn't speak, but we both examined the room and the space behind us. Someone wanted to do us harm and the people in this room wanted to keep their distance. Damn. I had been hoping Jerimiah's fears were the exaggerated fantasies of a mind scrambled by ill treatment.

Dressed in trail clothes, I was wearing my Army Colt .45 instead of my .38. This was my gun of choice, so I felt comfortable, but Sharp preferred a Winchester. I saw him look toward the stairs and knew he wanted to go to his room and grab his rifle. I wanted him to have it as well, so I nodded toward the stairs. He marched away while I kept a wary eye on the room, then I followed a brief moment later.

In his room we spoke for the first time since scaring Jerimiah away.

"What do you make of that?" I asked.

"Trouble," Sharp said.

"Should I warn Virginia?"

I was really asking myself, but Sharp answered before I did. "She's nappin'. Let her be." He picked up his rifle. "Let's see what we can learn."

With that we went back downstairs. I thought Sharp carrying a rifle would provoke some interest, but everyone continued to ignore us. We were shown to a table and ordered Irish whiskey and the restaurant's specialty, steaks with Béarnaise sauce.

Just after our drinks were served, four self-assured men entered the room and immediately surrounded our table. The easy manner of the men meant danger. Neither Sharp nor I made any provocative moves.

Sharp spoke first. "Gentlemen, if ya have business with us, make it later. We've been waitin' a long time for these steaks."

One of the men briskly said, "Someone wants to see you. We're escorts."

"In the mornin'," Sharp responded.

"Now. I'm afraid we must insist."

Sharp put a hand on the barrel of his rifle that he had leaned against the table. "And just how do you intend on insisting?"

"You want a shoot-out in the middle of a crowded restaurant?" the leader asked. He chuckled. "They won't serve you again."

Before Sharp could respond, I asked, "Who wants to see us?"

"You'll find out when you get there."

"In that case, don't bother coming back in the morning," I said. "I don't meet with people who keep their identity secret."

"Don't make this difficult."

Sharp scooted his chair enough to give him room to stand if necessary. He spoke evenly. "Mister, I plan on makin' it highly difficult."

For a long moment, everyone stared at each other. Two against four were long odds. Especially since these men appeared to know what they were doing. When I scratched my chair back a bit, I noticed no other noise in the crowded room. I'm not sure anyone even breathed.

"We have our orders," the leader said.

"Then by all means, carry them out," Sharp said.

When nothing happened, Sharp slowly stood. I slid my hand until only my fingertips were on the table. Nothing happened. Sharp reached his full height, leaning forward until he was eyeball to eyeball with the leader. His hand still gripped the barrel of his Winchester.

"It's time to fish or cut bait," Sharp said.

"You think you can swing that rifle around faster than I can shoot you? That's crazy."

Sharp said nothing. His calm intensity was breathtaking. Nothing happened. I thought they were on the verge of giving up when I felt motion behind me.

I threw myself backward, ramming my chair into the man standing behind me as I rolled to the floor on my left side and pulled my gun with my right hand. My roll took a second man off his feet and his gun went off in some random direction. I swiveled back toward the man who had been standing behind me. He had regained his balance and was swinging his gun toward me on the floor. I shot him in the chest and came up on one knee to see over the table. I saw the head of the leader explode in a cloud of blood. Sharp's rifle barrel had been under his chin. He had jerked his rifle straight up and pulled the trigger, the entire motion accomplished with his right hand as his left seized his opponent's pistol grip so he couldn't draw. I shot the man across from me who wanted to shoot Sharp, but couldn't get around the leader's body fast enough for a clear shot. I heard Sharp's rifle report as he shot the man I had swept off his feet on my side of the table.

The room had went from silence to ear-splitting booms and back to silence in a matter of seconds. Now, nothing happened. Everything remained still. The scene looked grotesque, with four dead men on the floor and blood and other matter sprayed across walls and patrons. Gun smoke with an acrid odor clouded the room and smarted the eyes. Just when I decided there was no further threat, chaos broke out. Women started screaming. Men groaned. Patrons who had been frozen in shock suddenly bolted from the dining room or slipped and fell, quickly scurrying back to their feet. Dinnerware and glasses shattered as they hit the floor. Men shoved women out of the way. One man leaned down to help his wife back up and slipped on the oozy floor to collapse beside his wife. In a flash, they were both up and out of the room.

In less than a minute, the restaurant was empty.

I looked at Sharp with a raised eyebrow. "Whole?"

He actually looked down at himself before answering. "Yep. Yourself?"

I nodded that I was okay.

Sharp glanced toward the kitchen. "Damn, I hope the cooks didn't run off. Sure could use that steak."

Chapter 13

After the fight, we picked up our glasses and moved to a clean table to wait for the marshal. No one came out of the kitchen with steaks—or more whiskey, for that matter. The first person to burst through the door was not the law, but Virginia. She looked relieved to see us alive, then horrified as she surveyed the blood-bath. After a quick hug for each of us, she walked over and examined the bodies.

She looked back at us over her shoulder. "Do you know these men?"

"Never laid eyes on 'em," Sharp said.

I nodded agreement.

She walked back to our table. "Any more whiskey?"

Sharp volunteered by traipsing into the kitchen.

Virginia sat down, staring back at the bodies. She appeared terrified and angry at the same time. She looked me in the eye and her expression turned worried.

"Would Jenny hire men to kill you?"

I shrugged. "I don't know. There was very little conversation before the shooting started."

She looked back at the bodies. "Were you lucky or good?"

"A bit of both. Sharp and I acted on instinct and somehow we each knew what the other would do." I reviewed the carnage in front of me. "It was close."

"Steve, how will you find out who's behind this?"

I waved at the bodies. "Not from them." When I saw she disapproved of my flippancy, I quickly added, "I hope the marshal will tell us something . . . or give us a clue."

She glanced at the door. "Where is he?"

"That, my dear, is a damn good question." Sharp said this as he returned from the kitchen with a bottle of Jameson's and a fresh glass for Virginia.

As he poured drinks, I said, "Four gunshots and dozens of panicky people scattering onto the streets. When I stayed here last, a guest threatened to punch the innkeeper and a deputy marshal was here within minutes. What do you make of it, Jeff?"

Sharp downed his whiskey in a single gulp. He thought. Poured another glass. "Either the marshal purposely made himself scarce . . . or he's outside waitin' for his deputies before confronting deadly gunfighters."

Virginia stood and squared her shoulders. "I'll find out." She saw I was about to object, so she added, "They won't shoot a woman, but they may shoot you two."

Her reasoning made sense, so I watched her go. She returned almost immediately.

"They're massing an army out there. Stay put and I'll tell them you'll come out unarmed."

"Will we?" I asked Sharp.

"Yep. No real choice."

"We could sit here and finish that bottle."

"We could, but I want to see mornin'."

We looked at each other a moment, and then nodded at Virginia. With no further words she again left. I noticed she had not taken a sip of her drink. Probably better not to have whiskey on her breath when she talked to the marshal. I checked my pocket watch. If she did not come back in ten minutes, I intended to go out and get her.

She returned in five minutes.

"You're going to have to spend the night in jail. Probably no more, he said. The marshal hasn't gotten a single witness to tell him what happened." Her eyes turned pleading. "He gave his word he would keep you safe."

"What do ya think?" Sharp asked her.

"He seems genuinely befuddled." She paused. "I don't know. He could be lying to get you locked up." She looked at the door and repeated. "I don't know."

Sharp stood and left his rifle leaning against the table, so I unhooked my gun belt and laid it on the table.

Sharp started for the door, but I stopped him with a hand on his forearm. "Let Virginia go first." I turned to her. "Tell them we're coming out unarmed. Stand beside the marshal. Tell him you'll follow our party to jail. Be an obvious witness. Then as soon as we're locked up, go find Claude Jansen. He's my lawyer in Carson City. He has an office in the building next door, but he'll likely be in the street with all this commotion. Find him and tell him to get over to the jail. I want to depend on more than the marshal's word for our safety."

She nodded understanding before saying, "I'll yell when it's clear for you to come out."

"Did I ever tell you I loved you?"

"You better love me. I'm facing twenty twitchy trigger fingers out there. I've been shot once and prefer not to revisit the experience."

We kissed lightly and she carefully approached the door. She yelled that she was coming out, and then I heard the marshal order his men to hold fire.

I turned to Sharp. "Now what?"

He poured another drink. "Like ya said, we finish the bottle."

Chapter 14

We only had time for one drink before Virginia yelled that it was safe for us to come out into the street. When we stepped onto the hotel veranda, I felt more vulnerable than when we were surrounded by four men intent on escorting us to parts unknown. Could this be my destiny: Winning gunfights against supposed experts and then getting killed by some nervous citizen helping out a baffled marshal?

No. At least not on this day. There were more than twenty guns aimed at us, mostly rifles. It seemed that every man who hadn't been in the dining room had come running with a trusty gun, eager for a little excitement. The marshal kept control with barked orders. As soon as his deputy confirmed we were unarmed, he told everyone to return to their business. Then he told us we were going to jail until he sorted things out. He was polite, but firm.

After he personally inspected the dining room, the marshal ordered the undertaker to clean up the mess. He then gave orders for his deputies to interview witnesses. With Virginia trailing closely behind, he alone marched us down the street to his office.

I had never seen the man before, so I asked how long he had been the town marshal.

"Four months," he answered. "But I know you gentlemen, you have big reputations." He walked about four paces before adding, "Bigger now."

"Did ya know those men we left in the restaurant?" Sharp asked.

"You mean those dead men? I've seen them around. Hired guns, I suspect. Talked tough . . . but I guess they weren't so tough."

"Know who they work for?" Sharp asked.

"No . . . but I have suspicions."

"Will ya tell us?" Sharp asked.

"Nope."

"Man or woman?" I asked.

"If I answered that, I'd be telling you, wouldn't I. I've got no evidence to back my suspicions."

He, of course, had just told us; in a way where he couldn't be held at fault if he was wrong. He was smart and confident. Good attributes for a lawman.

"What's your name?" I asked.

"Matt Wilson, but you can call me sir."

"Yes, sir," I answered.

The jail was a barred enclosure at the back of the marshal's office. Carson City must be tame because there was only one cell. The entire furnishings comprised two narrow beds with a bedpan set between them. Wilson waved us through the open door and then clanked it shut.

After locking the cell, he unceremoniously threw the keys on his desk.

"Sorry for the poor accommodation . . . and don't break out. I've been after the city to strengthen the jail with a new coat of whitewash."

Sharp laughed at the probably oft-repeated joke, and then made a show of rattling the bars as if to confirm their sturdiness.

Virginia had been quietly watching the whole proceedings. Now the marshal faced her, arms akimbo.

"If you intend to stay, keep away from that cell," Wilson said.

"Now that they're secure, I'll go find Mr. Jansen," Virginia said.

"Claude Jansen?" the marshal asked.

"He's my attorney," I said from the cell.

His expression showed contemplation. "So, at least the rich part of the rumors must be true. Claude's the most expensive attorney in Nevada."

"Yep, the rich part's true, but the rest is hokum," Sharp chuckled.

"I hope so, or you boys sure have a penchant for trouble." He returned his attention to Virginia. "You'll find him in his office next to the St. Charles. Tell him to get over here. I want to talk to him."

After Virginia left, the marshal sat in a wooden swivel chair behind his desk and put his feet up. Rocking gently, he continued to contemplate us.

No one spoke, which must have been a hardship for Sharp.

After a bit, Wilson said, "You both have a history in this town. I suppose that means you know all the highfalutin people."

"We do . . . including Jenny Bolton."

"Well, that's pretty highfalutin, to be sure." His rocking was as smooth as a metronome. "Make any enemies hereabouts?"

I wasn't buying the good ol' boy routine. Wilson was clever, but he slipped occasionally, like when he used the word *penchant*. He was educated, probably some college. He was also careful. He wanted information, but he wasn't going to give away anything until he got the lay of the land. He obviously knew about us, but I wasn't sure how much he knew. I expect he knew we were generally law abiding because he showed no fear in escorting us to jail while his deputies questioned witnesses. In point of fact, he had told his deputies to do the routine interviews while he questioned the key witnesses— us. Despite the casual, friendly demeanor, I realized that this was an interrogation. My respect for the man grew.

"Shooting Sean Washburn may have displeased some," I answered, lightly.

"Seems a long time to hold a grudge." His measured rocking continued unabated. "Do anything else to anger anyone?"

"Ya mean like rescuin' our friend Jerimiah down in Pickhandle Gulch?" Sharp said. "Never knew for sure who was behind that."

"Really?" He just swayed back and forth before following up with, "Any inklings?"

"I don't repeat loose talk," Sharp answered.

"Well, you boys think on it. Somebody wanted to do you harm."

At that moment, Virginia and Jansen burst into the office. Jansen appeared overly pleased to see us, which raised an alarm because he certainly didn't need paying clients.

"Jeff, Steve, it's good to see you safe. I heard you had some trouble, but I don't think you'll be in here long. Right, marshal?"

"We need corroborating witnesses and we can set them free until trial."

"Good, because we need them free to help us," Jansen said.

"Free to help who?" I asked.

"Me, Governor Bradshaw, a few others. . . . Richard used to be one of us, but he was killed. Is that what brought you back to Carson City?"

"We got a telegram from Jerimiah about it," I answered. "Claimed he was in danger as well."

"Jerimiah?" Jansen waved his hand. "No one cares about him. No matter, it got you back here. I don't know why we didn't wire you ourselves."

"What's goin' on?" Sharp demanded in a stern voice.

"Jenny Bolton. Jenny's what's going on. She's out to take over the state. Got her hands on everything except the governor. Bradshaw brought in Matt here to help, but it's not enough." He shrugged. "Hell, half of his deputies are on her payroll. Problem is which half."

Now I knew why Wilson took us to jail by himself. He didn't trust his own deputies. I asked myself if I wanted to get involved. If Jerimiah was safe, I didn't need to get dragged into the quicksand of Nevada politics. The state had been nothing but trouble for me and nothing stayed resolved. Bad apples kept popping up like targets at a carnival shooting booth.

While I wallowed in regret, Sharp asked a good question.

"What're the chances of a fair trial?"

Wilson and Jansen looked at each other with forlorn expressions.

Jansen gave us the bad news. "There's nothing fair in this state."

Chapter 15

The marshal released us the next morning, but the reprieve would only last a few weeks until our trial. Jansen promised to try for an extension, but his expression didn't convey hope.

In fact, it took the governor's intervention to set bail because the town council wanted us locked up until proven innocent.

Sharp, Virginia, and I met the governor and Jansen for the midday meal after our release from jail. The St. Charles restaurant had been scrubbed spotless and the table cloths gleamed as white as sheets freshly delivered from a mill. Despite the hard work of the hotel staff, Bradshaw had arranged a private room for our luncheon.

After taking our respective seats, Bradshaw opened by saying, "I hope this meal is less eventful than our last."

"Me, as well," I said. "I'm not sure we'd be so lucky a second time."

"I didn't mean yesterday," Bradshaw said. "I was referring to our meal when you convinced me to run for governor."

"If I recall, ya turned us down flat," Sharp said. "Sean Washburn convinced ya to run."

Bradshaw smiled. "Afterwards, you did a fine job of dispatching Mr. Washburn. We may need services of that particular nature again."

"That's not why we came to Nevada," I said, irritated. "In fact, now that we see Jerimiah's safe, we have no further business here."

"You may wish that were so, but you know it isn't," Bradshaw said. "Like it or not, you're in the thick of it. With the courts in this state, you'll have a better chance of leaving Nevada if you put away that damn Jenny Bolton before the trial."

No one spoke for a long moment.

Finally, I asked, "What does *put away* look like?"

"Jail or the graveyard . . . makes no difference to me. All I know is that for you to go free, I need to be back in control. I need the senate and assembly pliable to my will again. Right now, they're scared shitless—of someone else for damn sake. That I can't abide. I can repair the courts, but I need my nominations confirmed. I can make this state lawful, but I need my appointments and budget approved. I could call on Federal resources, but Washington believes this entire state is a hopeless mess. In other words, I need Jennifer Bolton out of my way."

Sharp shook his head. "Beggin' yer pardon, governor, but even if we *dispatch* Jenny this very afternoon, none of that's gonna help us."

"Oh, ye of little faith," Bradshaw chuckled. "You'd be surprised how fast a bunch of cowardly politicians turn. With the legislature behind me, the judges will kiss my ring. Your case will never go to trial. Trust me. Corral that wench and all of our problems will be behind us."

"How old is that wench?" Virginia asked.

Bradshaw looked annoyed at the interruption. "I'm not sure, ma'am." He smiled kindly. "I'm not sure anyone really knows."

"I heard she is under twenty . . . with no formal education," Virginia said, innocently. "How did she manage to emasculate you?"

I thought lunch might be over. Bradshaw turned crimson. Spittle sprayed the table as he sputtered incomplete sentences. After a moment, Bradshaw laid his hands flat on the table and visibly struggled to regain control.

"Mrs. Baker, I believe?"

"Yes, sir."

"If I may, these affairs are best left to men."

"Governor, my fiancée and I work together . . . or not at all," I interjected.

Bradshaw didn't look pleased, but his expression turned resigned when I kept firm eye contact with him. I believe we were past the moment when Virginia decided to throw salt into the wound she had inflicted.

"Leave it to the men, you say? It appears a wee girl has made mincemeat of your famed political organization." She flipped a napkin onto her lap. Looking up again, she added, "Perhaps you need a woman on your side in this brawl."

Jansen tried to lighten the mood. "A woman's perspective might be helpful, governor. Heaven knows, we men have had a tough time figuring her out."

"I don't need to figure her out," Bradshaw said angrily. "It's obvious. She wants the state and everything in it. She owns the largest ranch hereabouts and the Cattlemen's Association kowtows to her. The legislature is in her pocket after Richard's killing. They're all a bunch of cowards. A company she owns has interest in several Virginia City mines, and she's out to collar the timber industry which will give her leverage over the other mine owners. She even started a detective agency to compete with the Pinkertons, but I believe it's just a subterfuge to hire thugs. She may be shrewd and relentless . . . but she *is not* mysterious."

"Did she acquire it all legally?" Sharp asked.

"Legal? Damn it, Jeff, that woman came from nowhere and in two years became the most powerful person in this state. How could she have done it legal? You saw her handiwork in Pickhandle Gulch: corrupting local politics, stealing businesses, beating people. Hard to pin anything on her, but it was Bolton all right. Now she's picking up speed like a locomotive halfway out of the station. That's too much power in one person's hand. It's not natural." He banged the table with the flat of his hand. "Women don't know how to wield power!"

Virginia's eyes never wavered from Bradshaw. "Except in this case, as I think you just made clear."

"Jennifer Bolton is no ordinary woman . . . and she hasn't *emasculated* me." Bradshaw caught himself before he launched into another tirade.

He took a deep breath and suddenly wore the calm façade he had shown during our encounter with Washburn. "This contest will eventually work out in my favor, but I'm concerned for your fiancé who only has a couple weeks. The purpose of this meeting is to protect him, not me."

"Governor, I remember our last meal in this hotel," I said. "You were confident Washburn could never wrest control of this state from your hands. You said you were going to wring that strutting peacock's neck. He never intimidated you. Yet Jenny succeeded where Washburn failed. My fiancée may have used an indelicate term, but her question is valid." I waited a beat. "Sir, how did Jennifer Bolton grab the reins of power away from you?"

An unusually proud man suddenly looked beaten. He spent an inordinate amount of time smoothing out the table cloth in front of him. When he spoke, he sounded downhearted.

He muttered something, but the only word I heard clearly was ruthless.

"Excuse me?" I said.

"I said she's ruthless. She'll do anything. No scruples whatsoever. She's mad. Nothing restrains her: not morals, not ethics, and certainly not gentlemen's rules. Political niceties mean nothing to her. She just knocks everything out of her way—all the while wearing that goddamn sweet little smile that says be nice to me and maybe we can go to bed together." He shook his head. "She grabbed the reins of power because I underestimated her. I was stupid. Stupid. I saw her as a pretty, lascivious little girl who didn't have a brain or even a rudimentary education." He slammed the table again, this time with a fist. "Yes, if you need to hear it, she made a fool of me."

"She wants something. Not just power, something more," Virginia said to herself.

I answered Virginia's musings. "Revenge. She wants revenge. She's been treated shabbily . . . worse. She's like a steam engine building pressure enough to explode." I softened my tone. "You were fooled, governor, but so was I. She may act like a flirty young girl without a care, but behind that guise is a disturbing force. She's steadfast . . . unwavering. I fear she's out to get even with a world that has used and abused her."

"But that still doesn't answer how," Jansen said. "Governor, capable men have possessed her ambitions, only to be brushed aside with the back of your hand." He looked at me. "You know her. How do you think she pulled off this usurpation?"

"She's clever as hell, but more important; her three tutors gave her an education unobtainable in the finest schools."

"What three tutors?" Jansen asked.

"Her husband, her mother-in-law, and another

woman also named Jenny who taught her to read and write and figure."

I explained that Jenny's husband, John Bolton, had been a shrewd businessman as well as president of the state senate. He spurned risky mining ventures to concentrate on timber, banking, and railroads; all things mine owners needed to extract their ore. Washburn, the largest mine operator in the state, had hired an assassin to murder Bolton when he declared his candidacy for governor.

Her mother-in-law, a bitter woman, ran the family's ranching empire, which showed Jenny that women had the wherewithal to boss tough men doing tough jobs. The older Mrs. Bolton also treated Jenny with such contempt that it fanned her anger until it encompassed not just men, but the entire world.

Finally, a tutor, who had taught the children of the rich and powerful, gave Jenny private lessons. Jenny was an eager learner and her book smarts should not be underestimated.

From a business perspective, her husband hardly acknowledged her existence, but she was always around because John Bolton would never leave his wife at the ranch with his mother. Unbeknownst to her husband, she was watching . . . and calculating. Nevada was not much more than rock, except that Virginia City and a few other districts possessed a very special kind of rock. To date, over three hundred million dollars of gold and silver had been mined from the Comstock Lode, and that wasn't counting the other mines scattered around the state. Many guessed that nearly half as much more may have been secreted away from the government and shareholders. Big amounts of money attract carnivorous predators. Jenny intended to devour them all.

After I finished, Virginia said, "Jenny's more than a power broker."

"What do ya mean?" Sharp asked.

"I mean she's dangerous . . . lethally dangerous."

Chapter 16

As soon as we closed the door to our suite, Virginia exclaimed, "I can't believe you supported that puffed-up nincompoop for governor?"

"At the time, I thought I needed someone beholden to me in the governor's office. Bradshaw was the only candidate that had a chance of winning on short notice. In the end, I didn't need him because I found a different solution."

"You mean you gunned down Sean Washburn."

"He hired an assassin to kill me and would have again. I had no choice. I told you all about this. Why are you angry?"

She stomped around, and then whirled in my direction, arms akimbo. "That man is a sore on the planet, but that's not it."

"Then what is it?"

"Your relationship with Jenny. I want the truth. If you tell me the truth, I can live with it, but I won't abide deceit. Did you go to bed with her? And if you did, was she still married?"

"We never went to bed together. I was infatuated with her, but nothing came of it. Not even a kiss on the damn cheek. I went to her ranch to court her, but she turned me away. I saw her again when I brought her mother-in-law's body back to be buried, but that time I spurned her. It took a while, but I realized I was attracted to the person I believed her to be, not the person she really was. I never gave her another thought after that . . . except to run away when she started to take over the state. That's when Sharp and I rode down to Arizona Territory."

"You have no feelings for her anymore? Is that what you're telling me?"

"That's what I'm telling you. Virginia, I love *you*. I never loved Jenny. I was smitten for a time perhaps, but no more." I did some pacing of my own. "In truth, I still retain one feeling for her. Fear. You're right, she's dangerous. Really dangerous. The kind of danger I may not be able to defeat with guns or wits or wealth . . . because she has all three as well . . . maybe more than

112

me." I quit pacing and looked into Virginia's eyes. "I think we should get the hell out of Nevada. I have a bad feeling. I'm afraid terrible things will happen if we don't leave. Let's catch the morning train."

"You can't. The trial."

"I'll never come back to Nevada. They won't chase me. Let's go. Now. We'll head for Durango and get married. We don't need this."

"Don't fool yourself. If Jenny runs this state, they'll come after you. Didn't she already send four men to fetch you? I'm sure she has others at hand."

"Those men came after us because she believed Jeff and I returned to help the governor, otherwise she doesn't care about me. We can't underestimate her, but we shouldn't overestimate her either. She wants power, not some personal vendetta against me. I never did anything to harm her."

"I thought you spurned her."

"So what? She didn't care. Besides, she rejected me first."

"This woman might be crazy. You have no idea what rejection meant to her. She—"

A loud rap at the door stopped Virginia midsentence. When I threw open the door, I backstepped twice in shock. Standing before me wearing a fetching smile was Jenny Bolton.

"Are you going to invite me in?" she asked with a teasing tone.

She wore a chirpy yellow patterned calico dress with short puffy sleeves and a daring two-piece neckline held in together with delicate drawstrings. She looked ready to snatch a beau at a barn dance.

I remained in shock as I waved her into the suite.

She bounced into the room with all the joy of a teenager being allowed out on her own for the first time. She looked young and fresh, perhaps mid-teens, but I knew she must be approaching twenty. Her delicate complexion was set off by excited emerald eyes. Fetchingly pretty, any man would instantly want to know her. Like the first time I saw her, she beamed wonderment with an openness that suggested unsoiled innocence, but this time I knew it was a façade. I had seen her kill and birth a calf with equal indifference.

"Mrs. Jenny Bolton, may I introduce my fiancée, Mrs. Virginia Baker."

To my surprise, Jenny flew to Virginia and hugged her like a long lost friend, all the while exclaiming how happy she was I had found someone to marry. Then she pushed us together, shoulder to shoulder, saying she wanted to see us together. Standing with an outstretched hand on either of our shoulders, she went on about what a handsome couple we made. Finally, she dropped her hands to her side and exhaled slowly and smiled at us like we were three friends reconnected in the very best of circumstances.

"I'm so happy for you, Steve," she said. "Mrs. Baker fits you like a glove. I hope you have a chance to be happy together."

"A chance?" I asked.

"Oh, you know, the trial and all." She brushed the difficulty away with the back of her hand like it was a pesky fly. "You *are* beautiful, Mrs. Baker. Steve's a lucky man."

"Thank you," Virginia said. "I'm pleased to meet you, as well. Steve has talked so much about you."

"Really?" She adopted a naughty glint. "Considering how close we were, I'm surprised he mentioned me."

Virginia cocked her head. "He said you never were . . . shall I say, physically close."

Jenny laughed uproariously. When she calmed enough to speak, she asked, "You mean sex?" Then she laughed some more. "Sex isn't close. Look around. It's happening all over. Raising livestock depends on sex. My ranch would go bankrupt if my animals weren't so eager to copulate. No . . . sex is nothing special. Just nature. What Steve and I had was much more intimate."

"And that was?" Virginia demanded.

Stunned, I could hardly wait for the answer.

"He killed for me," she said, matter-of-factly.

"Killed for you?" Virginia sounded incredulous.

"Two men. He killed them right off for having

115

sex with me without my permission. Three men, if you count Sean Washburn . . . and I do. You can have sex hundreds of times with one man or once with a hundred men—it's all meaningless. It's nature's way of keeping us animals coming down the chute. The act is short. A brief moment of lust, and then it's over. But killing . . . killing's permanent . . . the most intimate act imaginable. Nothing shows greater affection for another person, and Steve has done it for me three times." She smiled coyly at me. "Go ahead, take him to your bed, but I know the truth. He cares for me far more than you."

"If you cared for him, why did you send men to kill him?"

She laughed again. Not a cackle, but a laugh of merriment. She saw the question as genuinely funny.

"I would never kill Steve. We're too close. Weren't you listening? Steve and Jeff killed those men for no reason. No reason, whatsoever." She laughed some more. "I would never kill one of my bulls. Never. They're far too valuable. A cow is a different matter entirely. If a cow fails to behave properly, I kill and eat it. That's nature's way. I've witnessed it in every kind of animal." She winked at me. "The strong eat the weak. Always have, always will."

"And you're determined to be the strongest?" Virginia asked.

She looked surprised at the question. "I don't intend to be eaten." She twirled, billowing her dress. "Now, if you'll excuse me, I have business to attend to."

She waved a friendly goodbye and almost skipped out of the door.

We both stood stunned for a long moment.

Finally, I asked, "What do you think?"

"She's loonier than my aunt . . . who we put away in a home."

Chapter 17

W e need to find Jeff so we can get out of here," I said, heading for the door.

"No," Virginia said.

I whirled around on her. "We're not staying. Didn't you hear what she said? She's not after me now, she's after you."

"I heard. I'm not stupid. I'm supposed to be the cow failing to behave properly. But that's why we need to stay. You said it yourself; she's relentless. If she wants me, she's going to come after me. I'd rather face her than look over my shoulder."

"And how do you propose we fight her? Politically? As you say, our only ally is a puffed-up nincompoop. Attack her businesses? As far as I can tell, her businesses are not vulnerable and anyone with commercial stature is aligned with her. Guns? Sorry, I can't just walk up and shoot a girl . . . and neither can you."

"You're underestimating us. We're a good pair. That nincompoop *is* the governor. Jansen's the best lawyer in the state, and I think the marshal will support us. We have Jeff and his friends. We can even wire McAllen if need be." She started to get excited. "We can beat her if we fight her way. First, we show no animosity. We're all just friends. Then we focus on making the governor stronger. I don't know how, but I'm sure we can figure something out. Scout out the businessmen in town and find allies. Ask Jansen what crimes she may have committed. Next, see the local Pinkerton agent and get us some detectives and a few guards."

I felt exasperated. "It would be easier to skedaddle."

"She would hang over our heads forever . . . and you might end up getting hung." She hugged me and nestled her head in my chest. Her voice was muffled, but I heard her next words clear enough. "Steve, I want that bitch's head hanging over *my* mantle."

I pushed her out to arm's length. "She riled you, didn't she?"

"That was her intent . . . and she succeeded. This is a feud, and like all feuds, it won't go away easy. It's better to win than to run. It's the only way to end this."

"I'll go along on one condition," I said. "When this is over, we leave Nevada and never return. Okay?"

"Okay."

I pulled her back to me and we embraced for several minutes without another word. Slowly I pulled her arms from around my chest and started to pace. She watched me without interruption.

"The key is to put her away for her crimes," I finally said. "I can't shoot a woman, so the Washburn solution won't work, and despite what the governor said, it'll take months to shake her tentacles free of the political apparatus. So . . . Jansen, the Pinkertons, and the marshal are first on the list."

I stopped pacing in front of her. "I know that's what you just said, but I'm getting it straight in my own head. Bradshaw said Jenny opened a detective agency. I need to talk secretly with the local Pinkerton agent and have him bring more men to Carson City. He can say it's to protect his turf against this interloper agency, not to protect us or investigate Jenny. That way we can continue to pretend we're all friends. I'll talk to Jansen and by the time they get here, I'll have a list of crimes for them to investigate. What am I forgetting?"

"The marshal," Virginia said.

"Good. He should have a bead on Jenny's troublemaking. Anything else?"

"Talk to Jerimiah?"

"Can't hurt. Maybe a loon can tell us what another loon is up to. Besides, I need to say hello proper." I paced the tiny room again. "This gives Jeff and me a full plate. What about you?"

"I've been around politicians all my life. I understand them like an insider."

"City or state?" I asked.

"Mostly state and national. The elitc of Philadelphia considered it their duty to guide the political class."

"Do you know people on the national scene?"

"Why?"

"The best way to bribe a local politician is with national office."

"Steve, the men I know would be obligated to inform my family about any contact. I'm not sure I can accept that."

She looked anxious for the first time. Like me, she was estranged from her relatives. We each had run away from our respective families for similar reasons. Virginia had married outside her class and followed her husband to the wilds of Leadville, Colorado. I felt drained by my family's financial shenanigans and attempts to marry me off to a society heiress to increase the reach of the Dancy clan. Virginia's family had disowned

120

her for cavorting with a man below her station, while I had disowned my family for trying to dictate every aspect of my life. Actually, to be more accurate, I hadn't disowned them so much as ignored their existence.

"Is there no one who sympathized with your choice of husband?" I asked.

She sat down with her hands in her lap, sitting erect, like a child waiting to be reprimanded for breaking her father's favorite pipe. She remained still so I left the room to let her be alone with her thoughts.

When I returned from using the hall privy, she appeared more relaxed.

All she said was, "I need to send a telegram, but we need to talk first."

"How uncomfortable does reconnecting with your family make you?" I asked.

"Less uncomfortable than dying or seeing you die. Don't worry, I've been intending on mending this fence for months. This just gives me the courage to do what I should have done all along." She gave me a direct look. "My uncle is chairman of the House Ways and Means Committee."

That took me aback. "Boy, your family really is connected. That's the most powerful committee in Congress."

"As a child, I was his favorite niece, but he sided with the family when they ostracized me. It hurt. It still hurts. I cared about him more than I cared about my mother or father. Saw more of him. I guess I thought he'd understand."

"What are you going to say?"

"That's what we need to talk about, Steve. I finally came to understand that my uncle harbored ambitions far beyond what a child could grasp. He loved me, but he loved power more."

"I understand," was all I could think to say.

"But you don't know the price of getting back in his good graces."

"Tell me."

"I need to announce that I'm engaged to a Dancy."

I opened my mouth to object, but slammed it shut. If I encouraged her to use her family, how could I object to her using mine? But I didn't want my family to know I intended to marry someone with the qualifications they desired for my spouse. It would be admitting they won. But Virginia was in the same predicament. Damn it. My rebellion would be for naught.

Then I had a thought that made me smile. They would only think they won. Virginia did come from a society family, but she carved out her own space in this world. Except for blood, she was nothing like what my family wanted for me in a wife. And what did it matter anyway. They lived on the east coast and we intended to traipse around the frontier. Besides, I treasured imagining my mother's expression when she learned Virginia came from a Philadelphia family with haughty credentials, especially after her rudeness to her when we had visited New York. If we ever returned east, Virginia and I could enjoy a private game of pretend. They had pushed, used, and manipulated me my entire life, and it was time to get something from them in return.

"Why are you smiling?" Virginia asked. "I thought you'd be livid."

"Tell them. It can't change our lives. We don't like our families, but they're ours. It's how we grew up. We can run away, but nothing will change that. We are who we are . . . and yet we love each other. I'm happy for the first time since my father died." She smiled now. "Listen, I just realized that I no longer get satisfaction from snubbing my mother and the rest of them, so we might as well reconcile so they can do us some good for a change. Besides, it gives us an advantage over Jenny."

"What advantage?"

"Remember I said she has guns, wits, and wealth, just like us. But she's alone. She has no family. No one she can draw on."

"Our families may not appreciate us barging back in."

"Bull. They'll welcome us with open arms because they'll think we're doing what they wanted all along."

"So, you're okay with this?"

I nodded.

"Walk me to the telegraph office?"

"Of course, I need to send my own telegram. It's time we announced our engagement to our families."

We locked arms and laughed our way to the door, but before I opened it, Virginia added another item to our list of actions.

"Steve, I want another shooting lesson."

That caught me by surprise. "When?"

"Today."

Chapter 18

After visiting the Western Union office, I decided to see Jerimiah even though I had previously decided that Jansen and Pinkerton were my first order of business. Jerimiah had been right about the danger in the dining room, so he might have something more to offer. I suggested to Virginia that she watch the Nevada legislative proceeding to get familiar with the politicians we had to convert back to the governor's side. She readily agreed, saying she missed the drama of politics. We're all creatures of our upbringing.

I found Sharp in the same room where we had lunched with Bradshaw. He had never left. He seemed content with an unfinished bottle on the table and a comely maid who had come in to clean up after us—the two things he loved most in life. When I entered, they were sitting cheek to cheek trading innocent lies and not so innocent suggestions. We're all creatures of our upbringing.

"Mr. Sharp, may I have a word?"

"Yep. Need to stretch my legs anyway."

The maid jumped up and scurried out of the room.

I had to wait until she disappeared around a doorjamb before Sharp's attention left her undulating backside. He grinned when he looked at me. The simple things in life made Sharp happy.

"Business concluded?" I asked.

"Will be." He stood, ready to leave. "By the way, I have dinner plans, so whatever ya got better be quick."

I waved him back into his seat to explain our surprise get-together with Jenny. Sharp agreed with our plans and volunteered to find his old security foreman that used to protect his mines and ore shipments. Sharp had heard he worked in Virginia City, so he didn't believe he would be hard to find.

On our way to Jerimiah's boarding house, Sharp asked, "Do ya really think Jenny would hire someone to go after Virginia?"

"Not sure. What scares me is that she throws around little threats like her mother-in-law used to. Veiled, but the meaning's clear enough. And the older Mrs. Bolton always followed through."

"Damn, I think yer right. Can ya get Virginia out of here? Maybe she could visit San Francisco."

"She said she wants to face Jenny rather than run. Hard to argue against with my history."

"Then we better get her some protection."

"Someone she knows about, and a few she doesn't."

"Good thinkin'. She's too proud to remain wrapped in bodyguards."

"I'm taking her shooting when we get back to the hotel," I said, offhandedly.

"She ain't as bad as she once was, but she ain't good."

"It makes her feel safer."

"Practice never hurts. Perhaps I should go with ya and give her rifle pointers."

"Good idea for another day. By the time we go, it will be late and daylight won't last. Besides, if I remember correctly, you have plans."

"Yep, slipped my mind."

"Not a chance," I quipped, to be rewarded with a chuckle from Sharp.

We stopped for a moment in front of Jerimiah's boarding house. The clapboard affair needed sweeping, painting, and groundwork. After we climbed the porch, a resident sunning himself directed us to the first room at the top of some squeaky stairs. I wondered if Jerimiah picked the room so he could hear anyone coming. It would be consistent with his skittish nature.

After knocking and calling out our names, I heard a creaking bed, footfalls, and then a key unlocking the door. If possible, Jerimiah looked more disheveled than before. He hadn't shaved or bathed and his clothes desperately needed washing. The room smelled of sweat, tobacco, and an unemptied chamber pot.

Without preamble, he waved us into his modest abode.

"Hell, Jerimiah, this place reeks," Sharp said, unconcerned about insulting an old friend. "And ya don't smell too pleasant yerself."

"I'm not sitting alone in that bathroom."

"Order a hot tub and we'll mind ya," Sharp said, lifting his rifle up so Jerimiah saw it. "They got a maid in this fine establishment?"

"I don't need a maid."

"Ya do, and sayin' ya don't leads me to question the wellbein' of yer mind. I remember when ya were a tidy man."

Jerimiah looked around as if seeing his room for the first time. "It'll cost two bits . . . maybe more 'cuz it's such a mess."

"I'll pay," I said. "You shouldn't live in this squalor."

Sharp leaned his head out the door and yelled for a maid. She came immediately from the room next door and he instructed her to heat water for a bath and then clean Jerimiah's room. When she looked doubtfully into the room, Sharp made a give-it-to-me motion with his hand, so I flipped him a silver dollar. The woman reminded me of a droopy-eyed basset hound, but Sharp set about charming her anyway, offering up the dollar as if he was presenting a precious pearl to a beautiful princess.

After she left to heat water, Sharp said, "Your room will be scrubbed with clean sheets in short order."

"Do you charm all women?" I asked.

"Can't say that I do." He paused dramatically. "Try like hell though."

Turning back to Jerimiah, I asked, "Do you have any other clothes?"

He pointed at a pile tossed carelessly in a corner. I told him to pick them up and we'd take them to the wash house around the corner. After he bundled them under his arm, we gratefully left his room. We made a stop at a general store and I bought Jerimiah a clean set of clothes to put on after his bath. I planned on throwing away what he was wearing at the moment. When we returned, the bath was ready, so Sharp and I drew chairs up to the tub and waited for Jerimiah to get settled into the scalding water.

"Why do you think Richard was murdered?" I asked. "There were plenty of errant shots."

"Those random shots were meant to disguise an

assassination," Jerimiah said. "The first shot was aimed carefully, and it hit Richard in the chest."

"How do ya know that?" Sharp asked.

"I know a man who saw it. Said the gunman weaved a bit, but looked to be playacting. Stopped, drew a bead through the window of Richard's print shop and fired once. Then he started lurching around like he was drunk and shooting every which way. Soon he mounted a nearby horse and rode off with all the skill of a Pony Express rider. Lickety-split, he was gone, never to be seen hereabouts again."

He sunk down to his chin and used two hands to scrub his face.

"What man told ya this?" Sharp asked.

"Gone too. Bet they kilt him 'cuz he saw it. If they know he told me, they'd want me dead too, so keep an eye on that door."

"What was his name? Who was he?" I asked.

"Ben somethin'. I just saw him around. Ranch hand, I think. Not a miner."

"Do ya have an inklin' who might have been behind this assassination?"

"Everybody knows. Jenny Bolton wanted Richard dead because he wrote 'bout her in ways she didn't like. She acts all pretty and sweet, but the devil's got a hold on that woman."

"Were you and Richard still friendly?" I asked.

"Only friend I had, but he got a big head, bein' a senator and all. We didn't eat or drink together.

He dined with politicians and newspapermen."

"Maybe ya shoulda bathed more often," Sharp said.

"I did before the shootin' . . . every week. I'm not crazy."

I wasn't so sure. "So people knew you and Richard were friends?"

"We didn't keep it a secret. Why?"

"Did it occur to you that someone wanted that story about the shooting spread around town?"

"Why would anyone want that?"

"To scare the bejesus out of the other legislators."

Chapter 19

O ur visit with Jansen went quick. He didn't sound hopeful, but promised to put together a list of crimes the Pinkerton reinforcements could investigate. Jansen doubted that Jenny had made a discoverable mistake because she kept herself separated from actual wrongdoers.

Good food, expensive lawyers, fine haber-dashers, and other *services* congregated around capitals, so we found the one-man Pinkerton office around the corner from Jansen. The Pinkerton agent introduced himself as Thomas Copley, and he displayed the ingratiating brand of congeniality common to politicians. In fact, he couldn't be more different than the taciturn McAllen, who could stop an assailant with a hard look. Copley, in his mid-thirties, had enjoyed far too many meals with politicians. He was soft and round and would never intimidate anyone.

His tiny office was spartanly furnished with a maple table, comfortable chairs, and walls covered with autographed photographs of state politicians. I made a quick survey, but didn't see Richard's picture on display. A single Winchester in need of cleaning and oil rested in a wall-mounted rifle rack that could hold a half-dozen rifles.

"What can I do for you gentlemen?" Copley asked after introductions.

"What do you know about the killing of Senator Richard Wade?" I asked to get a read on Copley.

"Not much. I understand you two were friends. You have my sympathies."

"You know who we are?" I asked.

"Of course. I'm new to this posting, but I've read the last two years' worth of newspapers. You two figured prominently in many stories. I've also heard gossip."

Sharp asked right out, "Do ya work for Jenny Bolton?"

"No. The practice of this office is mostly political. The Pinkerton agency has many friends in high places. We help the people across the street get things done, especially in Washington."

"We heard Mrs. Bolton started a competin' agency," Sharp said.

Copley smiled at us like we were children. "That ragtag band hardly competes with us. Her men aren't detectives nor do they possess political influence. They're just a bunch of ruffians. An odd lot, in fact. For the life of me, I don't know who would hire them. I'm not worried."

"We'd like ya to be," Sharp said.

"Excuse me?"

"We'd like ya to bring about a half dozen Pinks to town," Sharp said. "Say ya want to nip this upstart agency in the bud."

Copley shook his head. "I don't need them, and they would cost a lot of money. Chicago would never approve."

I handed over a draft. "We'll pay for the extra agents."

Copley examined the draft. "This will cover a full month."

"We know," I responded.

"Captain McAllen?" Copley asked with a raised eyebrow.

"Yes, we've done business with Pinkertons before."

"What will they really be doing?"

My respect for Copley immediately went up. He knew about our association with McAllen and deduced that we needed these agents for other business. That meant he had investigated us, probably after hearing about the shooting. A smart agent kept abreast of important happenings in his jurisdiction.

"We want them to investigate Richard's killing. Find out if it could have been murder disguised as a drunken shooting spree? We also will want them to look into potential crimes committed at the direction of Jenny Bolton. Jansen will provide direction on that score. Last, two of your men will be assigned to protect Mrs. Virginia Baker, my fiancée. One openly, the other discreetly, without her knowledge."

Copley sat for a moment. Then he said, "We'll set up the discreet guard as a magazine writer from New York City. We'll put him up at the St. Charles and charge the room and board to you. It would be logical for him to befriend you and your fiancée, the three of you being easterners and all."

I had another thought. "Can the open guard be a woman?"

"Why?"

"The threat to her safety comes from Mrs. Bolton. A man might hesitate to hit or shoot her."

"Whereas, a woman would have no qualms about harming another woman?"

"Something like that," I said.

He shrugged. "She would need to come from Chicago . . . or further . . . if we can find someone." He chuckled. "Too bad you sent our best woman agent to prison."

Copley had done his research. During a visit to Prescott, Arizona, I had helped to uncover a crooked husband and wife team that worked for Pinkerton. The husband ended up dead in an unnecessary gunfight, and his wife now resided in prison.

"There was an agent in New York who taught Virginia how to defend herself. If you can get her, I'll pay the transportation."

"Of course you will." Copley sounded slightly mocking. "I'll send a telegram and see if she's available. Anything else?"

"No, except the man who shot Richard and a supposed witness left town, so can you send descriptions to your other offices."

"As soon as I get a description. I'll work on it myself as the first order of business."

"After ya order up them new Pinks," Sharp said.

"That goes without saying," Copley said.

"Actually, it don't," Sharp said. "Hearin' ya say it makes me believe ya listen as well as talk."

Copley bristled, but only for a moment. "I'll send the appropriate telegrams within the hour. Is there anyone other than Jerimiah who saw this witness?"

"That's why we hired you," I said, getting up to leave. "Now if you'll excuse us, I have a lesson to give."

Chapter 20

I snapped the reins on the buttocks of the horse that pulled our rented buckboard. I hurried the mare along because we had left late for our shooting lesson and darkness now threatened. Our practice had gone better than I expected, but Virginia remained only an adequate shot. She no longer reflexively shut her eyes when she pulled the trigger, but anticipating the recoil produced a hesitancy that impaired her aim. She had improved enough that she was fair with her first shot, especially for targets inside of ten feet. Still, if the person trying to do her harm was close, she might be better off swinging that lead-filled purse of hers.

"Hungry?" I asked.

"Yes. In fact, I think—"

"Shsss," I hissed, as I pulled back on the reins.

We had only ridden about a mile out of town to shoot, so we were close enough that I could see lamplight ahead, but I felt something more. I sensed danger, but couldn't see a threat. I had no history of premonitions, so I immediately began to question myself. Did an ambusher wait down the road or had I grown paranoid? I held up a hand to keep Virginia quiet and listened carefully. I heard nothing unusual. I reached behind me and slowly pulled my rifle from behind the buckboard seat. I thought about asking Virginia to climb in back, but remained unsure about our predicament. I glanced at her and she held her Remington .38 pointed straight up with a two-handed grip. Good for her. When I first met her, she probably would have waved the pistol around with the trigger pulled half back. If only her skill at shooting had improved as much as her gun safety.

"What do you see?" she whispered.

"Nothing. I just felt danger."

The countryside between us and town was relatively flat, but a bushwhacker could hide behind the occasional tree or lay in a furrow dug by one of the creeks that meandered between us and Carson City. If I were an assassin, I'd pick one of the dry creek beds. I checked behind us and saw that the dark horizon wouldn't present us as silhouettes to someone close to the ground in front of us. If killers waited out there, they would have as hard of a time seeing us as we had in spotting them. Perhaps it had been fortuitous that we returned after dusk.

I slowly stood, rifle in hand, but still didn't see anything. My edginess wouldn't go away. I felt something. But what? Since I had never experienced this feeling of forewarning before, I didn't know if I could trust it. A while back, my friends and I had been ambushed on the porch of the St. Charles and I hadn't felt the slightest inkling that my life was about to be put in jeopardy. I sat down carefully so as not to make a noise. I shook my head. Jenny's threat against Virginia must have made me jumpy.

I was about to snap the reins when I heard a stone tumble down an embankment. What could have loosened a rock in a creek bed? A footfall, a prairie dog, gravity. Again, I scanned the terrain. Nothing.

I examined my surroundings to see how I would set up an ambush. I would lie in wait at the next creek bed because it was deeper than the one closer to town. I would aim up the road, rather than wait for the buckboard to pull into the bed because that way I could prepare a rest for my rifle and have cover in case one of the targets shot back. My preference would be to lie only a few feet to one side of the road so I had a clear shot up the road. Which side? I looked behind me again. Assuming I didn't know the ambush would occur after dusk, I'd set up to the right because distant trees on the other side might make it difficult to distinguish my target from the background. So, if there was danger, my guess was that it would be on the right side in the next creek within a few feet of where the road crossed the dry bed.

I decided I needed more shooting practice. I

pulled my rifle butt tight against my shoulder and squeezed a shot in the general area I would have picked. I saw a puff of dirt, but nothing moved or made a sound. I fired twice more, once slightly to the left of my original shot and once to the right. Now I distinctly heard scampering: boots hitting against small rocks that lay just beneath the surface soil in a creek bed. Someone ran down the wash in a low crouch. I fired once more to hurry them along.

"Are you a sorcerer?" Virginia asked.

"Did I forget to tell you our children will be able to set a barn on fire with a hard glance?"

"Be serious. Has that ever happened to you before?"

"Never. It scares me a little."

"Not me. You can repeat that piece of witchery anytime." She had been searching the dark horizon, but now looked at me. "Do you feel it's safe now?"

"Yes. My sense of foreboding is gone."

I snapped the reins and the mare immediately went into a trot. The horse hurried along with no further prodding; he probably wanted supper as much as me. As soon as we started moving, I handed the reins to Virginia and positioned my rifle with the butt against my leg, so I could bring it into play at the slightest provocation. My eyes scanned in front of us, and I whipped my head back and forth as we crossed the creek bed. I saw nothing and no bullet came zinging out of nowhere to ruin our little excursion. In less than ten minutes we approached the outskirts of Carson City. The light provided a sense of safety, but I reminded myself that we had been attacked in a crowded restaurant in daytime. The thought reminded me that Virginia might be in danger if I dropped her off at the hotel, so she accompanied me to the livery to return the buckboard.

Since we had been shooting, we were heavily armed. The uneventful short walk to the hotel made me feel better. If someone had waited on the road to ambush us, a second assassin in town was unlikely. Inside the St. Charles, we marched directly toward the small bar next to the dining room. As we walked past the dining room entrance, someone inside startled me. Jenny Bolton sat at a table in the middle of the room. Her chair had been positioned to face the door and when she noticed us, her face slowly evolved into a sensual smile, probably meant to anger Virginia. At least, I assumed that was the intent. I believe Virginia read the coquettish expression the same way because she hooked her arm through mine and gently tugged me on toward the bar.

After we received our drinks, Virginia softly said, "I'm not sure what makes me angrier . . . her trying to kill me or her trying to steal you right in front of my eyes."

"To hell with her and her games. I still want to

leave right now. I have no reason or obligation to fight her. The people of this state made their own mess. Let them deal with it."

I expected another refusal from her to run away, but instead encountered silence.

"What does your silence mean?" I asked.

"It means I'm thinking."

I let her think.

When I signaled for a second round, she said, "You're right. I let my curiosity about her sway my judgment. She's intent on making this your fight. Let's go before she succeeds."

I felt elated. I wanted to find Sharp and tell him we would leave tomorrow, but decided it could wait until we finished our drinks. I needed to cancel the Pinkerton crew and tell Jansen, but since I'd be running from my bail and trial, I'd send a telegram after I was safely out of Nevada. After supper, Virginia could pack while I saw Jerimiah to offer him a chance to go with us.

We needed to disguise our intentions from Jenny, so after Virginia and I had a brief discussion, we preceded arm in arm to Jenny's table to set her mind at ease that our plans had not changed. She didn't look the least surprised to see us standing over her.

"Hello, Jenny," I said. "I hope you enjoyed your meal."

"Not entirely. I have a good cook at the ranch, and he knows exactly how I like things. Here, I send my food back time and again, and then it's cold."

I found her answer discomforting. My rhetorical comment didn't deserve a real response, but more disturbing; her complaints reminded me of her mother-in-law. Had something hardened her since I last knew her, or had I been blind to her shortcomings?

"I'll take whatever they have ready in the kitchen," Virginia said, easily. "We've been out in the countryside shooting and I'm famished."

This hadn't been part of our planned conversation. Evidently, Virginia wanted to engage in a little intimidation of her own.

"Really? I have such a fear of guns. Are you an expert shootist?"

"Hardly an expert, but I'm good at close quarters. Within ten feet, I can shoot the neck off a bottle. Several, in fact . . . in rapid order."

"How impressive," Jenny said, sounding anything but impressed. "I abhor guns." She pointed at two capable-looking men at a corner table who glared menacingly at me. "That's why I hire hands to protect me. Even after months of practice, I could never come close to their skill."

She smiled to convey she meant no threat, which she did, of course.

"Perhaps we should hire someone to watch our backside," I said. "Someone tried to ambush us on the way back into town."

"I'm glad they failed," Jenny said with an engaging smile.

"So are we. I guess we ought to find Jeff. We're supposed to have supper together."

"Good to see you again, Mrs. Bolton." Virginia offered her hand.

Jenny shook it without hesitation. "It was nice of you to stop by to say hello, Mrs. Baker."

As we walked away, I said, "So . . . fast and accurate, are we?"

"It doesn't hurt for her to believe I can protect myself. So what if I exaggerated a bit. I presume you told her about the ambush to hear her response."

"I didn't see any reaction. Did you?"

"Not a twitch. Maybe it was just a highwayman."

"Perhaps. Could I be completely mistaken about her?"

"Do you really want to hear what I think?"

"I do."

"You're a poor judge of Jenny. She's complicated . . . yet very simple. Inside her head, you'll find a twisted mess. That'll make it hard to anticipate what she'll do, because she'll do anything. But her goal . . . that's simple. She needs power over other people. She must have it. Other people have controlled her in the past, and now she wants control over them because if she gets it, they no longer have power over her. At the

142

moment, she's playing the queen—center table in the best restaurant in Carson City. She's holding court. You should have kissed her ring."

"Excuse me?"

"You want to lessen her fears about us, don't you?"

"Yes."

"In the past, men have abused her, now she's out to get even. That's what drives her. In her mind, you're one of those men. Next time, show deference."

"There won't be a next time." I was angry. "We're getting the hell out of here."

I approached the innkeeper. "Have you seen Jeff Sharp this evening?"

"Yes sir. He went out about two hours ago with a couple gentlemen. I haven't seen him return."

"What men?"

"Oh, they came back. They're sitting in the corner table in the dining room."

"The men who work for Mrs. Bolton?" I asked.

"Yes, sir, I believe they do."

I whirled around and marched back into the dining room. Jenny was still sitting at her table, hands folded in front of her, looking as innocent as a teenager at a church social. The expression on her face was what scared the hell out of me. Smugness. More disturbing, she appeared to have been waiting for our return.

When I reached her, I asked as evenly as I could

manage, "Do you know where Jeff Sharp is?"

"He's in my custody," she said simply.

"Custody? What does that mean?" I asked dumbly.

"In my protection, if you will. I knew bail wasn't enough to keep you around. You have more money than sense." Her expression turned sympathetic. "Don't worry . . . he'll be fine . . . unless you're found innocent."

Chapter 21

We left the St. Charles immediately. Virginia knew where we were heading without me mentioning our destination. We needed McAllen, so without a word we marched directly to the telegraph office, which scheduled a night operator on every evening except Sundays. The other Pinkertons we ordered could help, but McAllen's long friendship with Sharp meant he needed to be told immediately. He deserved no less. That thought reminded me of something I had forgotten to tell Virginia.

"Joseph resigned."

"Did he get his thousand dollars and stock contract?"

"He did."

We walked on a few paces before Virginia

added, "That means we're depending on Thomas Copley. He runs a one-man shop. Can he lead a team of agents?"

"We'll find out soon, but McAllen leaving the Pinkertons won't make any difference. If need be, he'll convince Copley to do things his way. Besides, even by himself, McAllen's someone I want on my side in a fight."

"Do you still think that ambush was Jenny's doing?"

"Been thinking on that. I believe she set it up, but not to kill us. She wanted to slow us down so her men had time to abduct Sharp. She's playing with us."

"She's not playing. She just doesn't want you killed by a bullet; she wants you strung up in front of the whole town. The supposed hero humiliated. I'll bet she even likes the injustice of you being hung for killings she set in motion." She looked at me. "By the way, I'm safe for the time being. I'm getting to know her, and I'm pretty sure she wants me to watch you hang. Only then will she shift her sights to me. Probably has something horrid in mind."

I stopped walking. "What do you mean?"

"She may want to get even with men, but she wants to shame women the way she was shamed."

"Good god."

"Possibly not so good," she said, absentmindedly. She started walking again. As I caught up, she added, "The trial will be rigged. Nothing will be left to chance. It won't help your case that Sharp ran. It will be portrayed as a sign of guilt. I'll bet she intends on being the key witness. She'll testify that those men were sent merely to escort you to meet with her. She'll be pretty, sweet, and enticing. The jury will believe her because they'll want to believe her. Other diners present that night will support her testimony out of fear." Her expression turned anxious. "Steve, if you step into that courtroom, you'll be sentenced to death."

"Then we need to get the charges dismissed," I said.

"Time's running short. This day is practically over."

Chapter 22

Virginia and I stood on the station platform waiting for the Denver train, hoping McAllen would change the course of events. I knew I'd feel better with him around. I looked at the other people on the platform, but no one appeared in the least threatening.

I felt nothing but frustration for the last few days. As the trial date came closer, we made no progress in getting Sharp or me out of trouble.

The judge would not grant a postponement. Jansen found no witness willing to testify that the four men in the restaurant had even threatened us, no less made a play for their guns. None of the four had committed a prior crime, nor did any of them have a reputation as a gun for hire. Marshal Wilson couldn't find Ben, the supposed witness to Richard's killing. Most of the Pinkerton team had arrived the prior day, but it took no time at all to notice that Copley lacked leadership abilities. The team scattered around town with conflicting or vague directions. The one who played the role of a magazine writer didn't fool Virginia for a minute, but she never objected to a protector. Virginia made a few inroads with politicians, but without a response from her uncle she had no way to persuade any of them to assist us or the governor. And in three days, I had not discovered a single clue as to Sharp's whereabouts. Worst of all, Jenny continued to regally preside over her sycophants right in the middle of our hotel dining room.

I wouldn't entertain the idea Sharp might be dead, so I concentrated on finding out where they had stashed him. The Bolton ranch, Virginia City, Carson City, or on the outskirts of one of these locations? I didn't know how to go about finding out. He could be held captive anywhere. The Bolton ranch came first to mind, but I decided Jenny was too clever for such an obvious hideaway. I took the train up to Virginia City the prior day—after the Pinkertons arrived to protect Virginia—but discovered nothing helpful. I left after talking to Sharp's old head of security, who promised to use his sources to investigate further.

On a good note, the Pinkerton National Detective Agency had promised to send the woman from New York City who had trained and befriended Virginia.

When the train arrived, I expected to see McAllen leap from a car before the train came to a complete stop. He hated crowded spaces and concern for Sharp would cause him to get off the train at the earliest possible moment, but I couldn't spot him anywhere, even after most of the other passengers had dispersed. I hadn't received a telegram alerting me that he had missed the train, so maybe he had run into trouble. I worried. Then I spotted him. Oh, damn. He wasn't alone.

McAllen proudly escorted a young girl off the train—a poised girl in her teens, wearing an outfit more appropriate for a boy, but somehow she remained feminine. I knew her, of course, and I knew Maggie hated dresses. Why would McAllen bring his daughter into a deadly situation? He knew Richard had been killed, he knew Sharp and I had killed four men, and he knew Sharp had been abducted. This was no place for a young girl . . . or a doting father for that matter.

We needed a hard man, seasoned by encounters with dangerous outlaws. We needed Captain Joseph McAllen, not this smiling, pleased parent with the only love in his life hanging onto his arm. As they sauntered toward Virginia and me, they looked affable and harmless. I wanted mean and terrifying.

A thought suddenly struck me. With Sharp missing, I was practically surrounded by women. Virginia, Jenny, Maggie, and soon a female Pinkerton. Thank goodness, McAllen had arrived. My few years in the West had been dominated by men. Ever since I left Pickhandle Gulch, Sharp had been at my side and McAllen close at hand. We drank, brawled, gambled, and charged into trouble unworried about the consequences. Now the toughest man I had ever encountered approached us with a silly grin. McAllen looked no more dangerous than a leaping sheepdog happy to see his master come through the door.

I had placed high hopes on McAllen's arrival; now I was uncertain. Despite my misgivings, Virginia and I rushed forward to greet him and his daughter. Maggie gave me a big hug, which I returned in kind. Virginia had never met McAllen's daughter, so I introduce the two women. I was about to add some banalities, when McAllen grabbed me by the elbow and guided me to a quiet corner on the train platform.

"Any word on Jeff?"

"No. Why did you bring Maggie?"

"Not important right now. We need to save Jeff, but findin' him solves other problems. If he's held by someone in Jenny's employ, then we have our crime to send her to prison. We need Jeff . . . alive."

McAllen's brisk, no nonsense manner restored my confidence. Evidently, between bantering with his daughter, he had been thinking through the possibilities.

"I spent some time in Virginia City and I poked around Carson City, but found nothing, learned nothing."

"Sharp's at the Bolton ranch," he said matter-of-factly.

"How do you know?"

"She locked him up in the same shed where we held Bill Sprague."

"What? How do you know that?" I asked incredulous.

"I don't *know* it. It's a guess, but a good guess knowin' that girl."

"You don't—" I decided not to argue. "Let's go get him."

"Not that easy. She has lots of men. They're probably waitin' for us to trespass on her property. We need to think this through."

"Jeff and I hired a Pinkerton team. They arrived yesterday. We can go in force."

"Pinkertons won't charge onto private land and

start shootin' people. We need to know he's there for sure, and only then make a plan."

"How?"

"I'm going to ask Jenny. Do you know where she is?"

"At our hotel."

"Let's get over there."

He left me to return to his daughter's side. Maggie and Virginia were chatting away as if they had known each other for years. Maggie was a spirited tomboy who loved horses. I thought she was fifteen, but she could have had a birthday since I last saw her. It had been over a year since she had been held captive in a scheme to force her father to rob an ore shipment out of Leadville. Although Sharp and I had rescued her, I didn't become friendly with her until Sharp ran into trouble in Prescott, Arizona. She was a handful, with a tart tongue on occasion. Like at the moment.

"Mr. Dancy, why did you let Mr. Sharp get into trouble again?"

"He got caught up in my feud, I'm afraid. Mr. Sharp is a tough ol' codger. If someone can make it through this, he can."

"Well, you needn't worry anymore, my father's here. In no time at all, he'll find the bad men and put them behind bars or belowground."

Maggie idolized her father and believed him infallible. I wasn't so sure. Her comment about bad men told me that McAllen had not confided in his daughter that a woman had concocted this villainy. I wasn't sure it was smart to keep her ignorant. Hell, only a few years separated Jenny and Maggie, although they could not have experienced life more differently. Without forewarning Maggie, the two teen-aged girls might end up getting chummy. That wouldn't be good for us or her.

"I thought you were in Durango," I said, trying to discover why she was here.

"My father asked me to come to Denver to help select stallions for his breeding ranch. We bought some fine horseflesh. I can't wait to get back to Durango and start working the stock. Did my dad tell you his idea for breeding a new line?"

"He did. He wants to breed a line for the Pinkertons that can out-carry and out-last any horse ridden by outlaws."

"We're going to interbreed Spanish Barb and Indian horses. I helped choose two Spanish Barb stallions. They're magnificent. We'll buy Indian ponies from the Utes."

I looked at McAllen. "So she was with you when you received my telegram?"

"She was. It was faster to bring her along. Besides—"

"Yes, I know," I interrupted. "But she's here, so she needs to know it all."

He looked confused, so I said, "Jenny and her are close in age."

McAllen's bewilderment vanished in a flash. "Virginia?"

We both turned to Virginia. She nodded and said she would explain everything to her.

"Explain what?" Maggie demanded.

"At the hotel," her father said in the tone he used to end conversation.

He picked up a bag and began to walk toward the hotel, but I whistled over a cab and he reversed direction and threw their bags into the buggy. We helped lift the women up into their seats and sent them on ahead to the hotel. We would walk to the St. Charles. This would give Virginia a chance to talk privately with Maggie while McAllen and I discussed our predicament.

"Why the ranch?" I asked.

"It sends a message."

"But it's obvious."

"Meaning you dismissed it, right?"

I hadn't dismissed it entirely, but I nodded.

"This is all personal . . . and she'll do things in a personal way. She's the richest person in Nevada, so it's not about money. She has enough of the legislature and judges on her side to keep the government out of her way, so it's not about politics. She has suitors aplenty and I hear she entertains them all, so this is not about blindly hating men. So what's it about?"

"I get the feeling you have an answer," I responded.

"It's about control. She probably believes if she can control everything around her, she'll never be helpless again. Men and women won't be able to take advantage of her. If she loses control, the whole world might rush in to crush her."

"Virginia has made similar observations," I said. "But who did you talk to before leaving Denver?"

"Who says I talked to anyone?"

"You always study a situation before arriving."

"I talked to a Denver doctor who studies mental philosophy. I described her history, and he told me she's probably driven by fear of bein' thrown off this great steed she alighted on. She was born and raised dirt poor. Now she's a newly minted baroness. It don't feel natural to her, doesn't fit her comfortably, but she'll refuse to give it up. Never. Not on her life. She fears being weak again. She fears people doin' what they will with her." McAllen looked directly at me as if to emphasize his next point. "She's driven by inner demons she can't control. Rage, not reason drives her."

"That's what the doc told you?"

"That's what the doc told me. Plus he said you are her special foe. She really didn't want you, but she can't abide you rejectin' her. It proves she lost control of you. What she can't control, she destroys."

I walked half of a block before asking, "Are Virginia and Maggie safe?"

"I didn't think to ask."

"I'm asking."

Now McAllen walked awhile before answering. "I suspect Jenny would like to put Virginia in her place. She's got to be jealous. I also need to worry about Maggie once Jenny knows I'm helpin' you."

"Should we send them away?"

"Yep." A few more paces. "They'll never go, of course."

"Your woman agent can't protect them both."

"No she can't. We better deal with Jenny straightaway."

Chapter 23

As we entered the St. Charles, McAllen started to ask where he could find Jenny, but stopped mid-sentence when he spotted her at her usual table. He immediately walked up to her and took a seat. Evidently, straightaway meant straightaway.

I quickly followed suit and sat beside McAllen. Jenny didn't seem surprised or angry, just curious. Her guards didn't get up from their table, but they kept a wary eye on us, especially me. I assumed they worked for Jenny's detective agency, and the hate directed at me meant they had been friendly with the four men Sharp and I killed in this very room.

"Good afternoon, Mrs. Bolton. My name is Joseph McAllen. We've met before."

"I remember. The last time I saw you, I sent you packing."

"If that's the way you wish to recall it, fine. I'm here to fetch Steve and his fiancée. As you know, he has no chance of a fair trial, so he might as well bolt."

"Haven't you heard about his friend being missing?" she asked.

"Probably dead. Staying in Carson City will just get Steve dead too. I see things as they are, Mrs. Bolton, and there's no reason to dally further in this trap of yours. We're leaving on tomorrow's train." He nodded toward her guards. "If any of your men try to stop us, we'll kill them." He hesitated a beat. "You as well, if you're within sight. I killed your mother-in-law, so you know I won't hesitate to shoot a woman." He slipped a derringer on the table that looked exactly like the one she had used to kill Sprague. "This will be found in your hand." He folded his hands on the table and looked her straight in the eye. "Do you understand?"

"You're the one that doesn't understand, Mr. McAllen." She met his stare without a blink. "If you leave, Mr. Sharp dies."

McAllen made a dismissive wave. "Already dead." He stood to go. "Good day, Mrs. Bolton."

"Sit back down. I didn't go to all the trouble of getting you here for a few sentences of conversation. We have more to talk about."

McAllen showed no emotion. After a short staring contest, he sat back down.

"Why do you want me here?"

I noticed he didn't question her statement. I did. What the hell did she mean? I thought she wanted revenge against me. Did she want to get even with all three of us, or had all these events been arranged for the sole purpose of bringing McAllen to Carson City? And did McAllen believe Sharp was actually dead, or was this one of his stunts meant to throw an opponent off balance? Or was he trying to get her to drop a clue as to his whereabouts? I glanced at her guards and they seemed unconcerned about the tension between their boss and the rough-looking McAllen. In fact, they still seemed more concerned with me. I took that to mean she had forewarned them to stay calm if things got a bit heated.

Jenny didn't say anything right away, but looked very satisfied that McAllen had obediently followed her order to retake his seat.

Finally, she said, "Captain McAllen, you made me feel bad for saving Mr. Dancy's life. Oh wait; you're no longer employed by Pinkertons. Do you still insist on being called captain?"

"Why do you want me here?" he repeated.

"Because you made me a man-killer. I shot my husband's assassin, but you gave me no choice. You lost control of your prisoner. I righted the situation *and* saved a man's life. For that, I should have gotten thanks; instead, I got your scorn." Her expression became hateful. "*Mr.* McAllen, you were nasty and mean."

Her recollections weren't made of whole cloth. McAllen had insinuated that Jenny entered the confinement shed intent to do murder. Later, I came to believe McAllen had been right that she had manipulated the situation so she could kill her husband's assassin in a way that precluded arrest.

"I don't care about your resentment," McAllen said. "It certainly won't change my plans, so cuss me out and we'll be on our way."

"Mr. Sharp is *your* friend; has been for as long as people around here can remember. Stay or go. Now that you understand, it's your decision."

For the first time, McAllen didn't know how to respond, so I asked, "What does that mean?"

"It means," McAllen said, "that I can either run away with you and my friend dies or I can stay and watch you die. Do I have that about right, young lady?"

She smirked. "Either way, I crush your precious pride." If possible, her smirk became smarmier. "I'm going to enjoy seeing you helpless."

I thought McAllen might shoot her on the spot, but he displayed enormous self-control.

"You orchestrated this whole series of events to drag me to Nevada for your entertainment?" McAllen asked calmly.

Suddenly, everything became clear. I leaned as far back in my chair as possible to see around McAllen. With a hand wave, I got the attention of her guards at the other table.

"Hey, did you men know Mrs. Bolton sent your friends to be killed? She knew about our skill with guns. She had already made us worried about an attack. She wanted a fight . . . and she knew how it would end."

When I saw the knowing glances between the men, I knew they understood. They returned their attention to our table, but now with their angry eyes pointed at the back of Jenny's head. I returned my attention to our table and met unbridled fury. Jenny normally captivated men. Her seemingly boundless vivacity made her the center of attention wherever she went. Not at this moment. Her twisted features displayed so much rage that she looked more than shrewish, she looked grotesque. Was I seeing underneath her façade for the first time?

"Mr. Dancy, I know what you hold dear. That Philadelphia swell thinks she's better than us. If I were you—"

My gun appeared in my hand cocked and

pointed straight at her nose. "You're right, Jenny; Virginia's the most important thing in my life. That's why it's a grave mistake to threaten her."

"Ben, Tom," she yelled.

"They left," McAllen said. "You're alone."

"You'd kill me in front of all of these people," she said, uneasily.

"Did you forget the bind you put me in? I already killed two men in this room. They can't hang me again for killing one more."

She composed herself quicker than most men could draw a weapon. In complete calm, she said, "You're forgetting Mr. Sharp. If anything happens to me, he *will* die."

"Prove he's not dead already," McAllen said.

"What? You want me to bring him in and invite him for supper?"

She folded her arms across her chest and smiled confidently. Her demeanor impressed me because my Colt held steady at the bridge of her nose. I wasn't going to shoot her, so how the hell could I find an excuse to put my gun away?

Reading my mind, McAllen said, "Steve, get me a piece of paper with hotel letterhead from the front desk."

I gratefully holstered my pistol and went to the front desk. McAllen yelled after me to get a pen as well. I knew why he wanted paper. When his daughter had been abducted, we had insisted on a handwritten note from her to prove she was alive, and then we had followed the carrier of the note paper to discover her location. I presumed he thought the trick would work again.

When I returned, McAllen had evidently already explained what he wanted. Jenny was livid, shaking her head no.

"You must take my word for it."

"In my experience, abductors kill their victims immediately. Less hassle. If you want our cooperation, you need to prove he's alive."

"I don't want your cooperation! What do you think's going on here? I want you to feel pain, my kind of pain. It makes no difference if you stay or go. You'll have killed one of your friends in either case. But I'm not going to fetch a note for you. Make your decision and go to hell."

"You don't hate Sharp, do you?" I asked.

"What?"

"Sharp always treated you kindly. You wouldn't kill him. He's not part of our feud."

"I thought you were stupid when you fell in love with me after a single smile. I had no idea how stupid you actually are. You're right, I don't hate Mr. Sharp, but that's so unimportant. What's important is that you care about him. Killing him is a means to an end. That's all. If you think I'll let him go if you run away from your trial, you're wrong. *Dead* wrong. You flee, he dies. You stay, he lives . . . then you die."

"Do you remember how your husband died?" McAllen asked.

"What do you think? I saw his brains splatter against our ranch house wall."

"If I were in your boots, I'd keep a watchful eye on the horizon. More than one can play at vendettas."

We both stood up and marched out of the dining room.

Chapter 24

The final member of our Pinkerton team arrived. The female agent from New York used her real name, Elizabeth Channing, on this assignment. Virginia told people Channing was a college friend who had come to Nevada to be maid of honor at our wedding.

Elizabeth liked to be called Lizzy, and she could display a flighty personality that conveyed a lack of seriousness about anything. At will, she could brighten her rather plain face with an engaging smile, and use her lithe figure to move in a way that turned men's heads. Her real personality bordered on overly-serious and highly aggressive. She gave Virginia some additional defense lessons and Lizzy clearly liked to hit things— hard and often. The two never parted, which made me feel safe to venture out on short expeditions. Nothing useful had been accomplished in the last several days. We had no solid information about where Sharp was hidden and our legal defense had made no progress that I could detect. The Pinkerton investigative team had discovered nothing and Copley refused to allow his men to be used for a raid against the Bolton ranch. It became clear that Copley would never be influenced by a retired Pinkerton.

The morning after Lizzy arrived, we all met in my suite to figure out our next move. The three women sat on opposing settees, while McAllen and I paced the room or sat intermittently in straight-back chairs we had positioned at opposite ends of the small seating area. Virginia looked anxious, Maggie confused, and Lizzy ready to hit something.

After a long, slow breath, McAllen said, "I'm even more convinced they're holding Jeff at her ranch."

"How do we free him?" I asked.

"Not by riding in, guns blazing. I believe that might be her real aim. Kill us all when we assault her ranch. Besides, Copley will never approve any forceful action." He shook his head. "I'm afraid that after she takes care of us, she'll come for Virginia."

"That can't sway how you go about rescuing Jeff," Virginia said. "Listen, we all know she's clever, so she probably has multiple schemes. Every one of them ends badly for me, so pick a set of actions that has the best chance of winning . . . because winning is the only way you can really protect me."

McAllen gave Virginia an appraising look. "Steve, you've found a brave and smart woman." He turned to me. "Any ideas?"

"Yes." The answer came from Lizzy.

She got all of our attention.

"One of the other Pinkertons and I should rent a buckboard and ride out to that ranch. We'll playact husband and wife who need water for our horse and food for ourselves. We'll see if you're right, captain."

"Your job is to protect Virginia . . . and now Maggie," I objected.

"We'll be fine," Maggie said. "My dad's here and Mrs. Baker carries a gun."

"Virginia?" I exclaimed, startled that she told Maggie about her pistol.

She looked sheepish. "She asked if I was frightened. I . . . I shouldn't have boasted."

"She says you taught her how to shoot," Maggie said excitedly. "I can shoot a rifle really well, but I want to learn how to handle a pistol as well."

"No!" McAllen's firmness made Maggie pout and Virginia look chagrined.

"Jenny wants me to watch you hang," Virginia said. "I'm safe until then."

"You don't know that," I said. "Besides, she was after Joseph all along, so Maggie may be in danger. Lizzy should stay here."

"Steve, Lizzy's right," McAllen said. "We need information, and her idea is probably the only way someone can approach the ranch without a shoot-out. Jenny's biding her time for the moment. We need to take advantage of that."

I tried a different tack. "It doesn't make sense. She can't get back in time for us to mount an assault."

"Unless the ranch has a telegraph," Maggie offered. "Does it?"

"No, but Fort Churchill does." McAllen slapped his thigh. "Of course, why didn't I think of it? It's halfway. She has to have a man stationed there. She sends him a telegram and he can be out to the ranch inside of a day. The news would travel faster than our posse."

Lizzy nodded understanding. "We'll find out what's going on at that ranch, remove the relay at Fort Churchill, and send you a telegram in less than three days. Without her relay, she can't get word to the ranch any faster than your posse can ride." She thought a minute, and then added, "It can be done."

McAllen started pacing the small room. Soon I joined him. The two of us walked back and forth in opposite directions. The room was only five paces long, so we met each other in the middle repeatedly, but neither of us looked up from the floor directly in front of our feet.

"We need to distract her," I muttered to myself.

"Yep," McAllen answered. "Lizzy needs to disappear without suspicion, a posse needs to be formed and ready to go as soon as she sends her telegram, and whatever signals she trades with her Churchill man must be maintained until the last moment. The women must be kept safe. All the while, Jenny must concentrate on us and what we're doin' right here in Carson City."

"Lizzy's disappearance is easy," Virginia said. "I'll send her away in a huff. Steve and I'll stage a public argument, and I'll tell everyone the wedding's postponed indefinitely. Jenny may assume it's a charade, but it still works to get Lizzy out of town."

McAllen stopped pacing and faced the women. "Forming a posse without her notice won't be difficult either. Steve, you engage another Pinkerton team, but have it form up at Fort Churchill instead of here. The leader will report to Denver, not Carson City. They'll pretend to be inspectors sent by Congress to report back on the continued need for the garrison. It gives them a reason to talk privately with the commanding officer. Done right, they can spot Jenny's relay without raising any suspicions about themselves. They take him captive just before riding to the Bolton ranch."

McAllen renewed his pacing before adding, "How about four new Pinkertons? I'll give you names of trustworthy men. With Lizzy and her supposed husband, that makes six." He stopped. "Enough?"

"Probably . . . with surprise on our side," I answered. "But everything's got to go perfect."

"That leaves distracting her and protecting Maggie and Virginia. Any ideas?"

"We need to wreck her sense of control," I said. "Did you see her reaction when I told her men that she had set their friends up to be slaughtered?"

"We need something bigger. That made her hotter than a pistol, but she recovered fast."

"She didn't recover; she pulled a shield in front of her. I bet she's still steamed at me for meddling in her affairs."

"Steve, she's always been angry as hell underneath. We need to bring it to the surface for an extended period."

"Why now?" Virginia asked in a low voice.

"Why now what?" McAllen asked. "Are we havin' the same conversation?"

"Not exactly. I was thinking about something from earlier. She claims to have summoned you here. Why now? How long has it been since you last saw her—two years—more?"

"More," McAllen answered.

"So, why now?"

"What difference does that make?" McAllen asked annoyed.

"It makes a difference because she evidently had other things she wanted to get done before playing with you."

"She's not playin'. She wants to hurt me." McAllen's annoyance had not abated. "Let's not get distracted."

"Men," Lizzy said, shaking her head. "You think everything is about you. Well, it's not. Jenny's got bigger fish to fry. She's been at it for a couple years, and now that she's got things to her liking, so it's time for fun."

Maggie had been devouring our conversation, and her expression conveyed agreement with Lizzy. McAllen and I must have appeared dumbfounded because all three women laughed at us.

"We're entertainment?" I asked.

"I believe so," Lizzy said, with Virginia vigorously nodding her head. Maggie just grinned; apparently pleased that the women were dominating the discussion.

I remained unsure about what we were even talking about. "Are you saying she's putting us in all this trouble because she's finished sewing up the state?"

"That's my guess," Lizzy answered. "You weren't at the top of her list of chores. In fact, you were pretty close to the bottom."

"What about the governor?" I asked. "He's not

in her camp and wants to send her to prison, or worse."

"I presume she didn't kill *every* person not on her payroll," Virginia said. "Besides, the governor will be gone in a year or so."

McAllen resumed pacing. "So you're sayin' she feels secure that she has everything under control? Are you suggestin' that to distract her, we throw a wrench into those well-polished gears?"

Maggie shook her head at our slowness. "Dad, I knew you'd eventually catch on."

With a sly smile, Virginia added, "So what are you going to do, Mr. Steve Dancy? You have a crazed baroness intent on absolute control over her new empire. If memory serves, you've encountered this type of opponent before."

"You're suggesting I put my gun away and pull out my wallet."

"Don't be naïve." She sounded testy. "Pull out your wallet, but keep your gun on your hip. Distract her for the next week or so . . . after that . . . after that you'll probably need that gun."

"And I thought I was marrying a sweet, high society girl."

She literally huffed. "I ran away from that damn social register crowd, I'm certainly no longer a girl, the West knocked the sweetness right out of me, and if you keep this up, you'll be lucky if I ever marry you."

"I apologize."

"Accepted."

Her smile told me she had feigned anger at my flippant remark. We were fortunate to have bright women on our side. They had forced us to look at the bigger picture: to see that we were secondary. The way to attack her was to go after what was the most important to her. How to go about it? Virginia said Jenny was like other opponents I had faced in business, but she was nothing like them. She had an additional weapon. Jenny was a desirable woman, with the power to manipulate men.

I started cataloging her empire. "She controls the state's cattle, lumber, and politicians. She has heavy influence over mining, banking, rail transport, and newspapers. But . . ."

Damn. I had been fixated on Sharp, so I had no idea how her business and political empire worked. I reprimanded myself because I had wasted the last couple of days.

"I don't know where she's vulnerable," I admitted.

I looked at McAllen and he shrugged.

"We need a frank discussion with Jansen and the governor," I said. "They should be able to tell us something."

"Separately," McAllen insisted.

"You don't trust them?" Virginia asked.

"A lawyer and a politician?"

We all laughed, but I'm not sure McAllen

intended humor. He was right, however. We could only test their forthrightness by talking to each of them alone.

Lizzy interrupted my thoughts. "I'll get back issues of the newspapers to read as we travel. Maybe I can glean something. If I do, I'll telegraph from Churchill."

"You can read on a buckboard?" I asked.

"Headlines tell the story."

I had a revelation and it wasn't good. "Killing Richard had two purposes. She frightened other politicians and killed a competing newspaper." To Lizzy, I added, "I bet you'll find only positive articles about Jenny Bolton. I'll probably have to move newspapers to the control rather than influence side of the ledger."

"First step," Virginia said, "is a public fight. I presume the lobby will do."

"Depends," I said. "Anything to throw down there?"

"Barbs." She smiled. "All I need are barbs."

"Can I watch?" Maggie asked enthusiastically. "I can help make it real. Order me to go upstairs. I stomp up stairs really good."

"Joseph?"

"No secret who she is, so why not."

Maggie beamed with pride to be part of our conspiracy.

"Well, let's hustle down and put a noisy end to this engagement."

I said this in a lighthearted tone, but Virginia looked troubled. I asked what bothered her. She didn't answer right away, but when she did, she destroyed my newly-minted confidence.

"This entire plan assumes that Sharp's alive and at the Bolton ranch. If either of those is false, the wedding is off for real."

Chapter 25

Governor Bradshaw slapped the table. "I run this state!"

From the very first, he had been evasive or belligerent or both.

After Virginia and I staged a raucous breakup, McAllen and I had run over to the governor's office. Instead of having Maggie stomp upstairs, she became the consoling female companion. This provided a good excuse for them to stay locked up in Virginia's room for the remainder of the day. After the argument, Lizzy snuck out of the hotel and left with the Pinkerton guard who had pretended to be a magazine writer.

What had upset the governor were our pointed questions about Jenny Bolton's control of the state. His defensiveness told me she had more legislators beholden to her than Bradshaw would admit. That didn't concern me. She wanted political influence to keep the government off her back, but her power came from her business interests. I tried several times to steer the conversation away from the statehouse, but Bradshaw kept acting like a spoiled brat whose favorite toy had been taken away by the smallest kid in the class. I was just about to signal to McAllen that this conversation was fruitless, when Bradshaw said something interesting.

"Some people call her The Silver Queen, but they got it wrong. She's really The Bovine Whore. That child slept with every rancher in Mason Valley and contracted to buy every head of cattle they took to market. If you eat in Nevada, you pay that whore a pretty penny for every single bite. She has absolute control of beef, poultry, dairy, hogs, and every other animal you might want to bite into. She did some fancy contracting in Omaha and now she owns nearly all the grain that arrives by train . . . and that's most of it because we don't grow many crops in this state. You want to eat, you pay that bitch."

"When did she go after the food supply?" I asked.

"Hell, I don't know. Her husband started it, but she made him look like a pipsqueak. Not too long after you left, she traveled to Omaha. After her return, the price of grain nearly doubled. Several men have gone to Omaha to outbid her, but none of the co-ops would even talk to them. Knowing her, she probably slept with every damn one of them and threatened to tell their wives if they reneged on her contracts."

"You think that's the only way a woman can succeed in business?" McAllen asked, sounding more irritated than I expected.

"Hell, she's not a woman, she's a child. So you tell me, how else can she put together those kind of deals?"

"With money," McAllen said.

"And the Bolton name," I added.

"You think she's smart and rich enough for that? I doubt it. She's using wiles not available to men. You think she just waltzes into an agricultural hub like Omaha and throws her name around and everyone drops what they're doing to meet with this child? It doesn't work that way."

"No, it doesn't," I said. "You bring a letter of credit from a reputable bank. Your banker wires ahead to set up meetings. The Cattlemen's Association gives you a letter of introduction. You send telegrams in advance to introduce yourself. You arrive in style and stay in a big suite in the best hotel. You—"

"Damn it, I know how business is done, but how would she have an inkling?"

"Did John Bolton know how to do business?" I asked.

"Of course. But—"

"Was she ever out of her husband's sight?"

"No, but you're not telling me she learned by watching. Hell, John kept that girl illiterate."

"And as soon as he was killed, she hired a tutor to teach her how to read, write, and sum. She learned fast." I wanted to get back to her shopping trip to Omaha. "Did she take her foreman with her to Omaha?"

"You bet she did. That was the talk of the town for weeks."

"Damn it, you're not thinking like her. There's no relationship there. I know Joe and he's a capable foreman. I bet she had him lead the negotiations. Money, the Bolton name, and a seasoned rancher out front to talk man to man. She didn't need to sleep with these men. They'd jump at a contract that spanned multiple harvests at attractive prices from a reputable rancher."

Bradshaw looked furious, but said nothing.

So I did. "Governor, you're *still* under-estimating her. You believe she cheated . . . shamefully using sex to get what she wanted. She did cheat—is cheating—but through old fashioned intimidation, corruption, and violence. You can't admit that because those ways aren't foreign to you, and that would mean she's better than you. You prefer to believe her womanhood gives her unfair advantage because then you don't have to admit she beat you at your own game. If you

175

want to win, forget that cockamamie gossip and concentrate on how to defeat her as if she were a man."

His red face quivered in rage and his breathing was far too heavy for someone sitting perfectly still.

Finally, he spit out, "Good . . . then go over and shoot her like you did Sean Washburn."

I laughed, which made him angrier.

"You're right, governor, she does have some unfair advantages. I can't shoot a woman. We have to come up with another way."

His fury abated after I admitted being a woman gave Jenny advantages. In truth, Washburn had fancied himself a gunfighter of the first order, and he had a loaded pistol pointed at me. I shot him not because he was a man, but because it was a fair duel with a capable gunman . . . even if I had set it up. Although Jenny had once shot a man, she claimed she abhorred guns and went about town supposedly unarmed. I would never shoot an unarmed man, so her sex made no difference. I thought it would be best not to mention this to Bradshaw.

I found her control of food interesting. Break that hold and her attention would be jerked back to protecting her empire. I needed to figure out a way to get some of those farming co-ops to renege on their grain delivery contracts.

While I mused, McAllen had calmed the

governor by apologizing for my rudeness and disrespect for his office. I jumped in and reinforced the apology, making some general statement that the stress of the situation had unsettled me. In truth, I had tired of his incessant whining. If men played by different rules, one of them was to be manly. It always surprised me how misfortune turned outwardly virile men craven. The more bluster when things went well usually meant the more excuses when conditions took a bad turn.

I glanced at McAllen. I couldn't imagine him blustering or whining. I had witnessed situations that could have prompted either, yet he never boasted or complained. No matter the situation, McAllen just went ahead and got the job done. It was the same with Jeff Sharp. That thought broke my reverie and brought me back to the purpose of this meeting . . . rescuing our friend.

"Has anyone considered bringing grain and meat from Chicago?" I asked. "Might give her something to do other than make mischief for the people in this room."

The governor shed his negativity and looked intrigued.

"You mean flood the state with an over-supply?" he asked. "Drive prices down through the floor? No, or at least no one mentioned it to me."

"I know someone in Chicago," McAllen said.

"Retired from Pinkerton to run his family's butcher business. He can act as our agent."

I liked the way McAllen said *our agent,* as if he intended to contribute money to the endeavor. Then I realized it wasn't such a good idea because we didn't have enough time to pull it off. There was no way we could coordinate purchases and transport before my trial. Then I remembered something from my past.

When I first met Jenny, a silver tycoon named Sean Washburn threatened my life. In a fit of anger, I had Jansen write me a new will that gave my estate to the Pinkerton National Detective Agency with instructions to use my wealth to find and prosecute my murderer. Luckily, that eventuality had been avoided. But I could do the same thing today, but specify that my money be used to financially destroy Jenny Bolton. I could split my fortune between Virginia and seeking vengeance. In fact, I could even make her the executor of my little scheme of revenge.

"What are you thinkin'?" McAllen asked.

"That we don't have enough time to destroy her hold on food, but I can set it up to happen in case I do hang. Vengeance from the grave, so to speak."

"We can still do it. We bluff," McAllen said.

"What?"

"She doesn't know we just came up with this idea. You could have started buyin' when you first arrived . . . sooner. Hell, it's news to us that

Jenny cornered the state's food supply, but it ain't a secret. You could have learned about it while you were in Denver."

"Richard wrote a series of articles about it," Bradshaw offered.

"Were those the articles that got him killed?" I asked.

"If it wasn't an accident," he answered. "The articles sure made Jenny plenty mad."

A bluff might work, at least as a distraction. If we came up with a few other actions, she might take her eye off our search for Sharp. It was worth a try, besides, we had nothing else at the moment.

"Joseph, how do we make this deception believable?"

"First, I telegram my friend in Chicago." He thought a minute. "Has Jenny corrupted the Western Union office?"

"Doesn't matter," Bradshaw said. "The capitol has its own line and operators."

"It does matter," McAllen said. "I want her to read the incoming wires, but I'd be grateful for access to the state telegraph for my outgoing messages."

I could see the seeds of a plan and I liked it. I was about to offer some further suggestions when Bradshaw's aide came barging through the door.

"I'm sorry, sir, I know you said no interruptions, but Senator James Fair and Congressman William Morris are here to see you."

"Here? Now?" The governor seemed simultaneously startled, confused, and delighted. He stood. "I'm sorry to cut this short, gentlemen, but I can't keep our esteemed senior senator and the chairman of Ways and Means waiting. I'll be in touch when we can get together again."

McAllen stood to leave, but I remained seated.

"Mr. Dancy?" the governor said, lifting a palm to bring me out of my seat.

"I think we'll stay for this meeting," I said.

"I'm afraid that wouldn't be appropriate. Protocol demands that—"

"Governor, Congressman Morris is here to see me, not you. More precisely, he's here to see his niece, Mrs. Baker."

Now the governor looked only confused. "Your fiancée's related to Congressman Morris?"

"She is. We sent him a telegram announcing our engagement five days ago. It appears he decided to respond in person."

The governor harrumphed, and then declared in his stump voice, "Mr. Dancy, you are as yet unrelated to the congressman. He wouldn't be accompanied by our senator if it wasn't government business. I must insist you depart this office."

I slowly stood. "Very well. We'll wait in your outer office. You can call us back in after introductions."

"Go back to the St. Charles. I apologize, but I won't be inviting you back in."

"Perhaps not, but Congressman Morris will."

"And why would he do that?"

"To determine if I'm fit to be his niece's husband."

Chapter 26

In the end, Bradshaw allowed us to remain in his office. The senator and congressman initially appeared puzzled to find other men with the governor. Etiquette called for Bradshaw to excuse his guests through a separate door. I assumed we presented quite a sight. McAllen wore rancher trappings that were clean, but noticeably threadbare. My clothes were clean and relatively new, but more appropriate for a saloon or dusty trail. Perhaps I should have postponed this first meeting until suppertime when I would be dressed more formally. After all, in many ways Morris was comparable to a new father-in-law. He must take a keen interest in his niece to have traveled so far on short notice. The trip might have been a convenience, however, because a long train ride with the senior senator from Nevada might prove highly valuable to a congressional committee chairman.

Fair and Morris looked exactly like what they

were: powerful politicians, intent on becoming more powerful. They both wore tailored and pressed dark suits with ornamental vests over white shirts with stiff collars. Their shoes shined so brightly, I assumed valets accompanied them on the train ride, albeit in second class. Our clean-shaven faces also set us apart from these long-bearded politicians. It occurred to me that like the Smith Brothers, these men could sell cough drops or possibly elixirs for other maladies.

Introductions were made all around. If Morris had looked puzzled by our presence, he appeared baffled when told my name.

As we shook hands, he asked, "Did you know we were coming?"

"No, sir. We were meeting with Governor Bradshaw on a different matter when his aide said you were in the outer office."

"But you stayed because you recognized my name."

"I did, sir."

"How is my niece?"

"Her health is excellent. It may not be the best time to discuss it, but we were meeting here about a serious problem that involves Virginia."

"The best time to address problems is *immediately*." He took a seat next to Senator Fair, which required us to pull over two chairs that had been placed along the wall.

After we had taken our seats, Morris simply said, "Tell me."

It took nearly thirty minutes to tell the senator and congressman about our situation. Neither asked questions as we went, and both remained quiet after we had finished our story.

Finally, Morris asked, "Did you know all of this when you wired me about your engagement?"

"We did," I answered. "At the time, we planned to depart Nevada and leave these problems behind."

Morris sat bolt upright. "And you thought I'd allow my niece to marry a fugitive?"

"It was self-defense, sir."

"I don't doubt it, but until you clear your name, the law will pursue you. That's not the way to start a marriage. You should stay and face trial. You're a Dancy, for god's sake. Don't sully the name."

I was so hot I wanted to leave the office. What made him think he had any say in who Virginia married? Hadn't she already proven that she would marry whomever she wanted? Up until now, McAllen had remained fairly silent, except for adding a detail or two as I described our predicament. Now he spoke.

"Congressman, politicians have a reputation for talking . . . not listening. You evidently didn't hear Steve tell you—without objection from the governor—that the trial will be fixed. Steve will hang if he steps into that courtroom and Virginia's life will be put at risk. If we run, a good man dies. If we stay, a different good man dies. This is the type of villainy confronting us. We remain in Nevada not to stand trial, but to put Mrs. Bolton away." For a long moment, he treated Congressman Morris to the McAllen stare. "Do you intend to help or not?"

"Who are you?" Morris asked, stunned.

"My name is Joseph McAllen. Nothing else about me should concern you. If you're not here to help, I'm leaving. I have a job to get done and jabbering the afternoon away won't help."

"You can't talk to me that way!"

"I'll take that as a no, you're not here to help. Good day, sirs." He stood. "Steve, I'll see you back at the hotel."

He got up and unhurriedly waltzed out of the governor's office.

"Who was that man?" Morris demanded angrily.

"My friend . . . he recently headed the Denver Pinkertons, but resigned recently to start a horse ranch. He's not rich, he's not important, and he's not highly educated, but he's a damn good man in a fight."

"I don't like him. Keep him away from me."

"I don't think that will require much effort. Now, if we can return to the issue at hand, there's a way the two of you can help us and the governor."

"How's that?" This came from Senator Fair,

who sounded as wary as a deer that sniffed an unnatural scent.

"The Nevada legislature has been frightened by the shooting of Senator Wade. They're afraid to offend Mrs. Bolton, which means they vote her wishes, instead of the governor's. To handle Mrs. Bolton, we need the legislature beholden to the governor again. You gentlemen hold the keys to high political positions in our nation's capital. If you could—"

"Hell, no!" Morris exclaimed. "Listen here, young man, we're not here to hand out patronage. Senator Fair has business to attend to and I came to see my niece and her fiancé. I thought she had come to her senses, but after meeting you, I'm not sure. Where is she? I want to talk to her." He got up in a huff. "Now!"

"She's at the St. Charles Hotel," I said. "Are you staying there?"

"No. Senator Fair has been kind enough to invite me to stay at his home."

He stood and asked the senator the location of the St. Charles. Evidently, he found further discussion with me distasteful.

I rose and quietly left by the main door. As I walked out of the capitol, I felt more anger toward those buffoons than I ever felt toward Jenny . . . and she wanted to kill me. I kept marching until something on the St. Charles porch brought me to a halt. Two women in rocking chairs were sipping tea and chatting away as if they had known each other for decades. I stopped with one boot on the bottom step, but my motion must have drawn their attention. Virginia and my mother turned in unison and smiled at me like I was a fattened calf.

Damn, why had we invited our families back into our lives?

Chapter 27

Virginia and my mother knew each other from our recent visit to New York City. It had not been a pleasant encounter, and I never told my mother that Virginia came from an aristocratic family. I felt that was Virginia's choice and she never mentioned it either.

Both women had had huge influence on my life, and yet I couldn't imagine two more different people. My mother obsessed about what other people thought of her and her family. Virginia didn't care a lick about what other people thought. My mother craved money and influence. Virginia enjoyed money, but could be happy without it. My mother dressed for afternoon tea. I bet she was taken aback by Virginia's boots peeking out from under her run-of-the-mill calico dress. A fleeting expression of distaste made it certain she dis-approved of my attire, trail clothes set off with a Colt revolver on my hip. The West had changed Virginia and me. I only hoped that my mother wouldn't change the West.

"You should have wired me you were coming," I said, taking a seat in the next rocker. "I could have arranged quarters for you."

"I didn't want to ruin my surprise. Besides, Virginia already made your suite available to me. She's so gracious. She'll share a room with that cute little Maggie girl. My, I never imagined a state capital so primitive. This is one of the few decent hotels in town and suites are rarer than a properly dressed gentleman."

I tried to keep my face neutral, but I didn't like giving up my suite. The last time I found myself moving rooms, it had been for Jenny's bad-tempered mother-in-law. The parallels were frightening.

"I'm glad we could accommodate you," I said. "Where's Maggie now?"

"In our room arranging things," Virginia answered.

Virginia gave me a glare full of reproach to behave myself. I told myself to remember we reengaged with our families to gain an edge on Jenny. I thought I might call on my mother's financial or political prowess, not that she would show up in person. On the other hand, my mother

187

might be able to dispatch Jenny with one of those condescending looks that made people step out of her way.

"You have my sincere appreciation, even if the rooms are miniature. Your two rooms combined are actually larger than my suite, anyway, so you'll be far more comfortable." She used her condescending look on Virginia. "I understand these things, dear, but it's really inappropriate to share a room before the ceremony. People will talk."

My mother believed that appearances were all important . . . far more important than what went on behind closed doors. She always told me to close doors gently to avoid drawing attention to moments that could embarrass you in the light of day. In other words, it was okay for Virginia to join me in my room, as long as we maintained the pretense of separate rooms. On the frontier, it seemed pretty silly when houses of ill repute outnumbered churches, but I said nothing and garnered a faint smile of approval from Virginia.

"Let's get to the business that brought me to the far edge of civilization." She patted Virginia on the knee. "Mrs. Baker and I had a chance to really get to know each other while you were off gadding with your male friends. I approve of your choice in a wife. Well done, son. It was devilish of you in New York not to tell me your young lady friend was a Philadelphia Morris. Very wicked, indeed. You let us bicker and spar for absolutely no reason. It all could have been avoided if you had been forthright."

"I apologize. In truth, I didn't want to admit that I fell in love with the kind of woman you wanted me to marry."

"Of course, dear. Did you think I didn't know that already? You hate admitting error, just like your father, God rest his soul."

I wanted to strike back, but again held my tongue. Instead, I went to safer ground. "Were you on the same train as Senator James Fair and Congressman William Morris?"

"Only from Denver, dear." She possessively patted Virginia's knee again. "Your uncle is such a gentleman, we had a fascinating conversation. It seems that when it comes to living up to your family obligations, you've been as disobedient as my son, but that's all in the past. We're together now . . . both families, soon to be united in one grand amalgamation."

If holding my tongue before had been difficult, it was now a test of fortitude. There was a slight shake of Virginia's head that helped me hold my temper.

After a deep breath, I said, "I wasn't quite gadding with friends, I was meeting with the governor, Senator Fair, and Congressman Morris. The congressman objects to me marrying his niece. At least in my present circumstances."

Virginia leaned forward to see around my traumatized mother. "Uncle Billy objects to me marrying you?" she asked, incredulous.

"This is distressing," my mother gasped. "Stephen, you must dress and speak properly. You've been despoiled by the seediness out here. Thank goodness I got you moved into separate rooms."

I ignored my mother and answered Virginia. "He objects to you marrying an accused murderer and even more strongly objects to you marrying a fugitive. He counseled me to stay and face trial and he refused to assist with winning over the state legislature. To make matters worse, McAllen spoke bluntly to him, so he objects to my friends, as well. All in all, not a good first meeting."

"I saw that dreadful Mr. McAllen stomp through the hotel a few minutes ago," my mother said. "His mean visage should be against the law . . . if there are laws out here. The congressman's right, you need a better class of friends. But about this—"

Virginia interrupted before I made an angry retort. "Mrs. Dancy, please, Joseph McAllen is an honorable man who has saved your son's life several times. If not for that gruff man, Steve wouldn't be sitting beside you today. I grant you his normal expression is a scowl and he can't abide small talk, but he's a good man with your son's best interests at heart." She smiled sweetly.

"You'll grow to like him after you know him better."

"Doubtful, my dear, but be that as it may, I want to know why my son is going around shooting people." She swung toward me. "*Dancys* don't shoot people. Your father liked to play with those guns of his, but he never aimed one at a real person. We handle our enemies in a more civilized fashion. What have you to say for yourself?"

Another cautionary glance from Virginia. "It was self-defense, mother."

"Well, you shouldn't have given offense, then. But that's neither here nor there. What we need to do is get you acquitted." She got up from the rocking chair. "I'll have the best team of lawyers money can buy on a train within the hour."

I presumed her intent was to go into the hotel to compose a telegram that some boy would run over to Western Union. I couldn't imagine her walking over there herself. On second thought, she probably assumed the best hotel in Carson City had its own telegraph station. She would be disappointed.

"Mother, please sit down. I have the best lawyer in the state, but this is not a legal issue, it's a political issue. Nevada is corrupt beyond even your experience. All the attorneys in New York cannot get me a fair trial. That's why we were hoping the senator and congressman could help."

"How exactly?"

I explained the entire mess to her. She listened all the way through without comment, but showed more and more consternation as I went along. I told her everything. If she was to be of help, she had to know the details. And she was a considerable force when she set her mind to it. I knew she would throw everything behind me to help. My bet was that eventually, so would Congressman Morris. We were more important to our respective families than I had imagined. All of their harsh words could be discarded after considering one real fact; both my mother and Morris jumped on the first available train after receiving our telegrams. Earlier, we had said we didn't like our families, but they were still ours. It was how we grew up. Now I recognized that we were also theirs. They were being their normal, difficult selves, but in the end, if we didn't insult them, they would help.

When I finished, my mother sat quiet for a moment. Then she said, "I read news stories about a Steve Dancy, but I always assumed it was another man with the same name. Now I find out that those stories were true and my son is a notorious gunfighter, shooting people right and left. You're friends with vile men who practice violence."

"I won't argue about the shootings I've been in, but my friends are not vile and they use violence only as a last resort. This is not Manhattan where

192

grudges are settled with foreclosures and press releases."

"Steve's right, Mrs. Dancy," Virginia added. "These are good men . . . and it wasn't that long ago a United States Vice President shot and killed a former Secretary of the Treasury on the outskirts of your fair city. When last in New York, we ran into gang violence on your streets. Whether you believe it or not, the murder rate is higher in New York than on the frontier. In fact, killings are still news out here."

"I don't accept that," my mother said. "I've never witnessed any violence back east."

"That's because in the West violence is not quarantined to bad districts," Virginia said. "Classes intermingle out here."

"You seem such a gentlewoman to have such an unrefined opinion about the world."

"I assure you, my opinions have been refined . . . refined by experiencing life outside of my childhood cocoon."

"That's neither here nor there," my mother said dismissively. "What's important now is clearing Steve of these awful charges and getting you two happily married with the blessings of both families. Agreed?"

I recognized my mother's habit of setting clear goals before taking action.

Virginia and I caught each other's eye and smiled. In unison, we said, "Agreed."

Chapter 28

I had talked with my mother and Virginia for nearly an hour before Congressman Morris strolled in our direction looking every bit the peacock, begging for attention. When he spotted the three of us on the hotel porch, his features softened, and then turned joyful. In an agile move for someone his age, he bounded up the porch steps and lifted his niece out of her rocker to give her a long hug. I was impressed. His first unguarded moment showed genuine emotion. He unquestionably adored Virginia.

He held her out at arm's length and looked her up and down. "My goodness, you are a sight for sore eyes. I've missed you, Ginger."

"Thank you, Uncle Billy. I've missed you more than you can imagine."

"Oh, dear, we mustn't use that term in public." He winked. "At least not vociferously."

Despite his words, he looked enormously pleased that she had used a nickname reserved for her. Virginia didn't like being called by a nickname, but she had told me Ginger had been her uncle's term of endearment for her since she had resided in a bassinet. He was still a pompous, power-seeker, but at least he had one soft spot. Hell, it was the same one I had, so he couldn't be all bad.

After the emotion of the greeting diminished, I suggested we move indoors out of public view. Morris heartily agreed. The small stand-up bar wouldn't do, so I tipped the porter to use a room restricted to private supper parties. The porter immediately sent in the barman to take our drink order.

"Your arrival has caused quite a stir," I said. "It's unusual to have someone of your stature visit Carson City."

"Son, I've been buttered up by the best, so you can leave it be. I'm just a lowly congressman . . . and by the way, if memory serves, President Grant toured Virginia and Carson Cities not long ago."

"He did," I answered, "but Grant's retired. You, on the other hand, chair the most important committee in Congress. This is a political town, and politicians can spot a titan from a dozen paces."

"A titan?" he laughed, and then laughed some more. "Never been called that before. Son, when you're done here, you might find work in the great District of Columbia."

"If I may, sir, are you no longer peeved at me?"

"No . . . yes, a bit. The governor vouched for you, so I guess this incident . . . did it happen here?"

"In the dining room," I answered.

"After a few drinks, I may impose on you to describe the incident in minute detail. I've eaten tense meals with disreputable men, but none erupted into gunfire." He made a show of looking around. "So this is the Wild West. Looks fairly tame so far."

"Tame?" my mother said. "Ruffians everywhere." She glanced down at my Colt. "Guns, knives, fisticuffs. Hard men, like that awful Mr. McAllen. I know he saved your life, son, but you won't need someone like him when you return to New York."

"Or Philadelphia," Morris added.

"We intend on living in the West and visiting the East," Virginia said, as if she were commenting on the weather.

"Oh, dear, that will never do." My mother traded a conspiratorial glance with Morris. "The congressman and I think you should live close to family. You can pick between the two cities and as a wedding present, we'll buy you a fine townhouse. Although I'm sure, New York will be preferable to Philadelphia."

"Now, Mrs. Dancy, we agreed to let the young couple decide for themselves. If you don't stop lobbying, I'll be forced to throw Washington into the mix."

Virginia uttered some banalities to deflect the subject, but I wasn't paying attention. I was thinking, and what I was thinking made me apprehensive. How far had negotiations progressed for this *grand amalgamation* of our two families? Was there more than a business deal behind their visit to Nevada? I suddenly suspected that the common train ride from Denver had been no coincidence.

"Listen," I said, "let's talk about where we'll live after Virginia and I get a chance to discuss your generous offer. I'm afraid you're far ahead of us. By the way, if I may be so bold, are you a descendant of Gouverneur Morris or Robert Morris?"

"Yes, indeed," Morris said. "One of them is my great grandfather. Which do you prefer?"

Both had been Philadelphia residents, and both were important Founding Fathers. Unrelated, they had each played a major role in the Revolution and at the Constitutional Convention. It had never occurred to me to ask Virginia, in fact, the question just popped into my head when I needed a change of subject.

"The author of the Constitution or the host for General Washington during the convention? Tough choice. I think you should feel honored in either case."

"Very diplomatic, son." He smiled, but it wasn't friendly. "Well, my great grandfather was Robert Morris, the richest man in America during the revolution, but he died a pauper due to his speculation in western lands. Ever since then, none of us Morrises have been too keen on the West."

That didn't go the way I had hoped, so I decided to return to the *grand amalgamation.*

I asked, "Did you begin trading telegrams immediately after you received the announcement of our engagement?"

"We did," my mother exclaimed. "We made arrangements to meet in Denver so we could travel together to see you love birds. It was a beautiful trip through the mountains. My goodness, I've never before seen landscape so wild and majestic."

"Did you settle any other issues between the families?" I asked.

"Now, now," the congressman said, "we haven't bartered your souls for any accommodations. We merely discussed places for the wedding and where you children might live after the marriage. We assume it would be close to one of the two families. We both love you dearly and want you nearby. But the decision is yours."

"Well, let Virginia and me discuss it," I said, as flatly as possible. "We'll get back to you. Unfortunately, we have a prerequisite to resolve. If you remember, I have a murder trial coming up and time is fleeting. In Governor Bradshaw's office, you took offense to doling out patronage. Are you unwilling to use your position to help us?"

"Mr. Dancy, you may know how to handle guns, but you're unfamiliar with handling men, especially politicians. I'll use my position to help you, but I prefer being paid double. I'll help you and Ginger, but beyond your gratitude, I want the governor beholden to me. In politics, you never give anything away for free . . . especially when you can charge twice for it."

He laughed to give the impression he was not entirely serious. I knew he was.

"So, you and the governor came to an agreement after I left?" I asked.

"Yes . . . and the results of our little talk put the bounce in my step you may have noticed. Your governor will be the cock of the walk in no time at all, at least as long as he confines his walks to Carson Street."

"And in return, Senator Fair will . . ." I left the question hanging.

"That my soon-to-be nephew must remain mum. Best way to squelch a deal is to blab it about."

He looked exceptionally pleased with himself, so he must have gotten something highly valuable. I didn't care about the quid pro quo. Getting the political side of our plan in place was all I cared about. On second thought, I also cared about the price of my *gratitude*. I could guess, but if it remained unspoken, I could possibly get away with playing dumb. I steered the conversation in another direction.

"Thank you." I took Virginia's hand. "We love each other very much, but other than the engagement, we've made no plans. We need to get past the trial before we can get serious about our future."

"With trains, we can live almost anywhere," Virginia offered.

Both smiled indulgently at us. They were certain that in the end, we would come around to abide by their wishes.

"We should let you two discuss our offer of a grand town house," Morris said. "I gather Steve's a bright young man who realizes our families' good wishes bestow many benefits . . . and corresponding obligations. Your marriage is no small affair."

I was a bright enough young man to realize that in this man's world, unspoken conditions were unlimited conditions. Playing dumb would never work. My mother had negotiated the outlines of a deal and I'd regret leaving it in their hands.

"Congressman, before we proceed, we need to get the terms of our gratitude clear. What have you and my mother agreed to?"

"Agreed to? Why, nothing. Everything is up to you, of course."

"Dear," my mother said, "don't be difficult. Our offer is not a bribe, it's a welcome home gift. We want you to rejoin the family and leave this barren wasteland. What can you possibly find engaging here? New York and Philadelphia are beautiful cities with culture and manners. And a fair justice system, I might add. If you—"

"Fair justice system? How do you define fair? Money can bend it any way you—"

"Bend, not break," my mother said in a rare display of anger. "The world's not perfect, but it is certainly less imperfect in the East. Here, you might as well throw a rope around your own neck. This lawlessness may very well kill you, son. In New York, I could get this all brushed away, and I would never apologize for *bending* a few public officials to save my son's life. Justly, I might add."

I suppressed my first impulse to argue. People were the same all over the world . . . and throughout time. Corruption existed, was fought, disappeared for a time, but always returned. I had read that Benjamin Franklin had said that humans were badly constructed because they were more easily provoked than reconciled, more disposed to do mischief than good, more easily deceived than undeceived, more impressed with their own self than considerate of others, and that man takes more pride in killing than in begetting. Franklin said men assemble great armies to destroy, and when they have killed as many as they can, they exaggerate the number. But men creep into corners or darkness to beget. I liked the West because the corruption was unsophisticated; it was out in the open for everyone to see. And what you see, you can fight. The big cities of the East ran a grand game of pretend. Quarantine the bad stuff, and do ill deeds behind closed doors. But it was useless to argue with my mother. She believed pretend was reality. All of that didn't mean I didn't need to get the conditions of this agree-ment clear from the outset.

"Congressman, what are your political ambitions?"

"Son, I have my hands full with my district. I have no grand ambitions."

"I believe you do. In fact, I don't believe it's possible to gain the chairmanship of Ways and Means without grand ambitions."

Now, he looked peeved again.

I charged ahead. "I suspect you harbor presidential ambitions. That's a tough reach. The presidency requires national support. Support from even wayward states like Nevada. Support and money from New York." Before getting to my point, I gave him a moment to ponder what I had said. Then I added matter-of-factly, "I started by saying we needed to get the terms of gratitude clear. How do you intend to show your gratitude to me and the Dancy family for helping you establish residency at 1600 Pennsylvania Avenue?"

I thought he would explode, but only for a moment. He suddenly burst out laughing and then reached around Virginia to squeeze her shoulder.

"Ginger, you have landed quite a catch. A natural. Damn, if he didn't turn that one on me."

With a fond expression, he extended his hand to me. We shook. Then he smiled kindly at Virginia.

"I approve of your choice in a husband."

Chapter 29

The next morning, I left Virginia with her uncle because I needed to find McAllen. The political end seemed to be falling into place, and I wanted to check on the business end of our assault. I found him at the livery with Maggie, renting horses for a morning ride.

McAllen leaned against a wall as Maggie evaluated the stock like a seasoned rancher. The rare smile on his face had proud father written all over it.

After he acknowledged me, I asked, "Did you send a telegram from the capitol?"

"No. I tried but I couldn't compose a message that sounded plausible to my ears. It needs your business experience. Besides, the way I left the governor's office, I didn't think his assistant would send it for me anyway, and I sure wasn't gonna stick my head back in to ask the governor."

He reached into his pocket and pulled out a pencil and telegraph form. "Why don't you compose a message right now?"

"Good idea. I'll send it while you ride. Might even have an answer before you get back."

"I suggest you give him the exact wordin' for the return message," McAllen said.

I walked over to a stand-up writing shelf in the rear of the livery. The pencil in my hand hung over the form in indecision. The difficulty would be composing the return telegram. The instructions needed to be terse, yet comprehensive. The development of the telegraph had caused the Pony Express to disappear, taking with it the ability to send long messages with speed. People used to write long letters meant to entertain as well as communicate. The Pony Express made each page of paper expensive, and then the telegraph made every word precious. Civilization traded wordi-ness for swiftness. It made me wonder how we would handle this modern world of compressed space and time.

I tried to envision what an agent would send his client if he had contracted for great quantities of foodstuff. This was going to take longer than I thought.

Eventually, I had a telegram that sounded like one I would expect to receive from someone spending a great deal of my money. This reminded me that we had another problem.

I yelled over to Joseph, "How do we reimburse this man for the cost of a lengthy telegram? We can't wire money from the governor's office and we can't send money from Western Union without raising suspicions."

McAllen threw himself away from the wall he was holding up and walked the length of the barn to where I was standing. Then he tapped my form. "Tell him we'll wire him one hundred dollars in four days. He'll trust me."

"One hundred dollars?"

"Quit grousing. Your life's worth twice that."

He turned around toward Maggie and his intake of breath make me look over at her as well. Three men had gathered close around her, gradually crowding her into a stall. McAllen moved fast, but I was only three steps behind him.

"You men have only a moment to save your lives," Maggie said. "My dad's in the back of the barn."

"We know that sugar, but he ain't—"

A noise stopped all conversation. Neither of us had spotted a fourth man hiding in a closer stall. He stepped out with a two-barrel shotgun, but he had underestimated McAllen's speed. As he tried to bring the barrel up, McAllen was already a half-step from being parallel to him. Without breaking stride, McAllen drew his big Smith and Wesson .44 and clobbered the man across the head just above his ear. He collapsed like a scarecrow knocked from his post. With my gun in hand, I continued to chase after McAllen.

The other three men stared agape at us charging toward them. No one wanted to pull their weapon because McAllen's .44 was already leveled at them. From behind, I couldn't see his expression, but for sure it was scarier than the big sidearm. I anticipated an explosion from McAllen's gun, but it didn't happen. Instead, McAllen planted his pointed boot into the groin of the biggest man as he whipped the long barrel around and crushed the skull of the one standing closest to Maggie. I arrived soon enough to ram my pistol under the chin of the fourth.

"Should I kill him?" I asked, regretting the question immediately because McAllen may have been too angry to recognize my bluff.

"Not until I talk to him," McAllen said.

The man McAllen had kicked writhed around and groaned so madly that I was about to put a boot to his head. McAllen beat me to it.

I still had a gun on the fourth man, but McAllen brushed me aside. "What's your name?" he asked.

"Go to hell."

McAllen poked him hard in the middle of the chest and he doubled over wheezing. He then grabbed his hair and pulled his head up. "What's your name?"

"Jude . . . Jude Carlson."

McAllen released his grip on his hair and Carlson bent double again.

"Steve, take Maggie back to the hotel. She shouldn't see what's gonna to happen in the next few minutes."

"I warned you." Maggie spoke in a defiant tone, but she couldn't disguise the nervous crack in her voice.

McAllen asked me to tie up the other three before I escorted Maggie to the hotel. She disappeared into a stall and immediately reemerged with a long rope. After a threat as scary as she had just been through, she still thought clearly. Maggie was definitely her father's daughter.

I only knew basic knots, but Maggie helped me hogtie all three men with the same rope. When we finished, the one with the groin injury started to moan again. Maggie kicked him in the head and he quieted right down. Father's daughter, all right.

As we walked back to the hotel, I said, "We were bluffing about hurting Carlson. Your father told me to take you back to the hotel to scare him so he would talk."

"I know," she said. She walked on a few paces before adding, "I wish he would hurt him. All of them. They were going to do something worse than hurt me."

"You're right. And they wanted to kill your father. If you had screamed, he might not have reacted the way he did. He might have been so full of fury, he wouldn't have noticed that man with the shotgun. You were very brave."

"They didn't want to kill my dad; they wanted him to see what they were going to do to me. They told me so."

I stopped and looked at her. "They told you that?"

"They whispered it in my ear . . . and then that ugly man licked my ear."

"Why would they whisper?" I asked. "Did they want to give the man with the shotgun time to hide?"

"I don't think so. I never saw him. He must have already been hidden away. Now that I think of it, maybe they wanted me to scream."

That made sense. A scream would signal the hidden man that McAllen would start running toward his daughter and he would have been better positioned to force him to stop. Stupid. They didn't know McAllen. He would've made the killer use both barrels on him so the path was clear for me to save his daughter. He would never hesitate to sacrifice his life for Maggie.

"You were even braver than I thought," I said. "Did they say anything else?"

"They said you're all going to die, but not now. Now was time for my lesson."

Chapter 30

I left Maggie with Virginia and raced back to the barn where I found McAllen leaning against an outside wall looking angry as hell.

"Damn it, Steve, why'd you leave Maggie?"

"She's safe with my mother and Virginia. I told them to stay in the room. I came back to keep you off the gallows."

"I didn't kill them . . . not yet anyway. Carlson won't be pullin' a trigger or throwin' a punch for a while though."

I looked around, but saw nothing unusual in the street activity. "It's dangerous for you to stand out her in the open."

"It's safe enough. After that bastard got talkative, he said it wasn't time for us yet. 'Sides, I'm in the mood for someone to take a shot at me."

McAllen was not suicidal, so I assumed he wanted justification to shoot someone. He was in a murderous frame of mind.

"What did you learn?" I asked.

"Employed by Carson Investigations. That's Jenny's supposed detective agency. Carlson said that Jenny has nothing to do with running the shop, and this contract supposedly came from another source . . . a confidential source. Claims he was just following directions from his boss."

"Who's the boss?"

"A man named Dick Matting. I'm trying to cool off before payin' him a visit."

I hooked a thumb at the door. "Them?"

"Tied up . . . all four. They'll keep."

"Turn them over to the marshal?" I asked.

"No." McAllen was emphatic. "Once they're in jail, I can't get to them. Let them stay right where they are for the time being. I bribed the liveryman to turn a blind eye."

"Did he see anything?"

"No, he was gone . . . collecting an overdue horse hitched out by the train station. Doesn't matter, the three of us can testify against them if it comes to it." He pulled his revolver and loaded a sixth cartridge. "Load up. We might run into trouble."

I followed his example and loaded a sixth cartridge as I skipped along to keep up with his pace. Usually, I had no trouble striding alongside McAllen. He moved deliberately, and sometimes became as motionless as a possum—until he needed swiftness. Then he moved unbelievably fast. Opponents underestimated him because his languid manner promised a lumbering response. The explosion of speed caught them off guard. Yet even moving fast, his actions remained deliberate. There was no wasted motion. No miscues. Riled, McAllen was the most deadly man I had ever encountered. And he was riled now.

Carson Investigations occupied a building next to the Mint. We covered the two blocks in short order. I wondered how we would approach entering the office when McAllen just burst right through the door with more energy than a locomotive under full steam. Heads whipped around at the noise, and a couple men put a hand on their sidearm, but nobody pulled a weapon. I counted five men; two sitting at an oak table and three standing in the corner. A door in the center of the back wall indicated that this was probably an outer office.

"We're here to see Dick Matting," McAllen said.

One of the standing men stepped forward. "On what business?"

"Are you Matting?"

"No."

"Then it's not your business."

This was one of those times when McAllen went still. Not a single muscle flinched. He just dared this pretend Pinkerton to challenge him.

"I'll see if he's available." He turned and walked toward the back door.

The other four men struggled to appear intimidating, but I could see their confidence wither. One still had a hand on his revolver, but after the briefest of glares from McAllen, he slowly eased his hand away. I wished I could control men with my demeanor.

The man returned from the backroom. "Mr. Matting's unavailable. He asked me to set up an appointment for you. What's your name?"

"Puddin Tane," McAllen said.

"Listen, don't be—"

"You know my name, and you know who I am." He took a step forward. "I'm the father of the girl your friends tried to rape."

He looked unnerved. "I don't know what you're talking about."

"You better hope that's true . . . otherwise, I'll beat you until you wish I had just killed you." He pointed at the door. "Go back in there and tell him you made the appointment for right now." He raised his voice. "The rest of you, you have only this moment to decide if you'd rather be some-place else."

Nobody moved.

McAllen slowly lowered the hand that been pointing at the door. It now rested close to his gun.

"Wait!" one of the men yelled. "I want to go."

Another nodded that he wanted to desert as well. I threw my head to the side to indicate they could leave and then shifted around so I could watch them as they went out the front door. In all, three of the men ended up leaving the building.

McAllen stared at the man he had ordered to

return to the backroom. The man tentatively turned to reenter Matting's domain. Just as he twisted the knob, McAllen dashed toward the opening and shoved the man inside, and then he spun against the wall, ducking at the same time. I dropped to a knee and drew my Colt, pointing it at the sole remaining man in the outer office. There was an immediate blast that sounded deafening in the enclosed space. The man stumbled back with arms flailing. He collapsed in a bloody mess with a shocked expression. He had taken a double load of buckshot in the midsection.

The last man in the outer office pointed desperately at the door. I had never seen anyone so scared. I nodded and he scurried out as fast as his feet would carry him. After he was gone, I scampered in a crouch to the front door and stretched a leg over to kick it shut, all the while making sure I remained out of the sightline of anyone in the backroom. McAllen had watched my progress and nodded approval. Now it was us against whoever waited for us beyond the wall.

Suddenly, McAllen burst across the open doorway and rolled into the corner. Another shotgun boom splintered the pine paneling just to the other side of the doorframe, but McAllen was long past that point by the time the blast came. Damn. He wanted us positioned on either side of the door, but walking the space with a shotgun on the other side of the paneling seemed risky, so I waddled the length of the room until I rested against the back wall. I was sweating and I tried to control my heavy breathing so the noise didn't give away my position.

McAllen held up the palm of his hand as a signal to wait. He then pulled off his boots and scooted toward the front door in his stocking feet. After a nod from him, I did the same. Scurrying back and forth across the length of this room was getting tiresome. Now our backs were against the front wall. We were still within lethal range for buck-shot, but the additional distance made the shooter's aim more difficult.

McAllen pointed his face against the wall to help disguise his location. He yelled, "Matting, come on out with your hands up. There's no one left out here to help you."

"I have men in here to help me. I'd be pleased to introduce you. Come on in."

"I don't believe you. You're by yourself."

"I got friends here."

"Sure, shotguns, rifles and pistols. Too bad you're the only shooter."

"I'll wait for the marshal."

McAllen pulled a pocket pistol from behind his back and placed it on the floor in front of him. Then he pantomimed shooting at the wall with his .44. He pointed at me and used a crossing motion with his finger to indicate that I should shoot at the wall on his side. I had a moment of confusion until I realized he wanted to tear up the wall so we could see the target through the holes. It might just work.

I nodded understanding and he instantly fired at the spot where the previous shotgun blast had perforated the paneling. I let him empty his gun before shooting, keeping my pattern of shots close to his cluster of holes. I reloaded while we waited for the deafening noise to fade and the gun smoke to disburse. When I glanced over, McAllen had his .32 aimed toward the hole in the thin pine. When he saw I was ready, he laid the .32 down and reloaded his Smith and Wesson.

After we were both reloaded, McAllen scooted sideways, peering through the holes. He gave me a puzzled look before edging back and forth again.

"Matting!" he yelled. "Last chance to come out!"

No response.

McAllen waved his hand for us to move forward. This was less dangerous for me because the wall remained intact on my side, but McAllen approached a splintered and shattered wood mess that possibly made him visible. I moved not only forward, but also a bit to the side so I would be up against the doorjamb when I arrived. My ears still rang for the gunshots, but I don't believe we made any noise as we approached. Once against the wall, McAllen took a quick peek through a major hole and then jerked his head back. A moment later, he took a longer look and then stood erect, signaling me to do the same. He stepped through the doorway and I followed.

My ears must have been more than ringing because Matting looked to be screaming with two bullet holes in his lower torso. When we blasted away to see through the wall, two of our shots hit Matting.

I realized if I couldn't hear Matting, I wouldn't hear someone entering the building from behind us. I whipped around to see a man not more than three feet away.

Marshal Wilson stood behind us, gun drawn.

Chapter 31

Two deputies with raised rifles stood behind the marshal. I looked back at Matting when I heard his screams and realized my hearing had started to return. Both wounds were in the thigh, but for him to make that much noise, one of the shots must have splintered bone. The room was still a haze of blue smoke and the odor of gunpowder burned my nostrils. The man blasted with buckshot laid motionless, leaking more blood than I thought a body held.

"This action is over, marshal." I heard McAllen say this as if he were in the bottom of a well. He added, "Go away. I need a few minutes."

"I can't do that, Mr. McAllen. Please holster your guns."

I did immediately, but McAllen made a show of unhurriedly sliding his pistol into his holster. As soon as McAllen finished, Wilson put his gun away as well. Following the marshal's example, the deputies lowered their rifles. I wondered if either of these two had been corrupted by Bolton. I decided to keep a wary eye on them.

Wilson made a hand signal and the deputies carried Matting out the office, presumably to a doctor. I was glad to see him gone so we didn't need to yell over his screaming. I walked back into the front room and pulled my boots back on. McAllen followed suit.

When we stood, Wilson asked, "Why did Matting barricade himself in this room? Did he know you were coming?"

"He knew our askin' for him didn't bode well for his safety," McAllen said.

Wilson cocked his head and waited for an explanation.

I wondered if McAllen trusted Wilson. The deputies had left to carry Matting off, so it was only the three of us standing over a corpse. Whether he trusted him or not, he decided to tell the truth.

"Four of his men tried to rape my daughter," McAllen said. "Steve and I stopped them. I came to find out who hired them."

Wilson looked skeptical. "You think they were under orders?"

"I wasn't sure until he started shooting at the sound of our names." McAllen stared at the marshal. "I want to talk to him as soon as possible."

"Matting's in my custody. I'll do the questioning."

Now we had a contest of manhood. At first it looked evenly matched, but Wilson withered, and to disguise his defeat, he asked if the dead man was the only other person in the outer office.

"He had five men out here doing nothin'," McAllen said. "Three left before the shooting started, another left soon after." McAllen pointed at the bloody corpse. "This one barged in on Matting, so Matting unloaded into him."

The marshal picked up the shotgun. He felt the barrel to see if it was warm, and then checked to see if it had been reloaded. It was. Next, he looked around the floor until he found two spent hulls, which he put in his pocket.

"How'd those holes get in Matting?" he asked.

"Chance. We started firing back, but we couldn't see to the other side of the wall."

"Let's see if I got this right. Four employees of this agency tried to rape your daughter. You stopped them and then came here to find out who hired them. Matting killed this agent on the floor and his other men ran away, and you wounded Matting firing blind through a wall."

"You have it right," McAllen said.

Wilson turned to me. "Do you agree with all of that?"

I decided to follow McAllen's lead and answer as brief as possible.

"Yes," I said.

Wilson shook his head, and then asked, "Where are the rapists?"

"Tied up in the livery," McAllen answered.

It surprised me that McAllen answered truthfully, but Wilson wouldn't allow us to return to the livery to beat answers out of those men anyway. I guess McAllen decided we might as well try to gain some cooperation from the marshal. Besides, they already told us it was a confidential assignment and they didn't know the client. They probably didn't know any more.

"Well, we better go over there and—"

Wilson didn't finish because one of his deputies burst through the door yelling that Matting was dead.

As we all ran to the doctor's office, the deputy yelled out that Matting had bled to death. When we arrived, the doctor said a splintered bone ruptured the femoral artery. Without Matting, we could never prove that Jenny hired his supposed agents to rape Maggie. All of this fighting had accomplished nothing. Had the deputies delayed getting Matting to the doctor? Had they poked around in the wound to make it worse? Did the doctor suspect foul play beyond the bullet wound? My impatience grew. McAllen seemed apathetic.

As we left the doctor's office, we nearly bumped into Copley running in the door. Without greeting, McAllen grabbed his elbow and pushed him away from the marshal and his deputies. He must have squeezed hard because Copley winced and back-stepped immediately.

"What?" McAllen demanded once we were out of earshot.

"It's Jenny. She's with your daughter. At the hotel."

Chapter 32

The three of us ran to the St. Charles. Actually, McAllen ran like hell and Copley and I chased after him. When I burst into the lobby, I saw no one, but heard boots on the staircase. I followed close behind and heard Copley breathing hard behind me.

The door to my room was wide open; the room was empty. The door to Virginia's and Maggie's room was also wide open showing no one inside.

McAllen had evidently thrown each door open and then raced forward when he failed to find Maggie. I hurried after him so fast that I bounced against the wall as I made the turn in the hallway.

There they were . . . in my mother's suite.

McAllen looked like a madman towering menacingly over the four women who sat on facing settees. Virginia, my mother, Jenny, and Maggie had all reared back in fright, probably due to an apparition bursting through the door without knocking.

"Pa, what's wrong?" Maggie shrieked.

At first McAllen said nothing. He just whipped his head around, looking at the four women in turn. They all appeared to have been crying, but now were dry eyed. Even my mother's eyes appeared puffy. What happened here? I had never before seen a tear deface my mother's aristocratic deportment.

McAllen concentrated his attention on Jenny, demanding to know what she was doing here. Jenny started to answer, but my mother beat her to it.

"Mr. McAllen, this is my room. Please go back outside into the hall, gently close the door, and knock like a proper gentleman."

"I'll do no such damn thing. This may be your room, but Maggie's my daughter and this woman"—he pointed, or rather jabbed at Jenny—"sent ruthless thugs to . . . to . . ."

"I think rape is the word you are looking for, pa," Maggie said with a firmness that surprised me.

"What? Maggie . . . listen, you have no idea what that word means," McAllen stammered.

"I know what the word means. I'm not a child and I work summers on a ranch. But you're right, I don't know the hurt . . . the humiliation. I escaped that, but Jenny didn't."

My mother waved at us to step inside the suite. McAllen turned around and saw me and Copley for the first time.

"Tom, get out of here," McAllen ordered.

Copley shook his head no, but retreated immediately after McAllen took a step in his direction.

"Steve, get inside and close the door."

After quietly shutting the door, I stood close by McAllen's gun hand. I had never witnessed McAllen lose control, but he had never been this angry. I wasn't afraid of him shooting Jenny, but McAllen had a penchant for pistol whipping opponents. We had barely saved Maggie from a horrific assault, and then fought a nerve rattling gun battle. Rage made me want to continue fighting, and Maggie wasn't even *my* daughter. I couldn't imagine how McAllen felt. Despite our fury, the four women did not cower. I expected McAllen to explode, but he seemed thrown at a loss by the women's calm demeanor. His daughter's presence also deterred him from violent action or even a heated exchange. I understood. I didn't want the situation to get out of hand in front of Virginia either. Was that why Jenny was here? Instead of running away, had she sought protection by sticking close to the women we loved?

Maggie was the first to speak. "Pa, Jenny didn't tell those men to go after me. Someone else is behind this."

"What makes you believe that?" McAllen's voice sounded eerily calm.

My mother answered. "We know this because while you men were out doing who knows what, we've talked it all out. Jenny told us about her own rapes. She would never inflict that degradation on another woman. In fact, she—"

"You don't *know* any of this!" McAllen boomed. "That's just what she told you. For god's sake, she's a liar . . . a practiced liar. A damn good, practiced liar. Her whole life has been one lie after another."

"You're right," Jenny said. "I do lie, and I don't like you or your friends, but I didn't—"

"You didn't what?" McAllen yelled. "You own that damned agency. Those were your hands. They meant to hurt my little girl and you sent them. I should knock your teeth out right now. You think you can hide behind these women. You think I won't do anything in their—"

"Quiet!" This came from my mother. "You will do nothing in front of us except listen. Jenny admits she caused you trouble. She wanted to hurt you, Steve, and that other man. But she says she'd never harm your daughter, and I believe her. We all believe her."

McAllen paced with long strides and abrupt about-faces. I had never seen him so fidgety. Finally, he reached out his hand to Maggie. "Come on. We're gettin' out of here."

"No. Pa, grab a chair. You need to hear this out."

I feared the explosion would finally come, but McAllen meekly pulled a straight-back chair from along the wall and sat down. I did the same.

Since neither of us said a word, Jenny started the conversation.

"Mr. McAllen, I own Carson Investigations, and those men worked for the agency, but I did not order them to . . . attack your daughter. Maggie's the same age I was when my father sold me into marriage, a marriage that led to me being raped by two foul men ordered to teach my husband a lesson. My husband, not me. I would never do that to another woman. Never. I would never inflict that kind of shame on an innocent relative just to get even with another person. That's cowardly . . . and I'm not a coward. I'll come right at you." She nodded toward Maggie. "Your daughter's not part of our feud."

"Why the hell are we even in a feud?" I asked bewildered.

Silence.

Jenny slowly stood and met me eye to eye. "Mr. Dancy, you could have saved me, but you didn't. You couldn't be bothered. You killed those animals to protect Mr. Sharp. But not me. Not me. Then you acted like you did me a favor, but I knew you did it for Mr. Sharp. And you had the nerve to come waltzing around trying to court me. Then when I didn't succumb to your charms, you tossed me away like a used cigarette butt. I hate you." She wheeled on McAllen. "And you. When I take revenge against my husband's killer, you sneer at me. You belittle me. Like you wouldn't do the same. The two of you need a lesson in manners. But not Maggie. She's still a whole person and I'm not going be the one to break her. It'll be some man who breaks her, probably mean-like, the same way a shithole wrangler breaks a proud wild horse . . . all bit and no grit."

She was crying . . . and the other three women were once again misty-eyed.

There was some truth in what she said. I did witness her abduction by the Cutler brothers. I wanted to save her, but I was unarmed, and it would have been suicide to try to rescue her. At least that's what I told myself at the time . . . and every day since. I later killed both brothers in a street fight, but I wasn't protecting Sharp. Not entirely, anyway. I regretted not helping Jenny and that regret tipped the scale toward taking action before someone else got hurt. In truth, I needed to prove to myself that it hadn't been cowardice that kept me from helping Jenny.

I glanced at my mother and Virginia. Their expressions showed disapproval tinged with confusion and doubt. I couldn't let Jenny's accusations stand unchallenged.

"Jenny, I'm sorry. I wanted to save you, but I was unarmed. The Cutlers would have killed me and still taken you. There was nothing I could do."

"You helped Mr. Sharp."

"By that time I carried a gun . . . I carried a gun because of what happened to you . . . and I wasn't going to be caught unarmed again."

Tears were rolling down her cheeks. "You see it the way you want to remember it."

"I could say the same," I responded.

"Damn you. You could have—"

"Who the hell cares?" McAllen yelled. "Did Steve know you? Did he have any obligation to protect you? Hell no. What happened to you was horrible, but it wasn't Steve's fault. He didn't do it. And I don't give a shit if I hurt your feelin's after you killed my prisoner in cold-blood. Now, who do you have on your side, because if it's only you, I can end this so-called feud with a single bullet!"

I stood ready to interfere. I didn't want McAllen shooting Jenny in front of three women that appeared sympathetic to her side, but his threat must have been bluster because he made no move toward his pistol.

"No need," Jenny said. "I already ended it myself. It got out of hand and I want no further part of it. I've ordered Mr. Sharp released. He'll be here in three days."

"Three days?" I said. "Where did you hide him?"

"Belleville."

"His old home?" I asked incredulous.

"I own it now. Along with most of his old mining operations."

"Three days?" McAllen yelled at her. "Three days until we know if you're tellin' the truth? You're crazy if you think you can lie your way out of this."

"I'm not crazy. I didn't want to hurt anyone, just scare you. But—"

"Didn't want to hurt anyone?" I said angrily. "You had Jerimiah beat up so bad he lost an eye. You had Richard murdered. What the hell do you mean you didn't want to hurt anyone?"

"I didn't do either of those things. That wasn't me."

"Everybody says it was you."

"I've heard the rumors. I let them go because a tough reputation helps me in my business dealings. Besides, I'd rather people talk about how mean I am than keep harping on my past."

McAllen shook his head. "You abducted Sharp, but you want us to believe you're not behind these other violent acts. Who else could it be?"

"I don't know!" She was nearly hysterical.

Now I paced. "And you want us to wait for three days to see if we can take you at your word. Joseph's right, this is ridiculous."

'No, it's not," Maggie said. "We believe her and we saw the telegram. She wrote it right here and a bellboy took it to Western Union. She ordered Sharp escorted here immediately. It's not her fault that it's a three day ride."

"It *is* her fault," McAllen said, not mollified in the least.

I held up a hand to quiet everyone. Surprisingly, they obeyed. Something bothered me about this whole affair, but I couldn't bring it to the top of my mind. At least not while everyone was yelling at each other. If it wasn't Jenny, then someone else had something to gain. Who? The actions all worked to make Jenny's empire larger or more secure. Who would want that?

Jenny was staring at me. She swiped the back of her wrist across her eyes. They were red, but she was no longer crying. In fact, her expression conveyed fatigue, instead of anger. She suddenly looked like a little lost girl, not a villain.

"Jenny, do you have any relatives?" I asked.

"My pa. That's all. I have no brothers or sisters. My ma died birthing me."

"You're a rich woman with vast operations. Who gets it all if you die?"

The lost little girl disappeared in an instant. She seethed resentment.

"Why do you ask?" she demanded.

"Because if you are telling the truth, then someone wanted Joseph to kill you. If he had, who would gain?"

McAllen shed his own anger and looked intrigued.

"No one," she answered. "Or at least I don't know who would get it all. My pa sure won't. That forty dollars he got for selling me is the last nickel he'll ever see from me. Besides, he's probably dead, otherwise he'd come around demanding his share from putting his little girl in such good circumstances."

"You've never seen him? Never inquired about him?"

"I don't care about him."

"Doesn't matter what you care about," I said. "If he's your only relative, he could still claim everything."

"No he can't. My lawyer created something called a trust. I'm not sure what it is, but he said my father couldn't touch a penny."

My mother explained. "A trust is a legal entity to hold assets and it can survive the death of an individual. The rich use them all the time, my dear. You have a good lawyer. A woman of your means should keep her assets in a trust. You still have complete control, but relatives, the government, and creditors have a harder time getting to your money. Wise, very wise indeed."

"Mother, tell her about an executor."

"Why dear, that's someone who executes the instructions of a dead person."

Jenny looked puzzled. "I don't know that I left instructions. I don't plan on dying, so I didn't pay much attention."

"Then the executor will run the estate according to the bylaws written within the trust," my mother explained.

"What are bylaws?"

"Since you don't know," I said, "I bet you don't know the terms and conditions of your trust."

"Should I?"

My mother made a dismissive wave with her hand. "These trusts are all pretty similar, dear."

"Do you know the executor of your estate?" I asked.

"No. I . . . I don't know. It was never discussed."

"It's probably your lawyer, dearie. They inject themselves into other's affairs all the time. Nasty little people, for the most part."

"Who's your lawyer?" I asked.

Jenny looked at me with bloodshot eyes. "Claude Jansen."

Chapter 33

Claude Jansen? My lawyer. The governor's ally? The person who told me I could trust the marshal? Was it possible? I held up my hand and again everyone allowed me to think. This could all be innocent. An attorney has no obligation to tell other clients who else he represents, and it would be normal for Jenny to hire the best lawyer in Carson City. But what a great disguise to take over the state. Jansen could appear to be helping his client amass her fortune while in actuality, he would be building his own empire. Staying friendly with the governor would allow him to deflect questions and investigations. A lawyer of Jansen's standing could sway judicial appointments. It was perfect. Everybody's eye would be on the girl with a grudge, while her lawyer guided her actions and set himself up to be the eventual emperor.

My thoughts were interrupted by McAllen. "Is there a telegraph at Belleville?"

"Yes," Jenny answered.

"Then I want a message from Sharp. Ask him the name of the man who abducted my daughter last year. For your sake, the answer better be right."

Jenny looked at Maggie. "You were abducted?"

"By a horrible man full of scars. Big as a bear."

"Why didn't you tell me when I was telling you my woes?"

"It was nothing. My dad took care of the bad men, and they didn't hurt me."

I guess fathers get all the credit. I actually dispatched the *man full of scars,* and Sharp and I rescued Maggie, and then foiled a robbery that saved McAllen's life and reputation. He felt more beholden about the latter.

Jenny turned her attention to McAllen. "We need to rush down to Western Union right away. They could have already left Belleville."

"Let's go." McAllen took Jenny by the arm and pulled her toward the door.

"Stop, that hurts."

He let go of his grip. "It's goin' to hurt a lot more if I don't get the right answer from Sharp. Move."

The two of them hurried out of the suite while trying to kill each other with dirty looks. I'd call it a draw.

I took Jenny's seat on the settee, so my mother took the opportunity to lecture me. "You should have saved that poor girl from that horrid experience. Did you really not have a gun? It seems like you've been shooting up the West ever since you came out to this desolate frontier."

"I was unarmed, mother. At first, I never wore a

gun . . . and I had never shot at a man. Dad and I shot paper targets. Besides, don't get all soft for that girl. She may be innocent of some things, but she has killed, lied, bribed, and stolen who knows what. She uses people . . . and in the end, we may discover that she's truly crazy."

"I like her," Maggie said.

"She wanted you to," I said in a huff.

"I liked her too," my mother said. "She acted the only way she knew how, and she won't act any better with you berating her like she was the devil's mistress. She needs a friend, a mentor, someone to show her how to act in a civilized world."

"You're not suggesting yourself for that sort of role are you?" I asked.

"Perhaps. I need something to do while I'm here." She smiled to herself. "Making a gentlewoman from a stray . . . oh yes, that would be a challenge."

If my mother tried to get her clutches on Jenny, it would be like watching a badger and a rattlesnake go at it. I had seldom heard a more dangerous idea, but I knew better than to directly challenge my mother.

I said, "If she redeems herself by showing remorse and helping us, *then* helping her might be okay. For the moment, let's wait and see."

Virginia leaned forward. "She says she was not only raped by those two men, but also in her home by ranch hands. She claims it was her mother-in-law's doing. That can't be true."

"It's true, but I bet she didn't tell you I got her out of that bunkhouse and back into the safety of the big house."

"She told us," Virginia said, "but she believes you did it so you could have her to yourself."

I wanted to make a smart retort, but thought better of it. Jenny had already assaulted my reputation, no use adding smart-aleck to the list.

"She's wrong," I said. "Once you've been mistreated over and over, you start seeing any action you don't like as further mistreatment, even if no mistreatment was intended. Jenny doesn't trust anyone's motives. She believes everyone wants to do her harm."

"Not everyone," Maggie said. "Just men." Maggie moved uncomfortably in her seat. "I said I liked her, but she scares me. She's . . . experienced so much. She's more than angry, she . . . I don't know how to put it." She shifted in her seat some more, and then seemed to have new thought. "Like she said, she's like a horse broke bad. You hurt a horse, treat it mean, and years later, it will whip its head around to bite you. The anger's so deep, it never gets cleansed."

"Here's something odd," Virginia said. "I believed her when she was in front of us telling her story, but now that she's gone . . . I'm not so sure."

I kept quiet because Jenny had had a spell-binding effect on me and I didn't want to bring any more attention to my past infatuation with her. Jenny had an innate ability to mesmerize people, and evidently it extended beyond men to womenfolk. Did that mean she really was demented? She might be blameless, at least for the worst offenses, but the longer she was gone, the less confidence I had in her assertions of innocence.

"Let's get back to Jansen. Mother, you know more about trusts than I do. Could he be manipulating Jenny?"

She took a moment before answering. "My prejudice is to say no. Attorneys are clever enough for that kind of fraud in New York, but out here, in this wilderness? How could a yokel small time lawyer get that shrewd? But who am I? Just an old lady who thinks all the smart people live on the other side of the Hudson." She got a mischievous grin. "I could be wrong, but with my track record, it's unlikely."

"But say he was, how would he set up the trust?"

My mother appeared pleased that I asked her opinion. "He, of course, would be the executor, and the bylaws would stipulate that the trust would last into perpetuity. A companion will would bequeath all the assets to the trust and for good measure specifically exclude her father from any inheritance. It's that simple."

"It doesn't sound simple to me," Maggie said.

"Just big words, dear. A reasonably competent lawyer could put it together in his sleep."

"And how would he get Jenny to sign all the papers?" Virginia asked.

"That girl's smart as a whip," my mother said, "but she doesn't have a lot of training in legal matters. I bet she signed whatever papers were put in front of her."

"If she would sign anything, why didn't he just make himself heir?" Virginia asked.

"Because if someone came forward to challenge the will or trust, he could lose it all and possibly end up in jail. Lawyers are not brave souls, so they hide behind legal arrangements."

"But how would Jansen benefit?" Maggie asked. "He wouldn't actually own Jenny's stuff."

"People confuse ownership with personal benefit," my mother said. "The top officials in government don't legally own the money they manage, but I assure you they benefit as if they did. Probably more. The rich are concerned with reinvesting to build wealth, while government officials only spend. They buy themselves nice offices, expensive carriages, and use government funds to pay for their extravagant needs so they can use their salaries to buy a nice home. Believe me, top government officials live well. Same with trustees. They live just as if they were rich because they control untold wealth. People do them favors because everybody wants a piece of the pie. All the while, these supposed big shots pretend to get along on a mere stipend." She smiled, before adding, "By the way, I'm sure he charged her a pretty penny to steal her estate."

"That sounds like you've come to believe Jansen is the big villain in this drama," I said.

"Interesting observation," she said. "I suppose I have. Jenny's not an innocent, but Jansen may be using her as ruthlessly as those Cutler brothers. Besides, I admire her. That's one tough girl. She'll make something of herself . . . and this wilderness."

For me this was a fascinating discussion, especially since I had had few civil conversations with my mother. Some of my attraction to Jenny had been the expectation that my mother would strenuously object to her. Instead of disapproval, my mother actually said she liked her. Ironic. In truth, I knew my mother admired her as a self-reliant woman who knew how to build wealth and position, but I also knew she would never allow her into the Dancy family until the actual grubbing for an estate rested at least two generations in the past.

Virginia looked at me as if she could read my thoughts. I smiled for no reason other than I was happy with the way things had worked out.

Just then, there was a soft knock on the door. Before I could get up, Maggie bounded to the door and threw it open with a big welcoming smile. Neither of the men standing outside the door were her father.

"Is Jenny Bolton here?" the man in front asked.

I carefully pushed up from my seat, trying to appear calm, but my heart raced. I didn't know the man in the rear, but I recognized the one asking for Jenny. He was dressed in black with his suit coattail tucked behind a nickel-plated Peacemaker with a walnut grip. The last time I had seen George Carson, I had hit him until he fell to the floor. What was he doing here . . . and why was he asking for Jenny? If she was hiring gunmen, then her protestations of innocence were probably false.

"She's not here, George," I said to show I recognized him.

He gave me a hard look and turned to go.

"George, what do you want with Jenny? I'm her friend."

Carson turned slowly back in my direction before saying, "That's a disappointment. You and I have a score to settle, and as my new boss, she might object." He smirked. "That's okay. Waiting to kill you will just increase the pleasure."

"Do you have the rest of my money?" I asked.

"What?"

"That pot in Denver was light. You owe me."

"Go to hell."

"Not in your lifetime."

I closed the door.

Chapter 34

W ho was that man?" my mother asked.
"A card cheat," Virginia answered. "And an arrogant ass."

Her answer surprised me because despite working around crude men in the lowliest district in Leadville, Virginia seldom used profanity. Her description was accurate, however. Carson cheated, stole, and bullied. I worried that his arrival might complicate things.

"The last time we saw that man, your son knocked him to the ground," Virginia added. "While in Denver, we helped Pinkerton shut down a rigged poker game. Mr. Carson played a key role as one of the fraudsters."

"George Carson fancies himself a gunfighter," I mused. "If Jenny told the truth, why would she hire such a man?"

"Son, why do you annoy gunfighters? When you play with fire, you get burnt. No wonder you're involved in so many shootings. I really don't understand this courting of violence."

I walked the small room, intent on disregarding my mother's comments, but she never allowed herself to be ignored.

"Steve, you must return east. Get far away from these awful men. If a townhouse isn't inducement enough, think about the safety of your children. Philadelphia, New York City, or Washington. Quit these silly contests of manhood. You owe it to Virginia and your children."

"I'll talk about it after the trial," I said absent-mindedly, still in thought.

Another knock at the door.

I lifted my Colt slightly and let it drop back into my holster to make sure I could draw it clean. Standing to the side of the door I asked who was there. The relief I felt upon hearing McAllen's voice surprised me. Carson shouldn't frighten me. Real dangerous men don't expose their guns like a porcupine lifting its quills. Carson was all bluff.

I opened the door and stood aside to let McAllen and Jenny back into the room.

"Well?" I asked with arched eyebrow.

"Bane," McAllen responded without further explanation.

It occurred to me that Bane didn't actually abduct Maggie, but he certainly acted as her captor until we rescued her. It didn't matter. It would be unlikely that anyone other than Sharp would know about his role in Maggie's ordeal.

"They're leaving now. He won't be harmed," Jenny promised.

"They better not . . . or I'll take revenge on their boss," McAllen said.

"How many escorts?" I asked.

"One," Jenny answered.

"Then I'm not worried about Sharp," I said. "You, on the other hand, ought to worry about your man."

She shrugged. "If he lets Mr. Sharp get the drop on him, then he'll only get what he deserves."

"Steve, I think you should trust Jenny," Virginia said.

She let affection seep into her tone. I suddenly became angry. "You told her that our fight was staged, didn't you?"

"It makes no difference now." Virginia sounded unsure of herself.

"Well, you women got right friendly, didn't you?" McAllen said. "What else did you spill?"

"That ruse doesn't matter anymore," Virginia said.

"Damn it, you could have put Lizzy's life in danger!" McAllen remained angry.

I motioned toward the bedroom. "Joseph, we need to talk."

McAllen didn't wait for an explanation, he just trudged into the bedroom wearing a scowl. He thought I was going to upbraid him for talking angrily to Virginia, but instead, I told him about our visitors. He said nothing, but his scowl lines deepened. He walked over to the window and surveyed the street below. I let him think.

Without turning around, he said, "I don't like

this. None of it. Jenny has won over our women, we know Jeff is alive, but it's a long way from Belleville to Carson City. The lawyer you hired to save your neck may be the real scoundrel behind these shenanigans, the marshal might be complicit, and now a couple of supposed bad men show up to work for our reformed villainess. Is she pretendin'? Hell, I don't know. If you put this in one of your books, your readers would never believe it."

"I don't know what to believe myself," I said.

"We need to expose the truth."

"How?"

"Ask Jenny? Gauge her response."

"Is that wise? It'll just give her the opportunity to deny it in front of the women. She's already won them over for the most part and she's a practiced liar."

Before he responded verbally, McAllen's expression told me I had said something stupid. "Steve, what do you think those women have been talkin' about ever since we left the room?"

Damn. I didn't want to make a bigger issue about my lapse in common sense, so I just motioned in the direction of the door. McAllen smiled as he stepped toward the parlor, but the grin vanished as he opened the door.

With his scowl firmly back in place, McAllen said, "Mrs. Bolton, please explain why you hired gunmen from out of town."

"Mr. Jansen suggested I need personal guards. Professionals, not my ranch hands or those sham detectives at Carson Investigations. I argued against it, but he insisted, so I let him hire them. He told me he got the best."

"They're far from the best," McAllen said. "We met one of them in Denver. He's a cardsharp. The last we saw of him, he was on the floor because Steve punched him for cheatin'."

"I don't need men like that; besides, if you're right, I'll be paying those men, but they'll work for Mr. Jansen. I'll give them return fare and send them home."

"Do that," McAllen said.

I couldn't tell what Jenny thought about Jansen's betrayal. Probably about like me. Jansen didn't want to take everything I had, just my life, but it irked me just the same.

"Anything else?" Jenny directed her question to McAllen.

She had asked for advice. That was interesting. Perhaps she had reformed. A bit, anyway. If she had drawn away from her more nefarious schemes, it might be more of a recess than a termination. She may have been put off by the attack on Maggie, but she still hated us.

"Steve?" McAllen asked.

Now McAllen was asking me for advice? This was even more interesting.

"Jenny shouldn't talk to Jansen. It's possible

our suspicions are false, and if they're not, we don't want to forewarn him. She should also eave Carson and his friend alone for the time being. Sending them home might set off alarms. We need to figure out what's really going on before taking action."

"So you're not going to fire Jansen?" Jenny asked.

"Not immediately, but maybe we should see Jerimiah to get names of other lawyers. Jeff and I still have a trial next week." I thought about how to express my next request. "Jenny, I can't tell you what to do, but I'd considered it a sign of good faith if you waited here until our return."

She nodded concurrence.

Without another word, McAllen proceeded out the door with me at his heels.

When we got out in the hall, McAllen said, "Good thinkin', Steve. I don't trust that girl yet."

"Do you think Jeff will make it back in one piece?"

"Yep. I agree with you. Jeff will work at it until he gets the drop on his escort. He'll put him off guard with good humor, and then probably put him down with a single punch." McAllen smiled because he was ribbing me for needing three hits to put Carson on the floor. "That man can be charming as hell when he wants something."

"Especially with women."

"Especially with women," he repeated.

Chapter 35

A clean-shaven Jerimiah opened the door to his newly tidy room. His properly fitted clothes even made him look as if he had lost a few pounds. Last time Sharp had accompanied me, so McAllen had never seen him as a saloon bum. In fact, since it had been over two years since his single visit to Pickhandle Gulch, I didn't expect McAllen to recognize Jerimiah.

McAllen proved me wrong with his first words. "Howdy, Jerimiah. You look good."

Jerimiah formally shook hands with McAllen. "I didn't until Steve and Jeff came along." He shook my hand as well. "Thanks, Steve." He looked behind us into the hallway. "Where's Jeff?"

We told him. At the end of our story, Jerimiah rubbed his chin and said that he wasn't worried because Sharp could handle a single man in the wilderness. It was funny how all three of us came to the same conclusion. One day, Sharp might disappoint us, but hopefully, not this time.

Jerimiah had no opinion about the culpability of Jansen, but sat down and wrote a list of lawyers I could hire to replace him. When he handed it over, the list included eight names.

"How do you know these men?" I asked.

"I know only one." He looked uncomfortable. "I had nothing else to do, so I read every issue of Richard's paper and every other paper I couldget my hands on for free. I developed a good memory for names. These lawyers were mentioned in news stories about trials here or in Virginia City . . . mostly Virginia City. Hard men, wanton women, money, and gambling in over a hundred saloons ignites like kerosene-soaked tinder."

"Which one of these lawyers do you know?" I asked.

"Myers, but you don't want him."

"Why not?"

"I used him a couple of times when I was arrested for public drunkenness. If I could afford him, he's not any good. Besides, he's a drunk himself . . . although I heard he's on the wagon."

"What can you tell me about these other names?"

He rubbed his chin again. "Not much." He paused. "In fact, I take back what I said about you not wanting Myers. If he stays sober, he's a damn good lawyer. Hates Jansen too. The others require a train ride up to Virginia City. If you go up there, interview the first three on that list, but talk to Myers first. He's right down the street."

I changed subjects. "The Pinkertons haven't been able to find that Ben character who witnessed Richard getting shot."

"No surprise. He's dead or three states away. Did you find witnesses to testify in your shooting?"

"Everyone's too frightened. Fifteen people must have seen the gunfight, but none will testify in our defense."

"Who told you that?" McAllen asked suddenly.

That question brought me up short. "Claude Jansen."

"Hell, Steve, if we're right about him, maybe he never searched hard. A new lawyer might find cooperative witnesses. I bet he didn't even give you a list of who was in the dining room that evenin'."

"Damn."

"Yep. Not gonna be easy for a new attorney to find you witnesses at this late date. And the marshal won't help if he's in Jansen's pocket."

"Joseph, that doesn't feel right," I said. "He seemed like a straight shooter to me. Maybe Jansen stays close to him like he does with Jenny and Bradshaw."

"Don't assume Jenny's telling the truth. It's too damn early for that."

"Whether Jenny's lying or not, it's possible the marshal's not part of this scheme. After all, the governor brought him to Carson City, not Jansen."

"Okay, while you talk to Myers I'll talk to Copley and the marshal. I'll get a read on him."

"Don't take Copley with you to see the marshal," I warned.

"I didn't intend to, but why do you say that?"

"I don't like the way Copley has been handling the investigation. He's an amateur . . . or secretly works for Jansen."

"Jansen can't have corrupted every official in this town, especially not a Pinkerton," McAllen said defensively. "We gotta trust someone."

"The marshal's a good man," Jerimiah interjected.

We both looked at him for a moment. My gut told me the marshal was not beholden to Jansen, but the two did seem to work together. On the other hand, Jansen seemed to have no connection with Copley. Jansen could have both or neither on his payroll. I wondered if he had recruited Copley and then kept his distance. That would be the smart move.

"Why do you think the marshal's a good man?" McAllen asked.

Jerimiah shuffled his feet. "I've had occasion to deal with the marshal. He's always treated me square."

"What kind of occasion?" McAllen asked.

"Drunkenness." He shuffled some more. "More than one occasion I guess. Spent a few nights as his guest, so to speak. Nothing serious, but like I said, he always treated me fair."

"Ever see him with Jansen?" I asked.

"Sometimes, but Jansen prefers to visit the marshal's office in the mornings, when Doug or Sam are in charge."

"Ever overhear their conversations?" McAllen asked.

"Always. The jail's just a barred area of the office."

"Anything suspicious?"

"Not really. Sometimes they took coffee outside to a bench on the boardwalk. Can't imagine they talked about anything secret out in the open."

"I can," McAllen said. He smiled before adding, "Steve, I think we've might've found our corrupt deputies."

Chapter 36

John Myers did business from an office barely larger than a closet. The furnishings consisted of a beat-up Wooton rolltop desk with a worn swivel chair. The peeling wallpaper hadn't been attractive when new and a faded map of Nevada hung in lonely isolation on the soiled walls. Myers' threadbare, but clean brown suit looked as if at some point it had been tailored for a prospering attorney. Bucking fashion, Myers was as clean-shaven as me, but his unruly hair needed a cut. He also wore the puffy, blotched complexion of an alcoholic, but appeared sober at the moment.

Once admitted, I pulled over a spindly, straight-back chair to sit down.

"What can I do for you?" He sounded weary.

"My name is Steve Dancy and I have a trial in a few days for killing some men at the St. Charles. It was self-defense and—"

"Yes, I'm familiar with the incident," Myers said. "I understood you had engaged Claude Jansen as your attorney."

"I had, but now I want a different attorney. Jansen may have a conflict of interest."

"A conflict of interest, huh? You sound educated. Can you pay?"

I took out my wallet and laid three hundred dollars on his desk top. "Will that do?"

"As a retainer . . . if I accept you as a client." He left the money on top of the desk. "What conflict of interest?"

"Is that important?"

"Only if you want my representation."

"I learned that Mr. Jansen also represents Mrs. Bolton. She's implicated in the incident."

"How?"

"Mr. Sharp and I were together in the hotel dining room. She sent those men to take us somewhere against our will."

"Do you know where?"

"No. Never found out. We refused to go."

"Quite adamantly, I hear."

I shrugged and waited for his next question.

"Where is Mr. Sharp?"

"On his way back to Carson City. He was abducted sometime later by agents of Mrs. Bolton."

He looked genuinely puzzled. "Why?"

"Bail would not deter me from fleeing the state. She knew holding my friend would keep me around."

I explained the major elements of our feud and possible reconciliation.

When I finished, I said, "Now, may I ask a question?"

"In a minute. Did those men draw weapons on you?"

That was a tough question. The man behind me had made a sudden move, but I didn't know for certain that he had actually drawn a gun. There had been a verbal challenge, and in a tense situation, the code of the West said any sudden movement could be interpreted as a reach for a weapon. If one party waited until the other party clearly held a pistol in their hand, that party would shortly be dead. I believed we had acted reasonably in the face of a lethal threat. I answered more positively.

"They were in the process of drawing weapons."

"You're sure?"

"I'm sure."

"How many people were in the dining room?"

"I'd guess about a dozen."

"Did any of them see the altercation?"

"All of them. There were verbal threats before the gunfire. I'm sure we had the attention of the entire room. That doesn't mean any of them will be brave enough to testify, however."

He asked dozens of additional questions. I described the entire sequence of events since we left Denver, explained how Jenny had manipulated us to send for McAllen, and how she claimed never to have ordered an assault on McAllen's daughter. I omitted our suspicion that Jansen might have been manipulating Jenny all along or that he may have been the one behind the attack on Maggie. I didn't want to provide too much information until Myers and I came to a formal agreement.

Finally, he said, "Now, you had a question?"

"Yes. How long since you had a drink?"

"Two months, three days," Myers answered immediately.

"Any plans to drink in the next few days?"

"No."

His unadorned answer made me feel confident that my lawyer would remain sober through my trial. So far, I could judge Myers only on the worth of his questions, and they seemed astute and penetrating. I had one more issue to clarify.

"What's your relationship with Claude Jansen?"

"We hate each other. He thinks I'm a drunk. I think he's a criminal."

"How so?"

"Well . . . I've seen him falsify contracts and take advantage of clients who are ignorant of the law."

"Do you think he would establish himself as trustee of an estate contrary to his client's wishes?"

"Are you referring to Williamson?"

"Never heard of him. I'm asking in reference to Jenny Bolton."

"Whoa! That's interesting." He rocked back and forth for a long moment. "That's a substantial empire. Are you sure?"

"Somewhat."

"Does she suspect?"

"She does now."

"Is she looking for a new attorney?"

"I'm looking for a new attorney."

"Of course. Discourteous of me." He picked up the three hundred dollars. "I'm willing to defend you."

"Do you think you can put a defense together in time?"

"Already have. You'll be acquitted."

I ripped the money out of his hand and stood to leave. "I'm sorry to have wasted your time."

Myers laughed in a pleasant, self-confident manner. "I understand your skepticism, but I wasn't making light of your case. You and Mr. Sharp will be exonerated."

When I didn't respond, he quickly added, "I was in the dining room that evening. I witnessed the altercation. I must admit, until now I thought you and your friend were common gunmen. Well, perhaps not so common. You handled double your number without mussing your hair. After this conversation, I see that there is more to you than a quick hand. I'd be pleased to represent you and delighted to steal a client from Jansen."

"How can you defend me and be taken seriously as a witness?" I asked.

"My key witness will be my wife. We were eating supper together. Once she testifies, I'll stipulate to the accuracy of her testimony."

I was stunned. This kind of good fortune seldom came to defendants in a criminal trial.

"Did Jansen seek you out as a witness?" I asked.

"No. Nor anyone else to my knowledge. Once I let it be known that my wife will testify, others will talk without too much arm twisting. There's safety in numbers, after all."

I shook my head as I handed back the money. "What was Jansen up to?"

"I suppose he was up to seeing you hang."

Chapter 37

Copley's corrupted," McAllen said. "So are Doug or Sam, but the marshal appears honest. By the way, he already suspected Doug and Sam." McAllen looked mad as hell. "By the time this is over, Copley won't be able to eat solid food for a week. That son of a bitch."

We had met up outside of Myers' office. McAllen no longer worked for the Pinkerton National Detective Agency, but he remained loyal to the firm. It would anger him if any agent accepted a bribe, but it especially rankled him that an office head despoiled the Pinkerton reputation. I, on the other hand, was not surprised. McAllen's honor and integrity came from McAllen's character, not the Pinkerton organization. He never noticed that as the firm grew, quality waned. It was probably best that he left the agency before the Pinkerton badge became tarnished.

"That explains the slipshod investigation. Did you confront Copley?"

"Not yet. He may be more valuable believin' he's still trusted. Matt feels the same way about Doug and Sam. He wants them to believe their relationship with Jansen remains unnoticed. What about you?"

After describing my meeting with Myers, he concurred that Myers' comments added weight to the idea of Jansen acting as puppet master. I asked what we should do next.

"Check on Maggie."

Without waiting for a response, McAllen charged off in the direction of the hotel. It took me several steps to catch up.

"Joseph, what about my Pinkerton team? Do I terminate the contract?"

That stopped him.

"It's your money, but I doubt they'll do us any good."

"Until we fully trust Jenny, I think we need protection for the women."

"That might be forever." McAllen gave me his closed-mouth smile. "Got enough money?"

I ignored his weak attempt at humor. "Let's keep Elizabeth Channing and her partner. I bet Lizzy will ignore Copley and take direction from you. I'll tell Copley to dismiss the rest. What do you think?"

"Don't do it until Lizzy gets back from her fool's errand. Tell Copley to stop the investigations. Say they aren't discovering anything useful and because of the attack on Maggie, you want them to protect the women. Tell him to have someone stationed in the lobby all hours of the day. When Lizzy gets back, cut the rest loose."

I nodded and headed down the street toward the Pinkerton office while McAllen returned to the hotel. Since Copley worked with Jansen, I wasn't sure if he really wanted to protect Virginia and Maggie, but fear of McAllen's notorious wrath might incent the agents to do the job properly. I would be happy when Lizzy returned with her pretend husband. After working with her in New York City, I had more confidence in her than I did for the rest of the team. She was sharp, tough, and fond of Virginia. After Sharp returned, they could send an army and we could probably hold them off. At least, that's what I told myself.

I kept my meeting with Copley brief. The more I talked, the greater the chance that I might give away our true intentions. He seemed amiable to a reassignment. Too amiable. Was I paying the salary of our own assassins? I doubted Copley or Jansen could corrupt Chicago agents enough to harm one of their own. Most likely, he feared even a misdirected investigation might turn up something of real benefit to our defense.

By the time I returned to my mother's suite, McAllen had succeeded in turning a companionable group of gentlewomen into a tizzy of screeching and agitated motion. McAllen seemed ready to dodge bric-a-bracs as he futilely pleaded for order. He looked as befuddled as any replacement teacher facing a raucous class. Virginia whirled around the tiny parlor exclaiming that she refused to be held captive, while Maggie literally stomped her feet in defiance of some McAllen directive. Jenny kept saying something about a ringmaster. Master of what? My mother remained seated, but the scowl on her face frightened me as much as when I was a child.

I stood helpless, but my mother as usual put her imprint on the situation with a single word. She yelled *stop* with such force that everyone shut their mouth and stood motionless. If a mouse had scurried across the room, we would have heard its footfall.

After she had everyone's attention, she said, "Mr. McAllen, you may boss your daughter, but not me, my future daughter-in-law, or Jenny. The three of us are not staying in this hotel one more day. We will attend the Montgomery Queen Circus tomorrow. Jenny has been selected as an honorary ringmaster, and Virginia's uncle will speak at the opening ceremony on the capitol steps and we *will* attend in our best attire. No more discussion. You may do what you will with your daughter, but take it from me, it'll be a grave mistake to keep her cooped up in this hotel room until you see fit to let her see sunlight again. If you become her jailer, that fine, strong-willed young woman will no longer hold you in such high esteem."

"What? A circus?" I asked, incredulous. "Mother, you hate circuses."

"I don't hate circuses," Maggie nearly yelled. "They never come to Durango, and I want to see one."

I waited for the foot stomp, but it didn't come.

"I may not enjoy circuses, but I'll enjoy this one because Maggie's so keen on it. It'll be great practice for when I have my own granddaughter." She beamed at Virginia. "Besides, I can hardly attend the evening gala at the capitol if I shun the day's events, especially the speeches by the congressman and senator. It's the congressman, after all, who will be hosting all of us. We'll be the toast of the party. For heaven's sake, there's little else going on in this town."

I didn't want to tell her about the wrestling; or prize, cock, and dog fights; or the gambling that went on with each, or the thirty-six saloons in Carson City. There was entertainment aplenty here and in Virginia City, but it catered to rough men with too much money and too little sense. For entertainment, westerners bet on anything, especially when drunk. One time I witnessed men wagering on the weight of a pig running loose in the street. Definitely not my mother's cup of tea. She might like the horseracing track outside of town, but it was primitive compared to her private box at Saratoga Springs.

I put my thoughts away and said, "Mother, there's danger outside this hotel."

"Oh son, didn't you and Mr. Sharp kill four men inside this very hotel? We might be safer in public."

"Mrs. Dancy, you're right about dangers lurking downstairs," McAllen said. "That's why I want you to stay inside this suite or one of our rooms."

"I said there will be no more discussion," my mother said sternly. "We're going . . . and if we attend the political rally and the evening gala, we might as well see the circus, even if it is only one ring. I'm certain I'll find the show more entertaining than the wallpaper in this room."

I quit arguing and started thinking about how we could deploy the Pinkertons to greatest advantage. McAllen, not knowing my mother as well I did, started to say something, but as soon as he uttered the first syllable, my mother hushed him like a dictatorial schoolmarm. He got the message and retreated out to the hall. I followed.

I had noticed the handbills spread around town announcing the circus, but paid little attention to them. I had seen circuses in New York and I doubted that Montgomery Queen could outdo Barnum & Bailey. I liked circuses, but preferred Buffalo Bill's Wild West show. In fact, that extravaganza had made me eager to explore the frontier. I found the real Wild West grittier than

Buffalo Bill playacting, but the energy and excitement were real enough.

After we were out of earshot, McAllen asked, "Any suggestions?"

"Give up trying to keep them holed up. They've made up their minds. If we give them tomorrow's entertainments, we might have a chance to keep them in their rooms until trial."

He nodded. "Okay, but we need to think about how to protect them while they're outside." He leaned against the wall and bent one knee to rest his boot against the wainscoting. I assumed the hotel would prefer he found a different stance. "First, we all go together and we stay together. I want Jenny close to Maggie . . . close enough to be in the line of fire. You and I will provide the close protection and Pinkerton agents will keep an eye on things from a distance. Last, we carry rifles."

"My mother will get us reserved seating for the speeches. Ought to be safe until the crowd breaks up for the circus."

"Will there be private seating at the circus?" McAllen asked.

"Doubtful, but there's usually only one entrance. Should we sit close to it or away?"

McAllen didn't hesitate. "Away, a seat where I can watch who comes in." He pushed himself away from the wall. "Okay, I think we can keep them safe at both venues and the gala. The problem is moving between them. I hate to say this, but I'm concerned about the Pinkerton agents."

"I'm concerned about the bazaar."

"What damn bazaar?"

"Montgomery Queen sets up stands behind the big tent. A carnival. Mostly crooked games and cheap exhibits, but the women may want to wander through the area because the broadside said townsfolk can also sell their wares. There'll be pies, cakes, jams, homemade jewelry, and everything else that can be banged together in a kitchen or barn. In my experience, women love these things."

"Damn it."

"We need protection we can rely on." I pulled out my pocket watch. "If I hurry, I can catch the four o'clock V&T to Virginia City."

"What's in Virginia City?"

"Sharp's old head of security lives there. If I find him, he'll know how to pull together a team we can trust."

"Then you better hurry. You don't want to miss that train."

"Will you be safe by yourself with the women?"

"No problem. I'll use my charm."

"Oh hell, you *are* in trouble."

Chapter 38

The next morning, church bells woke the town early. Evidently a circus coming to town warranted an early rise by one and all.

The prior evening, I had had little trouble finding Sharp's man. His name was James and in the past he had run security for Belleville and guarded Sharp's ore shipments. He knew everyone in Virginia City and promised a reliable team first thing in the morning. The early train would arrive before the speeches started, so I felt confident about the day.

Virginia had dressed quickly and returned to her room to re-dress in her finest. Luckily, she had brought clothes from New York that ought to make all of the wives envious. I hated political speeches, but looked forward to the circus in the afternoon. Clowns bored me and exotic animals like elephants and lions didn't interest me either, but I enjoyed exhibitions of athleticism on the high wire and trapeze. I especially enjoyed women trick riding around the ring. That kind of skill required a well-trained horse and untold hours of practice. I didn't expect a Barnum & Bailey class show, but I hoped this troupe demonstrated reasonable talent.

I dressed in my best suit but ruined the drape by wearing my Colt and a pocket pistol. I decided not to carry a rifle as McAllen suggested because I'd look ludicrous at the political event in a finely tailored suit with a beautiful woman on one arm and a Winchester in the other. I didn't believe Jenny had any ill intent today, and Jansen should believe his plans remained undisclosed. No, today would be fun and games. Tomorrow, however, would be another matter.

I went downstairs ahead of Virginia because I was hungry and I knew she would take a long time dressing. To my surprise, James waited for me in the lobby.

"I didn't expect you until later," I said.

"They added a dawn departure to the V&T schedule because of the hoopla. One way or 'nother, everybody'll get their butt off Gold Hill to see this circus."

"Eaten?"

"Ah can eat again."

As soon as we took our seats and ordered, I asked, "Where's the rest of the team?"

"Ah sent 'em in different directions until nine o'clock. Didn't know if you wanted us to show force or be quiet-like."

"What do you recommend?"

"Both. Ah stay nearby, my other men play sentry."

"How many men did you bring?"

"Four, plus myself. What're we lookin' for?"

That was a difficult question. I doubted the remnants of Carson Investigations posed a threat. With their leader dead and four in custody, their depleted ranks had no direction. After I returned the prior evening, I found Copley and told him to terminate the services of his team with the exception of Lizzy and her partner. Copley seemed indifferent because Montgomery Queen wanted to hire protection for the circus and carnival. Still having the team around concerned me a little, but I had faith that the agents owed no loyalty to Copley, and probably feared McAllen. I didn't believe Jansen would do anything himself, and, at least for the moment, Jenny professed to be in a neutral corner. That left one threat. Jansen's recent hirelings from Denver.

"Anything unusual, but watch for two men in particular," I answered. "They may not stay together, so don't concentrate on men in pairs. The leader is named George Carson. He'll be dressed in a black suit, probably with his coattail tucked behind a nickel-plated Peacemaker with walnut grips. He sees himself as a dandy and a gunfighter. I don't remember his partner too well. Rough looking character, scraggly beard. That's all I remember. Also, the man who hired Carson, may have hired more men we don't know about, so keep a sharp look out."

James nodded in response, so I went on to

explain that there would be Pinkertons assigned to circus security. I explained that they used to be in my employ, but I fired them last night, so they may feel no obligation to protect us. He asked if they posed a threat and I said no, but described each to the best of my ability anyway. I explained that I had retained two Pinkertons, but they wouldn't return from an investigative errand until tomorrow or later. Last, I asked him not to initiate contact with the Pinkertons and to keep his team's presence quiet.

"Ah understand." After a moment of contemplation, he folded his hands on the table and asked, "Ain't you the guy that shot Sean Washburn?"

"I am."

"And ain't the famous Captain McAllen with ya?"

"He is."

"And ya had all dem Pinkertons." He waited a beat. "Why did ya need us?"

"The Pinkertons should have been enough, but they might not all be dependable. We have reservations about an individual, someone in a position to confuse or corrupt the agents."

James gave me a direct stare. "Ah guess I'm askin' if we might be fightin' Pinks. If that be the case, I want to talk to Mr. Sharp first."

I hesitated before answering. I had explained the prior evening that Sharp had been abducted and released, but wouldn't get back for a few days. I tried to look at the situation through his eyes. He knew we had a Pinkerton protective detail, yet I hired him to lead an additional team. It must seem farfetched that Pinkertons would pose an unwarranted threat to a retired fellow agent, especially someone of McAllen's repute. I had offered lavish pay, so even my generosity might have raised suspicions. To James, this would appear to be an odd assignment that paid very well from someone he didn't know who used a reference he couldn't verify. No wonder he was uneasy. If I said the wrong thing, he would probably bolt straight out the door.

"Did Jeff ever write you about Prescott, Arizona?" I asked.

"Naw, but Ah heard 'bout it."

"How about him saving McAllen's daughter in Leadville, Colorado?"

"Mr. Sharp don't write me letters."

"Damn, I'm trying to find a way to convince you I'm friends with Jeff Sharp."

"Did he ever tell you how he got himself swindled out of his importin' an' exportin' business?"

"His partner accused him of bringing young boys up from South America."

"For what purpose?"

"For sex . . . with rich men. It wasn't true, by the way. Just a way for his partner to ruin his reputation and exercise a turpitude clause in their agreement."

James smiled. "You know 'im, all right. Pretty close too, if he told you that story. Still don't feel right keepin' an eye on Pinkertons, though."

"Do you know Thomas Copley?"

"Sure do."

"He's the only Pinkerton we're unsure of, but he's in charge of the Carson City office, so he could misdirect the other agents without their knowledge. In any case, you're not to use force against Pinkerton agents. You have their description. If one of your men feels there's a threat, set up a signal between you and your team so you can alert me or McAllen . . . preferably before bullets fly."

"What kind of signal?"

"I don't know . . . a police whistle?"

"Hard to find . . . how 'bout a toy bulb horn like them clowns use? Saw a peddler sellin' 'em at the train station."

"All the kids will be honking them."

"We'll use a pattern. Should be okay 'cept for during the circus itself."

"All right. Any other concerns?"

"This Carson fella, can we just take him out of the picture for a few hours?"

"How?"

"If we get the opportunity, bop him alongside the head, dump him behind a building, and pour whiskey all over him."

I thought about it.

"No . . . not today. I know him from Denver and he's cautious. There'll be too many people around for him to try anything criminal. But he's a blow-hard, so if he gets a chance he'll taunt me. If he does, let it go. Just make sure he doesn't threaten or harm the women."

"So, find him and watch him. Same with his partner. Keep 'em away from the womenfolk. Signal if the Pinks look to be up to mischief. That about it?"

"Don't worry about the speeches, but buy tickets to the circus. Spread out inside the tent." After a moment, I added, "I'll pay for the tickets and the bulb horns."

James smiled. "Of course. Ain't nobody else gonna."

Chapter 39

We felt safe during the dull political speeches. We sat in the front row with armed men along the periphery keeping an eye on the crowd. State capitol security augmented its small staff with the town marshal and his men, plus deputies from the county sheriff and Virginia City. Allan Pinkerton started his detective agency by protecting Abraham Lincoln, and politicians ever since have measured their stature by how many guards protected their exalted personage. The presence of Nevada's senior senator and the chairman of the Ways and Means Committee meant even more protection than normal for a run-of-the-mill political chest-thumping.

James and his team were better than I expected. James sat beside us, but looked as unobtrusive as an aide standing to the side of a politician. The men he had picked blended in so well even McAllen had a hard time spotting them. As was typical for Sharp, he had chosen a good man to protect his mines and ore shipments.

Front row at the political event meant we ended up in the back of the chattering throng heading toward the circus. I glanced at McAllen and he signaled that we should hold back even further. In New York, I had learned that McAllen dreaded being hemmed in by mobs of people, so I didn't know if he wanted us to dally for safety or to assuage his phobia. The walk would take about twenty minutes because the circus had been erected on empty land near the train station. I thought about seeking a ride, but the mass of people spilling into the street would make a carriage slower than the desultory progress of the crowd. I worried about getting into the first show because of the number of people, and my worries grew as the surging crowd increased every block as we proceeded down Carson Street. Evidently, many people found the circus more interesting than hearing politicians drone on about reviving the silver standard and other false promises.

When we arrived, the circus surprised me. I expected a miniature scale compared to Barnum & Bailey, but the Montgomery Queen circus at least competed in physical size. The shows encompassed four huge tents; one for the circus, another for a hippodrome, one for a menagerie, and yet another for a caravan. One ticket admitted us to all the exhibits and performances. We were able to gain access to the first performance because people scattered to all four tents and some took off immediately for the carnival and bazaar set up behind the big tops.

Inside I found another surprise: Montgomery Queen was a two ring circus, and professional to boot. Four women, two per ring, dressed in scanty, sequined costumes rode in circles staying exactly opposite each other like the movements of a well-crafted clock. All four riders were paired with beautifully groomed white horses, but what they were doing could hardly be called riding. They barely spent any time on top of the horse. In unison, the women would twirl stiff as a board on the back of a saddle-less horse, and then bounce to the ground onto their feet and then bound back up onto the horse for another twirl before doing the same trick again with variations. First, one side, and then the other. All four riders in two different rings working in harmony. This looked like fun.

McAllen rudely elbowed his way around the arena until we found seats directly opposite the tent flap that served as an entrance. As we fought our way around the ring, we came within a few feet of the bareback riders. Viewed up close, one of the women in the close ring appeared much older than she looked from a distance. The second rider was young, perhaps not even out of her teens. This young girl performed all the gymnastics perfectly, but hadn't yet mastered the easy grace of the older woman. The features of the two women looked similar, so similar I guessed they were mother and daughter. I had been told by a friend who had at one time run away with the circus that circus people were so insular it was hard to fit in unless you were related. I presumed this pair had no problem.

Despite her telling me she would come, I was surprised when my mother actually joined us. With her, Maggie, Virginia, McAllen, and James, we ended up taking a full row of seats. Previously, I held a concern that due to their closeness in age, Maggie and Jenny might become friendly. Instead, it was my mother who attached herself to Maggie. I would have guessed that a woman four times her age would seem ancient to Maggie, but she appeared equally drawn to my mother. In fact, more than I ever was. Perhaps being of the same gender accounted for their rapport, or maybe the separation of a generation makes people feel comfortable confiding to each other. My mother and Maggie certainly had their heads bent together much of the time. I wish I could shake the notion they were talking about me.

The show wasn't scheduled to start for another fifteen minutes, but Montgomery Queen had devised enough distractions that nobody noticed the wait. After most of the people had been seated, clowns appeared to deftly switch places with the women riders. The clowns were as clumsy as the women were graceful. They imitated the same routine, but fell off and chased after their horse, rode with their head almost touching the ground, or charged right up the tail of the other horse in the ring. The clown's antics drew full-bodied laughter from the audience, but I was amazed at the athletic prowess required to make their carefully crafted buffoonery look haphazard.

A baritone ringmaster soon appeared to introduce the acts. His booming voice and staccato cadence drew my attention every time he announced a new act, and according to him, each and every performance was better than anything we had ever seen. I felt a tug on my arm and Virginia pointed down the bench to McAllen who had evidently been trying to get my attention. With a scowl, he pointed to the entrance, and then made a sweeping motion with one finger to indicate I should be keeping my eye on the crowd. He was right, of course, but I still felt annoyed.

For the rest of the acts, I kept my attention on the audience. Nothing threatened except a clown that blew a horn in my ear. Perhaps we were paranoid. Just as the thought entered my head, George Carson sauntered into the tent and struck a haughty pose at the edge of the bleachers. He acted as if everyone ought to be looking at him instead of the acts in the rings. I glanced over at McAllen and he gave me a nod that confirmed that he had seen him as well. He had come in alone, so I scanned the audience to see if I could spot his partner. No luck. I had no strong recollection of his appearance and the huge tent held hundreds of people. I tried following Carson's eyes, but he seemed to be looking at no one in particular. In fact, from my vantage point, he appeared to be watching the show.

When we filed out, Carson left ahead of the crowd. That worried me. If he meant to do us harm, he could set himself up where we would have difficulty spotting him. As we were about to exit through the tent flap, McAllen put a hand in the middle of my chest to halt my progress and whispered to hold the women inside for a few minutes. I stalled the women as McAllen and James went outside to scout the area. The crowd surged around us as we stood to the side. Instead of chatting, I kept my eyes and ears open to anything unusual. Nothing. Soon, McAllen came back into view and signaled that we could come out.

When we drew alongside, McAllen said, "No sign of him. I don't believe he even spotted us."

I said, "But he may have known we were inside and wanted us to see him."

"Yep."

"Meaning?"

"Meaning he's playin' a game of intimidation today. He means to rattle us."

"Well, I for one do not rattle," my mother said. "Let's see what's for sale at the bazaar."

Without waiting for our concurrence, my mother marched off in the direction of the carnival and bazaar. Damn.

"I agree," McAllen said, as he swiftly followed in my mother's tracks.

Scurrying to catch up, I yelled, "What?"

"Your mother's right. We need to show we're not intimidated. Besides, he wouldn't expose himself in that manner if he was goin' to do somethin' today, so let's have fun."

"Fun? I've never seen you have fun."

"I'll pretend. I want to see what Carson will do."

"With the women as bait?"

"Steve, they're goin'. Nothin' to be done about it, so let's make the most of it."

"*Yes* would have been a shorter sentence," I said.

McAllen ignored me. "Keep an eye out for Carson's sidekick."

Before long, we were barely able to move through crowds trying to get to canopied tables selling every manner of baked goods, implements, and crafted novelties. I looked in every direction, but saw neither Carson nor his partner. Thankfully, the women stayed together, moving from stall to stall to examine the merchandise. My mother bought Maggie a silver bracelet. Virginia, not to be outdone, bought her a home-tooled brooch decorated with a piece of turquoise.

Then we heard gunshots.

The shots were nearby, but not right next to us. They rang out sporadically, with a sort of regular rhythm. McAllen called James over and ordered him to investigate. He walked quickly in the direction of the gunshots.

Within minutes, he returned looking unperturbed. "Shooting contest," he said with a shrug.

"What kind of contest?" Virginia asked excited. "Steve, I bet you can win." If that wasn't bad enough, she excitedly added, "Do they have a category for women?"

"No!" McAllen's steadfast exclamation startled the women.

"Why not?" Maggie demanded. "I'm good with a rifle."

McAllen tried to stare down his daughter, but then I witnessed something I had never seen before: he acquiesced to someone else's wishes. I had never gotten McAllen to take an action he didn't want to take. To get around him, I proceeded without informing him of my plans. In the early days of knowing each other, this practice caused a strain between us. Maybe I needed to recruit a fifteen-year-old girl to change his mind. Of course, there was really only one fifteen year old who could bend the unyielding Joseph McAllen.

"Does it look safe?" McAllen asked James.

"Dozens of people around," James mused. "The gunfire is drawing more by the minute. I think it may be the safest area of the carnival."

"Okay," McAllen said. "Steve, go back to the hotel. Bring back Maggie's rifle."

I looked quizzically at Virginia.

"I have my pistol, but bring more ammunition," she said.

Her confirmation didn't surprised me, but I couldn't tell where she hid a pocket pistol in her form fitting dress. Perhaps in her purse, but that seemed small, as well. Nonetheless, I took comfort that she understood the situation and carried protection. Virginia overly prided herself on her shooting skills, and a contest might show her that she needed further practice.

In a bit of whimsy, I said, "Mother, would you like a weapon, as well?"

Without the slightest hesitation, she answered, "My, yes. Please bring your Winchester. It's been years since I shot. This should be enormous fun."

Chapter 40

I cussed under my breath as I traipsed back to the circus grounds. A shooting contest for god's sake. The women thought it would be great fun to blast away at targets that didn't shoot back. Did they forget real villains threatened our lives? This whole exercise was dumb. No good could come of it, and someone could possibly get hurt. Probably my mother. I used a Winchester '76, which shot a powerful .45-75 cartridge. The sturdy frame and twelve-cartridge magazine made the rifle heavier than Maggie's 1873 model which accepted a pistol-load .45 cartridge. It might serve her right if the recoil knocked her on her behind.

More than one passerby gave me a curious look because I carried a rifle in each hand and my suit jacket bulged with ammunition. My frown probably didn't help either. I must have looked like an angry recruit marching off to war. I forced myself to slow my pace and relax. This day wouldn't see an ambush; not in front of hundreds and hundreds of people. Maybe an exhibit of gun skills would give Carson and his partner pause. Then I realized what really bothered me. Virginia possessed a gross overestimation of her shooting skills. Even before New York, she believed she shot better than she did, but then I lied to her about hitting a murderer in a street fight, causing her to become inordinately proud of her marksmanship.

When I arrived back at the carnival, I found everyone in a distant corner where a shooting range had been set up. A barker yelled out encouragement to would-be contestants, and a carnival worker organized the actual shooting. McAllen stood off to the side where he could watch the entire crowd. We exchanged nods, and then he pointed to the left, where I spotted James. He made a motion with his hand to indicate that I should stay close to the women.

Dozens of people watched a young man in his mid-teens shoot a rifle at bottles two hundred feet away. The intermittent popping noise came from a British .22 Martini-Henry target rifle. Smart kid. The gun had the endorsement of the British National Rifle Association for club competitions. If this contest was judged solely on accuracy, a low caliber, competition rifle gave him an advantage.

A broadside nailed to a post displayed the rules. It cost one dollar to compete in each competition, and there were categories for rifles and pistols. Due to less contestants, the schedule called for only one women's contest, but it left the choice of weapon up to the contestant. To make it fair for women firing different weapons, rifles shot at targets one hundred feet away and pistols at twenty-five. The contestant hitting the most bottles won, independent of whether the woman used a rifle or pistol. A prize of fifty percent of the fees collected for each category assured the carnival organizers a tidy profit.

I spotted Jenny standing to the side and she seemed to watch the proceedings with interest. She didn't attempt to join our group, which was fine by me. Virginia followed the direction of my glance and then gave me a swift kiss on the cheek, probably marking her territory. Virginia had nothing to worry about, I loved her and she seldom looked as attractive as at the moment. She appeared flushed and excited. I guessed the exhilaration of the contest made her happy. As I leaned over to whisper an endearment, I felt a tug from behind on my rifle butt and whipped around. It was my mother.

"If you please, son, I want to examine your rifle before the contest."

I let go.

"And I'd like to see mine, as well," said Maggie.

As I handed Maggie her rifle, Virginia pull out her .38 revolver and pointed it straight up. Good, she remembered her safety instructions. She unloaded the pistol and then pointed it at the bottles in the distance as she cocked and pulled the trigger several times. She was used to a single-action revolver, so I understood her reacquainting herself with the double-action of the pistol I gave her.

To ease her disappointment when she didn't win, I said, "It's not fair that pistol shooters compete against rifles."

"That's what your mother told the carney—that's what she calls the carnival workers—and he said if we get ten contestants for each event, we can have separate contests."

I looked around at all the men gathered in the general area. "Not likely."

"Doesn't matter," she said. "It's just for fun."

"And a dollar," I said lightly.

Virginia laughed. "Yes, indeed . . . so I hope Maggie wins."

Before I could respond, my mother startled me. "Son, you changed the sight on this rifle. What else have you done to it?"

"What? How do you know?"

An exasperated sigh. "Dear, before you were old enough to shoot, your father repeatedly drug me down to that silly shop of his. We didn't always fight with each other, you know. There was a time when we enjoyed each other's company. He loved to shoot, and he loved to compete against another person. At one time, I could shoot well enough to beat him on occasion."

That impressed me. My father possessed exceptional skill with practically any type of gun. I had a vague recollection that my mother once practiced shooting at my father's gun shop and even hunted birds on occasion. I had an even vaguer recollection that they had once gotten along. Not at the end, however. By the time I reached my teens, my father and mother made a studious effort to avoid one another. Since I lived inside a house where a civil war raged, I unconsciously joined forces with my father. He took a keen interest in me, and besides, he owned countless guns down at his shop. That was a pull no boy could resist. After he died, I saw for myself why the Dancy family greed drove my father to run away to his store or bird hunting.

"Steve!" my mother exclaimed.

"Yes, ma'am," I answered.

"You didn't answer my question."

"I'm sorry. What was it again?"

Another exaggerated sigh. "What have you done to this rifle?"

"The new sight, of course, and a lighter hammer spring. It pulls very easy. Careful. I exchanged the factory lever for an enlarged one in case I wear gloves. The ammunition uses English powder for a cleaner burn." I thought a minute. "It's a bit heavy in the barrel due to the extended magazine. I made a couple other adjustments, but they won't be noticeable except for improved accuracy." I hesitated. "Mother, this is a .45-75."

"You think I don't know that?" She sniffed.

Without further comment, she deftly unloaded the gun by repeatedly working the lever to spill cartridges onto the ground. Then she checked the open breech to make sure it was empty before dry firing the rifle a half dozen times. Next, she brought the gun up, tucked the butt firmly into her shoulder, aimed out into the open field, and swung the barrel left and right.

It appeared my father had taught her well because she knew how to handle a big rifle. Since her arrival, we had gotten along better than at any time I could recall. Perhaps Maggie and Virginia had softened her, or maybe being away from New York made her forget her money-grubbing ways. Possibilities, but in truth, I knew it was my pending marriage to Virginia Baker, a member of the eminent Morris clan of Philadelphia. In her eyes, Virginia represented a far better catch than she had envisioned for me. A matrimonial tie between the Dancy and Morris families would create a powerful alliance of business and political interests that stretched from New York City to Washington, D.C. This blissful vision would be destroyed the instant Virginia and I announced we intended to make our home in the West. In the meantime, I might as well enjoy the unexpected rapport with my mother.

I learned the fragility our new relationship when she spoke her next words.

Pointing at the ground, she said, "Pick up those

cartridges, dear . . . and brush them off so there's not a speck of dirt on any of them."

I dutifully acceded to her command. When I stood up, I received a knowing nod from Virginia, who found our entire charade amusing. I found it tiresome.

I rubbed the cartridges clean of debris. Pouring the shiny cartridges into my mother's open palm, I asked, "When does the women's contest start?"

She smiled. "I don't know . . . and I don't care. I'm shooting now."

"Now? Didn't you see that kid shooting the Martini-Henry? He hit nine out of ten."

She calmly reloaded the rifle. "Then I need to hit ten out of ten."

I examined the targets. Different sized whiskey bottles stood crookedly on a log set out in an open field. The log lay at about a forty-five degree angle, with the bottles cleverly spaced so they looked equidistant from the toe-line. Each contestant was allowed one practice shot. The shooter might think he had the range figured out properly, but probably wouldn't notice that the first bottle was as much as ten feet closer than the last bottle.

I whispered a quick explanation of the illusion to my mother and she nodded understanding. Then she took a silver dollar out of her purse, and handed the purse to me, oblivious of my embarrassment at holding a woman's bag. She offered the barker the dollar and he said something I couldn't hear, but it presumably was about her waiting for the women's competition. I watched her shake head and tell the barker something that caused him to shrug and accept the dollar.

She stepped up to the toe-line and peered downfield a long time before raising the Winchester. When she pulled the trigger, the gun barked so loud, several people jumped. This was not the pop of a .22. The bottle shattered. Now she had everyone's attention. Her gray hair, matronly dress, bonnet, and lace-up shoes made her look like a teetotaler grandmother, except this grandmother expertly brandished a big bore rifle. The barker reached out and took the gun to hold while the bottle was replaced by a boy who jumped up from a ditch. My mother looked back at me and smiled wickedly.

Her accuracy startled me. I had assumed my natural ability with guns came from my father. It was disconcerting to discover that my mother may have had something to do with it. I could see my father's instructions reflected in how she shot because I had witnessed him giving the same instructions to countless customers. Some readily grasped his techniques, while others struggled to absorb and implement his advice. At one time, he told me that some just had the knack, while others didn't. Obviously, my mother possessed some level of innate talent. She handled the big rifle with aplomb and her aim was true. This whole episode made me uncomfortable. The next words I heard made me even more uncomfortable.

"I see you found your place with the ladies," Carson said. "Nice handbag, by the way. It looks good with your fancy suit."

Carson's smirk irritated me more than his words. Virginia stepped toward him, probably intent on introducing him to her lead-filled purse, but a cautionary glance from me stopped her—at least momentarily. Then another woman approached him with a raw anger I had seldom seen.

"Who're you working for now?" Jenny demanded.

"Not you, honey," Carson said with a nonchalant air.

"But someone . . . otherwise you wouldn't still be in town."

He threw his arm in a wide arc. "I love the circus. Good enough reason to stay."

"Claude Jansen? Does he pay you?"

"Why the hell do you care? I do what I want. Sometimes I'm paid, sometimes I'm just out for some fun." He smirked. "Do you want to rehire me for personal services?"

The slap came fast, hard, and with enough force to rock Carson on his heels. He stepped forward toward Jenny, but she had already done a pirouette and disappeared into the crowd of onlookers.

I thought that might be the end, but then Carson turned on me. "I owe you a beating." His expression turned menacing. "Perhaps I should do it here and now."

By this time, my mother had regained possession of my rifle and used the butt to gently poke Carson in the stomach. "Do it later. I'm about to shoot and I don't want a ruckus behind me."

"Whoa, now I know where you learned to hide behind women . . . at your mother's knee."

My first reaction was anger, but then I felt a touch of fear. He knew this was my mother, which meant that he had been watching us. I calmed myself, then used my hand holding my mother's purse to nudge him back a step to give her more room to shoot.

"Give her room," I said. "She's about to win this contest."

When he didn't immediately protest my effrontery, I added, "Are you shooting?"

"Of course, I need to honor my father's name. Don't worry, I'll let your mother stay with the leaders for a turn or two." He smiled. "That is, if she can do as well as the boy."

"Don't tell me," Virginia said, incredulously. "Kit Carson is your father."

"He is." He waved his arm around in a sweeping arc. "All of this carries my name. Carson City, Carson River, Carson Street, Carson Valley, just to mention a few."

Maggie inserted herself into the conversation. "This city wasn't named after you . . . or your father."

Carson puffed out his chest. "Oh, you'd be wrong about that, little lady . . . and make no mistake, I inherited my father's skill with a gun."

"He didn't have a son named George," Maggie insisted.

"How would you know?" Carson asked, annoyed.

"I studied the great trailblazer in school, and none of his children were named George. Not from any of his three wives."

Carson laughed. "You're too young to understand, young lady, but a man doesn't need to be married to a woman for her to bear him a son."

"Too young?" Maggie huffed. "I'm a year older than Mr. Carson's third wife. She was fourteen." She made a face. "He was old, thirty-something if I remember correctly, but he still managed to impregnate her six times."

"Well, well," Carson said. "If you're old enough, then—"

He stopped and glanced at McAllen who had come in from the periphery to protect his daughter. The scowl on his face would have stopped anyone from further comment. I thought McAllen might shoot him on the spot. Carson must have thought so too, because he looked serious as he flicked his coattail to make sure it was out of the way of his gun. Suddenly, I knew the approaching McAllen intended to punch Carson to the ground.

My mother stopped the altercation. "Gentlemen, quiet! I'm about to shoot. If you have a score to settle, do it later."

Chapter 41

I had been impressed with my mother's practice shot, but I didn't believe she could beat that clever kid with the Martini-Henry. After she splattered six bottles, I became hopeful. All during her shooting, I kept Carson in the corner of my eye. He behaved himself, and McAllen receded into the background again. I never spotted his partner, but I knew he was around. McAllen saw me scanning the crowd, and mouthed the word James. I felt better knowing James had him in his sights.

My mother's seventh shot blew the bottle in more directions than a dropped watermelon. Three more to go. The next bottle cleanly lost its neck, and the carney scored it a hit. Eight down. Then a miss. Darn. I saw her hesitate in a moment of doubt, which seldom worked out well. After that ninth shot, she looked anxious. I had never seen her unsure of herself, so she made me nervous. If she could get this last bottle, the contest would be tied, and the rules called for a shoot-off to determine the winner.

She wavered on this last shot, then lowered the rifle. Heavy sigh. Finally, she looked at me and said, "Son, do you want to bet me on this last bottle?"

Before I could answer, Carson said, "I'll bet you, ma'am."

"How much?" my mother said in a voice that did not instill confidence.

"Ten dollars," Carson said.

"Make it a double eagle, and you have a bet," she answered with a slight tremor.

A double eagle was a twenty dollar gold coin, essentially doubling his bet. Perhaps she did this to improve her concentration. When he agreed, she asked to see the double eagle. He pulled out a twenty dollar note.

"No good," she said. "Find gold to trade for that currency or the bet's off."

He cussed and looked around at the crowd. Someone stepped forward holding a gold coin between the fingers of his outstretched arm.

"Twenty-one dollars," the stranger said.

"How about twenty dollars or a bullet in the chest," Carson countered.

"Twenty-one dollars," the stranger repeated, not a bit intimidated.

As the two argued a bit more, I glanced at my

mother. She winked. Winked? Darn her, anyway. She didn't want the money. She wanted to embarrass Carson. That's exactly what I would have done. Suddenly, I felt distraught. Most of my life, I wanted nothing to do with my mother. She was snobbish, greedy, relentless, and often downright vindictive. My father was a generous man who channeled his competitive nature toward hunting and shooting, shunning the family businesses. In truth, he possessed a placid spirit: A spirit nothing like my own. I examined my mother anew. Damn. I was more like her than I wanted to admit.

Once the bet was settled, my mother resumed a confident stance, swung the rifle up, and with only a moment's hesitation, blasted the tenth bottle to smithereens.

I kept my eye on Carson. He seethed, but handed over the gold piece. Then he pulled a silver dollar from a pocket and handed it to the carney. With that, his partner materialized from the crowd and placed a rifle in Carson's out-stretched hand—a Winchester '73. I couldn't see any external modifications, but that didn't mean the rifle hadn't been customized. As he stepped up to the toe-line, Carson waved off his practice shot. He had a good stance and held a steady rifle tucked tightly into his shoulder. I expected him to shoot, but he lowered the rifle and looked at my mother.

"A double eagle says I hit all ten," he said.

"No," was all my mother said in response.

"Ha, you know I can do it, don't you?"

"I know you can't do it . . . and I have no intention of angering you further. Take your turn."

"Listen—" He stopped and collected himself. "I went out of my way to accommodate your bet. You should do the same for me. Fair is fair."

"What rubbish. Nothing's fair . . . but I'll see your bet. Just be careful of the wind. It's not blowing as hard right here as it is across from that tree break."

She pointed out about fifty feet away.

"There ain't no wind, lady, you're just trying to mess with my aim."

"Suit yourself," she said. "No sense in giving advice to a cocksure man."

Carson gave me an angry look. "When I was done with you, I always intended to show your woman a real man." He gave my mother a nasty look. "Now I'm inclined to teach your mother a lesson as well."

I stepped forward, but my mother raised her hand.

"We're not impressed with your bluster, young man," she said. "Just show us how well you shoot."

He angrily whirled toward the target cussing under his breath. Perhaps she got him heated enough to ruin his aim. Too much to hope for. Carson took a deep breath and forced himself to relax. He then proceeded to hit five bottles in a row, but then the distance grew greater with the optical illusion and the side breeze he chose to ignore caused him to miss the sixth. Carson had just lost a second double eagle, which would shake most men. I thought of Carson as a blowhard, but he gathered his composure and hit the remaining four bottles.

He was a damn good shot . . . and we had a three-way tie.

Chapter 42

Hundreds of people milled around waiting for the final shoot-out that would determine the winner of the contest. Word soon spread about the three-way tie and people, both women and men, gathered a dozen deep behind the toe-line. Most people came to see this grandmother who could shoot as good as that upstart Annie Oakley. At least I overheard many of them refer to her as a grandmother. As a categorization, Virginia and I would need to make that a reality.

A few years previously, I had seen the oft mentioned Annie Oakley in a shooting exhibition.

I thought she might be the best shot in the world, and I had grown up around exceptional marksmen. I had recently read in a newspaper that Buffalo Bill had hired her for his Wild West show. I'd wager she would soon be the star attraction. I had seen Oakley and her husband perform at the Ohio State Fair on my way west. At sixteen, she shot the tip off of a cigarette held between her husband's lips. At ninety feet, she could hit a playing card set on edge, and then shoot it several more times before it touched the ground. Her shooting convinced me that accurate shooting could be acquired, but exceptional gun handling requires something that comes to a person when they're born.

Several men paid their dollar and did their best, but no one even hit seven bottles. The contest looked to be between my mother, Carson, and the boy with the Martini-Henry. Oakley shot a variety of guns, but used a .22 caliber rifle for her most difficult shots. This made me think the boy had a clear advantage with his target rifle.

The three drew straws to see who would choose the shooting order. The boy won, and started first, which proved he was as clever as I surmised. If he hit nine or ten bottles, it would put undue pressure on the other two contestants. He hit ten.

My mother went next and hit ten as well.

Finally, Carson matched the other two's feat.

With ten hits each, wagering became wild. The

crowd pushed and shoved to offer and accept bets. Women also jumped into the betting, presumably due to my mother's performance. I spotted Jenny making a wager, and wondered who she bet on. She caught me looking at her and her expression turned none too friendly.

The carney, knowing a good thing when he saw it, held up the next round of shooting until the betting frenzy abated. For a two-bit fee, the carney would note the bets and hold the cash. As a supposed honest broker, he collected a lot of coin.

The boy fell apart in the second round. He missed his seventh shot, and then followed it with another miss. He pulled himself together for his final two shots, but if prior shooting was any indication, he would shortly be out of the contest. I wanted my mother to win, but felt disappointed that the boy let the hoopla rattle him.

My mother and Carson both hit ten bottles on their next turn, and the betting fever heated up even further. My mother walked over to me while the carney collected bets, making his notations on the back of a broadside. I handed her a box of ammunition, and she absentmindedly reloaded my rifle while watching the commotion.

"He's a good shot," she said.

"You could try another double-eagle wager, but I doubt you're going to shake him again."

"Suggestions?"

"Shoot straight."

She laughed. Then her face turned serious. "Did you do the work on this rifle yourself?"

"I did."

"Nice work, son."

She hefted the fully loaded Winchester into the crook of her arm and calmly approached the toe-line. As she waited for the next round of shooting, she kept her eyes straight ahead, looking neither left nor right.

Her praise surprised me. First, there was the shock of her understanding the extent of my modifications and second, I couldn't remember the last time she said something complimentary to me. Then I realized she was having fun. My socialite mother reveled in the attention she got from this frontier contest of skill and grit. Suddenly, I knew she would win handily, so I found a willing gambler and laid down a big bet.

She did win in the next round. She hit ten bottles once again, but Carson missed his eighth shot. From the prolonged cheering, it appeared most of the townsfolk had bet on my mother. To his credit, Carson took his loss graciously, or at least he didn't curse, threaten, or stomp around. He merely walked away and disappeared into the crowd.

I found Carson's reaction surprising, but my mother's behavior startled the hell out of me. She hugged me and Virginia, then took each of Maggie's hands in hers and danced in circles like a schoolchild. Virginia came over and looped her arm through mine. I even spotted Jenny smiling from the periphery, at least until she spotted me watching her again, then her expression turned sour.

"Proud?" Virginia asked.

"Puzzled."

"You didn't know, did you? You're surprised she can shoot as well as you?"

"That remains to be seen, but that's not what puzzles me. I could almost imagine she likes me."

"She loves you."

"I never questioned that, but neither of us liked each other much. The last thing I would have guess is that she'd have fun out here." I shook my head. "Look at her. Maggie's her first new friend in decades and she's enjoying herself . . . and . . . I think . . . our company." I shook my head again. "What happens now? Does she go back to tea, crumpets, and gossip?"

Virginia didn't answer because a barker shouted that the women's shooting competition would start in five minutes and contestants should pay their dollar to get a number. I saw my mother hand Maggie a dollar and she rushed over to be first in line. I fished around in my pocket until I found two half-dollar pieces. I offered them to Virginia.

She shook her head no. "I want Maggie to win," she said.

I doubted Virginia could actually challenge that outcome, but I didn't say anything. I smiled, and squeeze her hand. She smiled back . . . and then she gently hit me.

"I know what you're thinking," she said. "Maybe I'm not a great shot, but I can shoot straight when someone else is shooting at me. How many here can say that?"

She was right. In New York, she proved her bravery, but more important, she showed that she could and would fight in a life-threatening situation. Her aim might not be true, but her courage and character were tried and true. I felt enormously proud to have her at my side.

McAllen had again approached the contestant area to encourage his daughter. He stood over her for nearly a minute with his arm wrapped around her shoulder whispering in her ear. She said little, but nodded understanding or agreement. I wasn't sure who taught Maggie how to shoot. To my knowledge, McAllen had seen her only about once a year since his divorce from her mother. I also didn't think McAllen shot particularly well. His utter calm when under threat or attack gave him all the edge he needed to prevail in a fight. He attacked with such steadfast ferocity that he caused his assailants to hesitate or quiver. Either way, they soon found themselves dead, or more probably on the ground unconscious from a severe blow delivered by the barrel of his heavy Smith & Wesson revolver.

Whatever he told her, Maggie looked self-confident as she went up to shoot. Only three women competed, all of them used rifles. It wasn't close. Maggie won on the first round, hitting eight out of ten bottles.

Maggie and my mother hugged and congratulated each other. McAllen looked the prou father. Virginia gave me an indiscreet kiss on the lips. I remained flabbergasted at my mother's perfor-mance, until I heard a voice behind me.

"Your womenfolk did good," Carson said with a mocking tone. "Hurray for them, but soon it's time for you to come out from behind their skirts."

I turned, half expecting to see him with his gun drawn. His pistol remained holstered, but as usual, he had his coattail tucked back to expose his fancy Colt.

"Go away," I said.

"Can't. Already paid my dollar to compete in the men's pistol shoot. Are you competing?"

"No."

I took Virginia's hand and started to lead her away. I turned back at Carson's next words.

"If you're afraid, perhaps one of your women will compete." He pointed at Virginia as his typical smirk took on a lewd twist. "Maybe she'd like to test herself with me."

Without a word, I slapped a dollar into the palm of the barker.

Chapter 43

I told myself to remain calm. Carson thought of himself as an expert gunman, and I wanted to dissuade him of that notion before bullets flew in a harmful direction. The pistol competition had been scheduled last because it would be the most popular. Over twenty men had entered the contest, and many of the milling contestants appeared drunk. The combination of heady drinking, reck-less betting, and loaded guns made me nervous.

For the first round, bottles were set up thirty feet away from the toe-line, and a shooter needed to hit at least four bottles with five shots to remain in the competition. In the beginning rounds, each contestant would start with gun in hand, so speed of draw meant nothing. Carson and I both went five for five, but at least half the men found themselves eliminated in this first round. Not one of the drunk contestants made it beyond the first round. That should have been a lesson for anyone challenged to a saloon gunfight, but when whiskey dulled their senses, none of these men would remember their embarrassment at a carnival.

The boy next set up bottles at forty feet. The added distance cut the number of contestants to eight. Another round at fifty feet eliminated three more. Now we were down to five. Instead of moving the bottles further away, the carney said we should holster our guns because we now needed to draw and shoot.

"It's time for you boys to head on back to your womenfolk," Carson said. Although he used the plural, I felt Carson directed his comment specifically at me.

I kept my voice calm. "That's pretty bigheaded for someone who lost the rifle competition to an old woman wearing feathers and fake flowers on her bonnet. Perhaps you ought to bow out before you embarrass yourself further."

Carson made a show of looking over the remaining contestants. "I don't see any bonnets, so I'll stay. Perhaps you should ask for a recess to see if mommy can give you a little hug before you shoot."

His self-confidence annoyed me. "Let's make this interesting. One hundred dollars?"

He hooked a thumb at Virginia. "Throw in your woman and you have a bet."

I poked him hard in the chest with my index finger. "Touch her and I'll kill you."

He recoiled momentarily, but came back faster than I expected. "That'll be difficult when you're broken into pieces . . . and don't touch me again or I'll do it in front of your mother and woman."

"Virginia's not my woman, she's my fiancée.

If you mention her again, I'll make you a cripple for the rest of your life."

We tried to stare each other down. Then Carson laughed and his expression relaxed into his characteristic smirk.

"Hell, I know she's not your woman. You're her man. You toady up to her like she's got something special." He looked disdainfully at her. "I'll bet it's not so special."

I was about to lose my temper when the carney saw the intensity of the situation and yelled out that the next round was about to start. I was grateful for his interruption because I wanted to avoid a duel with Carson. I just wanted him to go away . . . but I knew he wouldn't. It was wishful thinking. A fight would come . . . sooner or later. My hope was that I could hold it off until my acquittal. A jury would probably not believe my claim of self-defense if I killed yet another man before the trial.

That realization brought up a different line of thinking. Why would Carson challenge me so aggressively when he knew I had previously killed hired gunmen in a lopsided fight and McAllen and I had bested Matting and his crew? Why taunt me as a sissy who hid behind women? He knew better. Was he trying to get me angry enough to gain an edge, or did he really believe he was that good? Was he being paid to irritate me? Cause me to do something stupid? Had Jenny really dismissed him, or did Carson still do her bidding? Perhaps he worked directly for Claude Jansen. I doubted he held that big of a grudge against me for knocking him down in Denver, and I doubted he needed to test his manhood. Something more was going on, and I needed to figure it out.

Before I could think it through, the carney called me to take my turn. The rules said I was to draw as quickly as I could and shoot one of the bottles lined up fifty feet away. Still somewhat distracted, I pulled my Colt and shot one of the bottles and re-holstered my pistol in one motion that was hard to follow with the eye. I had grown tired of Carson's game and wanted to show him that a duel would not end in his favor. The instant buzz of wonderment told me that I had succeeded in impressing the audience. Carson, however, looked smug as he approached the toe-line. With nary a blink of time, he instantly drew his weapon and fired what sounded like one long shot splattering five bottles to hell and gone. He proved to be far better with a pistol than a rifle. In fact, he was so fast and accurate, it jangled my nerves a bit. If nature gave undue shooting advantage to a few, then it would endow someone, somewhere with more advantage than it had bestowed upon me. Was George Carson that man? Suddenly, I didn't want to know the answer to that question.

Carson's shooting prowess so unnerved the

contestants that none of the other three survived this round. As we reloaded, Carson and I resumed our staring contest. I stepped up to the line, but the carney held up his palm to stop me. I couldn't figure out why until I heard the commotion behind me. The betting had grown wild and boisterous.

When the betting subsided, I looked at the bottles, and they had been moved to sixty feet. I relaxed and let my hand dangle as if I had no particular purpose for it. In less than a blink, I had brought the gun up to eye level and shot one of the bottles. This time I paused slightly before I re-holstered my pistol.

"Only one," Carson said. "I think I can do better than that."

In what looked to be equally as fast as me, Carson drew and rapid-fired, hitting four bottles with five shots. This was his first misstep. Perhaps he limited his practice to inside fifty feet. At any rate, it made me feel more confident that his aim was less than perfect.

Since his first shot hit a bottle, we remained tied. The carney again explained that we only needed to hit one bottle at this stage of the contest. Then he told us to be patient until the betting subsided.

"You missed," I said. "Perhaps you'd do better to concentrate on your first shot."

"If those bottles had been a man, he would have four bullets in his heart and one somewhere else in his chest. Putting five bullets in his heart wouldn't make a difference. He'd be just as dead with four."

"But if you miss that first shot, your make-believe man might put a hole in you before you shot again."

"One day, we'll find out," he said matter-of-factly. He remained far too calm for my liking.

I had to win this contest. If Carson developed an inkling that he could beat me, then he might very well try. I didn't want another gunfight, especially not against someone with Carson's skills. He loved to taunt me, but I cared nothing about him. If he suddenly caught a train back to Denver, I doubted that I would ever think about him again.

The bottles were moved further back, to about seventy feet, which was a challenging distance for a pistol shot, especially after a quick draw. This time, Carson went first. He missed his first shot, but hit the bottle and another in a flurry of shots that kicked up an enormous amount of dust. In truth, it was speedy as hell and potentially deadly. After all, a bottle is considerably smaller than a man's chest. I needed to end this contest . . . now. With one swift action, I drew my gun, brought my other hand around for a two-fisted grip and slightly squatted to bring the Colt's sight to eye level. A single shot sent glass shards flying in every direction.

To cheers from some of the crowd, the carney declared me the winner.

When I turned, I expected to see a scowl on Carson's face, but instead, he grinned as if he had won. As the betters settled their wagers, Carson kept grinning. I decided to ignore him and walked over to Virginia. She hugged me, while my mother kept her eye on something worrisome over my shoulder. When I turned around, I saw Carson reloading his pistol with that same inane grin. I considered knocking the gun out of his hand before he finished and beating him to the ground. Maybe even grinding his gun hand with the heel of my boot. Too late. He snapped the cylinder cover closed and then dithered menacingly before holstering his gun.

Jenny claimed to have dismissed Carson. As far as I could tell, he had no reason to challenge me. It seemed odd because I had won the shooting contest, and he knew I would not hesitate to kill if someone threatened my life.

What was he up to . . . and why did he find it amusing?

The answer might be right in front of me: Someone wanted to rattle me before the trial. Perhaps he hoped I would knock him to the ground again to show a history of undue passion. Even a yelling match might suffice to prejudice a jury. Jeff Sharp and I would face a prosecutor and jury next week. Someone wanted us to die on the gallows. Was it just me or both of us? Who wanted us to hang? Jenny had for a time. Did she still? Was her remorse only an act? She was certainly capable of a convincing performance. Or did Claude Jansen have reason to want us dead . . . and disgraced? My thoughts brought up an uncomfortable feeling. The circus and carnival had been a great diversion, but just below the surface, I worried about Sharp. Did he manage to escape? If not, would his handler let him go when they reached Carson City?

Where was Jeff Sharp?

Chapter 44

The five of us squeezed around a table intended to seat four. It was a celebratory lunch, full of laughter and comradery because Maggie, my mother, and I had won our respective shooting contests. The women also basked in the praise they received at the governor's gala the night before. McAllen said little, but his pride in his daughter's accomplishment was unmistakable.

When it came time to pay for our meal, my mother said that with the way events worked out, she believed Carson should pay.

"If only the hotel would put the charge on his tab," Virginia said. "He'd be mad as a hornet."

"No need," my mother said. "He can pay in

cash." With that, she slapped a double eagle onto the table. This provoked laugher all around. Without a doubt, we all thoroughly enjoyed heaping further humiliation onto the insufferable Mr. George Carson. I even heard a hearty chuckle from the normally taciturn McAllen.

"Judging by all the merriment, ya all didn't miss me much."

I was on my feet in an instant. "Damn, you're back!"

"Now, that's a hell of a greetin'." Sharp said this with a smile to show he wasn't really offended by my clumsiness.

Everyone stood and surrounded him with hugs, backslaps, and kisses from Maggie and Virginia. My mother nodded from the periphery. She cocked her head at Sharp like he was an odd specimen. His wet hair indicated that he had come straight from a bath, but his clean, tattered clothes failed to make him look the gentleman. Like always he appeared rough and ready. Just the way we liked him, but probably off-putting to my mother.

"When did you arrive?" McAllen asked.

"Last night. Late. Rode day and night, so I went right to bed." He looked out of the window. "Slept most of the day away, it seems."

"Hungry?" I asked.

"Yep." A waitress brought over a chair and he squeezed in between Virginia and Maggie. He looked up at the waitress and winked. "Young lady, bring me hot coffee, three eggs, plenty of bacon, grits, toast burnt till black, and a huge stack of yer famous hot cakes." Then he looked at all of us, obviously pleased with himself. "Want to know how I escaped the evil clutches of Jenny's minions?"

"They were bringing you back to Carson City to set you free," my mother said with a snotty air. "How you escaped is of little matter."

Sharp beamed as he reached over and took my mother's hand. "My, who's this beauty?" He looked at McAllen. "Joseph, is this your new woman-friend?"

"Certainly not," my mother huffed, but she couldn't completely hide her pleasure at hearing such a compliment. "Mr. McAllen is far too young and ill-bred for my taste. Tell me, does that crude flattery work out here in the wilderness?"

Sharp looked crestfallen. "I apologize if I offended. I had to guess because not one person at this table possessed the manners to introduce you."

"Jeff, this is my mother, Agatha—"

"You may call me Mrs. Dancy," my mother interjected as she withdrew her hand.

Sharp saluted with an imaginary hat. "Mrs. Dancy, a pleasure. You raised a fine son. Too fine for my taste. He stole my girl." Sharp winked at Virginia.

"Ignore him," Virginia said. "Three quarters of

what he says is blarney. He believes every woman is attracted to him because of his bucolic charm."

"Pay close attention to the other quarter of what he says," I cautioned. "It may save your life."

"And how am I supposed to figure out which is which?" my mother asked.

"That, my dear, is the fun of knowing me," Sharp said with an engaging smile.

"*How* did you escape?" McAllen asked, exasperated by the small talk.

Sharp looked smug. "They took me to my old home at Belleville. I guess they thought that would be ironic, except that I had hidden weapons all over that house. When we left that morning, I had a pistol and knife hidden in my clothing." He laughed. "Boy, did my guard look surprised when I got the drop on him. Poor soul, he's still out there in the wilderness burnt to a crisp, no doubt."

"Why would that be?" my mother asked.

"Because he took his clothes and boots," I guessed.

"Yep. He'll be walkin' right careful, I 'spect."

"Surely you left him with his underthings," mother said.

Sharp merely smiled.

"Knowing Jeff's sense of humor," McAllen said, "I'm sure he's tender-footing his way back to Belleville buck naked."

Sharp laughed. "And red as boiled lobster."

My mother seemed surprised by the analogy. "Is that something you eat often on the frontier, Mr. Sharp?"

"No, ma'am. Lobsters are pretty rare here, but I developed a taste for 'em at Delmonico's." His expression turned wistful. "I sometimes dream about Chef Ranhofer's Lobster Newburg."

"You've eaten at Delmonico's?" She couldn't have sounded more astonished.

Sharp laughed. "Even a Westerner wouldn't miss Delmonico's when in New York. I dined there so often I became friends with Charles."

"Charles Delmonico?" my mother asked, sounding even more astonished.

"Yep. Fine gentleman." He turned his attention to McAllen. "Now tell me what's been happenin' since I been gone. Hope you boys ain't had too much fun in my absence."

While McAllen explained our travails, I studied my mother. If her mouth had fallen open, she couldn't have appeared more astounded. Sharp had played her expertly, heightening his mischievousness by artfully turning the conversation in different directions. My mother knew Sharp was rich, but she assumed he was still a bumpkin who happened upon some gold and silver in the dirt. I wondered if Sharp knew her favorite restaurant was Delmonico's and she had maneuvered for years to ingratiate herself with Charles Delmonico. As McAllen talked, I couldn't help sniggering behind my hand, that is, until I spotted a severe reproach from my mother. Her stern, no nonsense countenance stopped my amusement as effectively as when I wore knee pants. Damn her, anyway. I was a grown man, and she shouldn't be able to control my behavior with nary a word.

When McAllen finished, I told him the good news about our new attorney, John Myers. I explained how he and his wife saw the shooting and she would be a witness on our behalf. I also relayed Myers' confidence that other witnesses would come forward after they learned that they wouldn't be the sole witness. I thought the news would make Sharp happy, but instead, he became thoughtful.

He sat for a long moment, then said, "I say we go find Carson and his friend and make 'em follow through on their threats."

"Goad them into a gunfight!" The proposal startled me.

"Call his bluff. Gonna happen sooner or later . . . hell, might as well be today."

Sharp stood to reinforce his seriousness. I was aghast. Reacting to imminent danger didn't allow time for forethought, but purposely instigating a fight meant you did have time to get nervous . . . and nervousness could tilt the edge in Carson's favor. He was an expert gun hand. I didn't know much about his partner, but I doubted Carson would associate himself with a slouch. Challenging Carson sounded like a lousy idea. I felt frightened, but before I could express my concern Sharp left to go upstairs.

"Where's he going?" Virginia asked.

"To get his rifle," I answered.

Chapter 45

S harp bounded back down the stairs in less than two minutes. In his absence, McAllen conveyed his approval of Sharp's plan. Sharp may have wanted revenge for his abduction, but he seldom went off half-cocked because of anger. If Sharp and McAllen thought a direct confrontation was the best way to resolve the situation, then I would stand alongside of them. Besides, one of Sharp's comments struck me as a solid argument. An inevitable fight loomed on the horizon. Carson made that obvious time and again. It would take gunplay, or the threat of gunplay, to end this dispute . . . sometime, somewhere . . . and until we eliminated the threat, the women were not only at risk, they presented a potential weapon in the hands of Carson and his associates. It was better to resolve it now . . . on our terms.

I did have one problem with Sharp's plan, which

became clear to everyone when he arrived at the bottom of the staircase.

"Where do we find these bounders?" Sharp asked cheerfully.

I shrugged and looked at McAllen.

"Hell, I don't know." McAllen sounded irritated that I had directed the question to him.

"Let's ask Jansen," I offered.

McAllen whirled and marched out of the hotel, with me and Sharp forced into an unnatural gait to catch up. When we got outside, I remembered a time when we similarly charged out of this hotel into an ambush. It had happened almost two years ago, but the memory made me swing my head back and forth to see if I could spot any danger. I noticed McAllen did the same.

We encountered no immediate problems, but after getting het up for action, we found Jansen's office closed and locked tighter than a drum. We pounded on the door several times, but no answer. I turned around on the boardwalk and inspected the street. Nothing looked out of the ordinary.

Finally, I said, "Let's see Myers. He seems to know what's going on in this town."

Unlike Jansen, we did find Myers in his office. We discovered him slouched in his beat-up old office chair, head lolled to the side because he was passed out from drinking. Damn it, this was our legal counsel? For a moment, I wanted to shoot him instead of Carson. The trial had no longer worried me due to Myers assurances that his wife and others would testify on our behalf. That presupposed that he would show up on the appointed day and be capable of properly questioning the witnesses. If this was how he prepared for our trial, Sharp and I were in deep trouble.

"What do we do?" I asked, dejected.

"Sober him up," Sharp answered, as he lifted him to his feet.

I wanted to slap him awake, but instead, I burrowed my shoulder under his other armpit so Sharp and I could walk him around the office. McAllen said he would go to the hotel and bring back coffee and food. After a few minutes, we got a grunt, but Myers' eyes remained shut. It took McAllen nearly fifteen minutes, and by then we had Myers half awake, but he remained incoherent. Sharp and I plopped him back onto his swivel chair which rocked tediously because he landed off-center. We each grabbed a side of the chair and steadied it to keep from dumping our esteemed barrister unceremoniously onto the floor. I suspected that he had been prone on this particular floor previously.

McAllen forced Myers to sip at the coffee. After he had finished half the cup, we got him up and started him pacing again. Two more cycles and Myers could speak a little. He stuttered, repeated himself, slurred his words, but we gathered he ate dinner with someone who persuaded him to drink a single beer with his steak. The one beer lead to another, which lead to whiskey.

McAllen decided he couldn't help, so he left to visit the marshal in case he knew the whereabouts of Carson.

After another hour of coffee, bread, and pacing, we brought him around enough so that he was somewhat coherent. Unfortunately, once conscious, a horrific hangover consumed him. He kept waving us away, but neither Sharp nor I had any intention of leaving him alone. His suffering prompted no sympathy from me, and his headache could keep pounding away for all I cared.

After another hour and a couple doses of salicylic acid, Myers regained his senses enough to answer questions.

"You promised me you wouldn't drink before our trial," I said. "What the hell happened?"

Looking down, Myers rubbed both temples with his fingers. Without raising his head, he said, "Nothing happened. When a drinker gets a taste of alcohol, all reason goes out the window." He lifted his head to look at me. "You just keep drinking until you can't anymore."

"If ya know that, then yer a dumb son of a bitch to take that first sip!" Sharp said.

"Guilty."

I shook my head. "Odd term, considering that may be our fate in two days." I felt fatalistic. "Jeff, we need to go find another lawyer. Right now."

"No. I can handle it. I just need . . . I just need time. Get my head clear."

"No," I said. "We can't trust you."

"Damn it, you have to trust me. Without me, you don't have my wife's testimony. I want this trial. I need this trial. I need to regain some level of respect in this town."

"Ya ain't got no respect for yerself," Sharp said. "Without that, ya can't get respect from others. Ain't my rules, just the way it is."

"I can do it. I've got depositions from six witnesses. I made a mistake, but I won't make another one. Stay with me." We must have looked dubious, because he added, "Listen, if it looks like you're going to be convicted, I'll play fallen down drunk in court. The judge will declare a mistrial."

"How do we know you'll be playacting?" I asked.

"I won't drink," he said firmly.

Sharp and I looked at each other. I shrugged, and Sharp turned back to Myers.

"Tell me, what mistake did ya make to get like this?" Sharp asked.

"Hell, what are you talking about? I drank too much."

"I know ya drank too much, but what did ya do to trigger the drinkin'?"

"I drank a beer. I thought I could control it. I couldn't."

"Before that."

"Before that? I don't know what you mean," Myers said.

"Ya got yerself in a temptin' situation. How? What was the mistake? If ya can't tell me, we're gonna find us a new lawyer."

Myers thought a moment. Then he said, "I let a stranger get friendly with me and join me for supper. I didn't know him, but I should have assumed he'd have a drink with his meal. Maybe I let him eat with me so I had an excuse to drink beer. I didn't think it out that way at the time . . . but maybe that's what I did."

Something occurred to me. "What did this stranger look like?"

Myers looked ashamed. Then he shook his head and said, "Someone I should've avoided. He looked to be a gambler . . . maybe a gunman."

"Why do you say a gunman?" I asked.

"Because he carried a fancy rig—polished black holster with a shiny Colt."

"Walnut grips?"

"Hell, I don't know. They were wood. Looked expensive."

"George Carson," I said.

"Who's George Carson?" Myers asked.

"An associate of Mr. Claude Jansen, Esquire," I explained.

Myers flew out of his chair. "Jansen! You mean to tell me Jansen got me drunk?"

"Ya got yerself drunk," Sharp snapped. "Ya can't blame it on nobody else. Nobody. Ya put yerself next to a gent that would surely drink so ya had an excuse to do likewise. Jansen knew yer weakness, but he didn't make it, so don't go chucking blame off onto someone else. It's yer fault. Nobody else."

Without another word, Myers sat back down.

"What do we do?" I asked Sharp.

"I think we leave Mr. Myers to his vices. Let's go."

"No. Wait." Myers stood shakily. "Let me ask you a question. What gives a man strength . . . strength of character or any other kind of strength?"

Neither of us responded because we knew Myers had his own answer.

"Strength comes from exercise or practice . . . or rage . . . and I can tell you nobody has more rage than me at the moment. Jansen made a fool of me. It won't happen again. Give me another chance, and I'll bury that son of a bitch."

"Ya won't drink again?" Sharp asked.

"No, sir. I'm done with drinking."

"Let me give ya a tad more incentive," Sharp said. "If ya mess up again and get us hung, I got a friend who will kill ya. Understood?"

"Understood, but I don't really believe you're that kind of man."

"Don't be a drunk and dumb," Sharp said. "We overestimated ya, don't underestimate us. I don't take kindly to gettin' killed for no good purpose. Good day, Mr. Myers. Ya got work to do."

Sharp spun on his heel and led us out of the office.

Chapter 46

W e burst out of Myers' office and almost knocked Jenny off the boardwalk. When she regained her balance, she looked mad as a hornet. Sharp had been the one to bump her, so I hoped her wrath wasn't aimed at me.

"Our apologies, ma'am," Sharp said, tipping his hat with a big smile.

She gave him a dirty look and started to continue on her way.

Sharp spoke to her receding backside. "Excuse me, Mrs. Bolton, do ya happen to know where we can find George Carson?"

Jenny wheeled on us. "I don't know where Mr. Carson is, nor do I care. Do you happen to know where I can find Claude Jansen?"

"Not in his office, ma'am. We already tried there," Sharp said.

"I know that." Her peevishness obviously hadn't started with our abrupt encounter. "He's not at his home, either."

I sensed that Jansen would regret Jenny finding him.

"Why are you looking for him?" I asked. "Perhaps we can help."

"Good god, are you trying to be my savior again? Well, no thank you. That attack on Maggie may have changed my plans for you, but I still wouldn't be disappointed if they strung you up."

"I'm asking for me," I said. "We want Carson and he's likely with Jansen. If we work together, maybe we can find them both."

Jenny took a hard gander at the rifle that Sharp casually held by the barrel along his leg. She purposefully raised her chin to look us in the eye. "I'll work with you under one condition."

"Just name it, darlin'," Sharp said.

"You do no harm to Mr. Jansen."

"I thought you no longer employed him," I said.

"That shyster's no longer my attorney, but if someone's going to shoot him, it's going to be me." She waved her finger at both of us. "You two leave him alone. Understood?"

Sharp smiled. "Agreed . . . unless he gets the better of ya. Then we just might shoot his pecker off for ya."

Jenny actually laughed, and a bit of her anger abated.

"Did you learn anything more about Jansen?" I asked.

Damn. The rage returned instantly.

"I don't know how, but he controls everything I own. I can't even sell my cattle without his signature. He told me he was taking care of me; instead he somehow weaseled his way into my affairs . . . and I paid that bastard to boot."

I pointed to the office we had just left. "Perhaps Myers can help."

"That drunk? He puked all over the floor of the Cattlemen's dining room last night. Ruined everyone's supper. No, thank you. I'll settle this score myself."

"Any idea where our dastardly pair may have gotten off to?" Sharp asked.

She looked up and down the street. "If they haven't hid in Virginia City, they must be at the capitol."

"Hell, it's a short walk. Let's go see," Sharp said.

When we entered the foyer, we found Senator Fair and Congressman Morris chatting with some men I didn't know. The congressman called us over and introduced us to a couple of the governor's assistants. Then he asked for a few minutes to conclude their business before he talked with us. He evidently believed we came to the capitol to see him. I decided proper manners required deference toward my future uncle-in-law.

Shortly, the congressman came over to where we stood. He looked none too friendly.

Without preamble, he asked, "Did you engage agents in Chicago to procure large quantities of foodstuffs for shipment to Nevada?"

What the hell was this about? And why would he care? I had completely forgotten about our ruse, but someone evidently hadn't forgotten about it. I looked at Jenny. She showed no recognition or interest in the congressman's query. In fact, she craned her neck to peer around the congressman, presumably to see if she could spot Jansen.

"Why is this of interest to you?" I asked.

Morris could not have looked more irritated if I had asked about the legitimacy of his birth. "Mr. Dancy, one of Senator Fair's important constituents has made inquiries about your business intentions. As we are soon to be related, I told the senator that I'd see what I could discover."

"I'm confused," I said, pretending not to be irritated at his audacity. "Does the Morris family generally sacrifice their business interests if a constituent complains?"

"Of course not," he responded huffily. "I only said I would look into the matter . . . as a favor for the senator."

"I presume this important constituent is named Claude Jansen?"

Jenny's head whipped around, suddenly interested in our conversation.

"Where is he?" she demanded.

"I don't like the tone of your voice, young lady. Excuse me, but it's impolite to jump into the middle of a conversation and make demands."

"Where is he?" Jenny demanded again.

"Do you know who I am?" Morris asked indignantly.

"*Congressman Morris,* sir . . . but who you are is not as important as *who* I am. I own the largest cattle ranch and timber company in Nevada and I have many interests in mining and banking. Mr. Jansen is my attorney, which makes him about as important as those pretend politicians you just introduced us to." She paused to enjoy the shocked look on Morris's face. "To make myself clear, Senator Fair cannot be reelected without me." Another pause. "Now, do you want to doom your friend's career or tell me where to find Mr. Jansen?"

"He's upstairs in the governor's anteroom," Morris answered immediately.

"Thank you, congressman," Jenny said as she headed for the stairs.

I started to follow, but the congressman held me back by gripping my arm. I signaled to Sharp that he should accompany Jenny. After all, we didn't want a killing inside the capitol.

"Was she telling the truth?" Morris asked.

"Every word," I answered.

"That pretty young thing. She's so young and so . . . alluring."

"This is the West, sir. Age, family, and upbringing mean less than determination and raw talent . . . and that's one capable woman."

"Woman?" He shook his head.

"Let me help you understand," I said. "The majority leader in the state senate married Mrs. Bolton when she was fifteen. He also happened to be the richest rancher and businessman in Nevada. If he hadn't been assassinated, he would now be governor. That *pretty young thing* would be Nevada's First Lady."

"Ah, that explains it. She inherited his estate."

Now it was my turn to shake my head. "Congressman, that's correct, but in the two years since his death, by my rough calculations, she has doubled the size of his empire. Her husband was a good businessman and an excellent politician, but she makes him look substandard. Do not underestimate that girl."

"Did they catch her husband's assassin?"

"Yes. In fact, McAllen and I caught him." Now I was the one to pause for dramatic effect. "Mrs. Bolton, that pretty young thing, killed him during an escape attempt. Shot him twice in the chest with a .45 Derringer."

The congressman's mouth dropped open. "That innocent-looking girl killed a man?"

"Face to face, and not just any man; the most dangerous and wanted outlaw in the state. You do not want her as an enemy. I should know."

"Mrs. Bolton." Recognition showed on his face. He finally remembered me telling him about her when we first met. "Oh my god, she's the woman that put you in this legal mess."

"She did, but I'd call it something other than a legal mess. That makes it sound like a dispute over a deal gone awry. As for that food in Chicago, I did it to knock her off balance. It's too hard to explain, but . . ."

"Explain it, anyway," Morris demanded. "I need to know everything."

I told him everything that had transpired in the last few days, except I failed to mention that the food purchases in Chicago were a ruse. The fiction might still be useful so I wasn't about to tell a blabbermouth politician. When I explained that Jansen had taken control of the Bolton trust, Morris nodded understanding. He seemed especially aghast when I told him that McAllen's daughter had almost been the victim of serial rape.

"My god, is that how they do business out here? I thought Washington was cutthroat."

"Jansen's a vile man . . . and he's certainly not someone that should be anywhere near Senator Fair."

"You're right," Morris said as he headed for the stairs.

"Stop . . . both of you."

I recognized George Carson's voice, and turned slowly toward the sound. His commanding order and belligerent posture were meant to intimidate. He was not alone. His nameless partner stood smirking right beside him. Morris sniffed and took a step toward the intruders. I felt certain he intended to repeat his *do you know who I am* refrain, so I reached out a hand to halt Morris from challenging what he probably saw as an insolent pair of nobodies. In the West, anyone with a sidearm was a somebody.

"What do you want, George?" I asked.

"Let's go outside. We can discuss it there."

"Why? Has Jansen heard that we have witnesses to clear our names? Has he given you orders to finish things another way so he can retain control of the state's food supply?"

"I don't know what you're talking about. It's you and I who have unfinished business. Now's a good time to settle accounts."

"On the capitol lawn? That seems unfitting."

He shrugged. "I want witnesses."

"Stay where you are," Morris said. "I'll get the police."

He ran off with no objection from me or Carson. After he had rounded the corner into a hallway, I nodded toward the door and said, "After you."

Carson and his silent partner headed toward the rear exit. Behind the statehouse a wrought iron fence enclosed a lawn where politicians liked to walk after lengthy meetings. Today, the square appeared deserted. While standing on the statehouse stoop, I examined Carson's sidekick. He made me nervous. He hardly spoke, but he wore a perpetual sneer that caused me to distrust him.

I pointed to the statehouse. "Go on back inside. This is between Carson and me."

"Naw, I wanna watch."

I didn't like two against one, especially since Carson handled his gun so expertly, but I didn't know how to get this ruffian to retreat back indoors. I wished Sharp would show up to even the odds. This thought made me think about how Sharp would handle the situation.

In a flash, I drew my Colt and coldcocked the sneer right off the sidekick's face. He fell straight-away and rolled down the three steps to the lawn. I holstered my gun.

"Sorry about that," I said, "but I'll tell him about the fight after he wakes up."

"He wasn't going to interfere," Carson said flatly.

"Perhaps, but now you have my total attention."

Chapter 47

With a wary eye on each other, we walked slowly to the center of the lawn. I remembered Carson only missed at long distance, so I traversed the lawn at an angle to put more room between us.

I had been in several gunfights, but never a one-on-one duel. This felt different. For one thing, there was time to think. Bad. Thinking interfered with reflexes honed by hours upon hours of practice. I washed all thought from my mind. Thinking would get me killed. I needed to simply react using all of my years of experience.

I relaxed. I relaxed my hand, my shoulders, and my mind. I just kept my eyes on Carson's eyes. His eyes would tell me when he decided to make his move. He waited. I realized that he had done this before and waiting put his opponent off balance. No. That was another thought. Get rid of it. I simply waited . . . and watched his eyes.

The tiniest of squints. Carson had committed himself to action. No conscious thought. The blast of my gun seemed to startle me out of a trance. I held it in my hand and I had fired it three times.

All three shots hit Carson in the middle of his chest.

His shiny gun with the fancy grips fell to the ground as his hand lost muscle control, but he wasn't dead. Recognition glinted from the same eyes that had betrayed his intentions. Then the glint faded until I could not believe he remained standing. Finally, his knees buckled and he fell forward, his face hitting the ground square on his nose.

George Carson would not get up again.

Chapter 48

I noticed my surroundings. Three men stood on the statehouse stoop, and another bent over the man I had clobbered with my gun barrel. A few others lingered on the other side of the fence. I felt exhilarated. I smelled burnt gunpowder, stale sweat, and grass. The gunpowder wafted away and the newly sheared grass smelled so good I wanted to pull a handful and bring it up to my nose. Instead, I reloaded my three spent cartridges.

"I thought we came here to do this together."

Sharp's voice shook me out of my reverie. "Hell, Jeff, I looked around and you were nowhere about, so I handled things myself."

"I see." Sharp looked at the people by the fence and around the stoop. There were now over a dozen in each location. "I better find out if we have any useful witnesses before everybody within a mile claims to have seen the legendary Capitol Lawn Gunfight."

"Try the four talking to each other by the door. They're the most likely witnesses. The others were drawn by gunfire." Sharp started to walk away. "Wait, where's Jenny and Jansen?"

"At his office, I think. She whispered somethin' to him and they left together in a big rush. He looked as if he'd seen a ghost."

I wanted to go after them, but Marshal Matt Wilson scurried down the statehouse steps with McAllen and a few capitol police close behind.

"You, again," Wilson said.

I just shrugged, so he went over and examined the body.

Without uttering a word, McAllen walked over to join Sharp at the statehouse steps.

"Nice shooting," Wilson said after he returned from his inspection. "There'll be an inquest." With a rueful expression, he added, "I'll see what I can do about getting it delayed until after your trial."

"Until then?"

"Hang here with these men until I speak to a few witnesses." He started to walk away, and then whipped around to bark at me once more to remain with the capitol police.

Wilson walked over to the fence and the policemen took a belligerent pose. I stood very still. There was nothing to be gained by frightening a nervous lawman. In a few moments, Sharp and McAllen brought over the two men I had seen outside the statehouse doorway after the shooting. Both talked a dozen words a second until the marshal returned from interviewing the people outside the fence. After a few minutes' discussion just out of earshot, Wilson sauntered over to where I stood.

"You can go, but don't leave town. You have three legal proceedings ahead of you: a trial and two inquests."

"How's it look?" I asked.

"Ain't for me to say . . . but I think you can safely invite me to your wedding."

He smiled and strolled away.

I turned to Sharp and McAllen. "We need to find Jenny."

"Why, for damn sake?" McAllen asked.

That brought me up short. I had my own problems. Why should I make her problems mine as well?

"Because when it comes to Jenny, I always do something stupid. Now let's go."

Sharp laughed and waved me ahead with his rifle. McAllen scowled.

We found both of them in Jansen's office huddled over a pile of legal papers. Both glanced at us to determine who had barged into the office, and then ignored us to resume their work. Jansen still looked ashen and he wrote furiously. Jenny stood a respectable distance behind him and held no weapon in her hand. Good. It appeared she had found a legal way to regain control of her trust.

"Leave." She said this without turning around.

I ignored her command, but didn't speak. Sharp did.

"What ya get on him?" he asked.

"He murdered my father and Senator Richard Wade," she said matter-of-factly. "Jansen paid an itinerate sodbuster to kill my father. Once I found him, he was more than happy to talk for a few dollars and a quart of rotgut. I cared not a whit for my pa, but he's finally proving useful. His death does me a grand service . . . it will hang this son of a bitch."

Jansen swung away from his papers. "You said if I set everything right, you'd let me leave Nevada."

"Don't worry, I'll keep my word. I'm a rancher, not a lying lawyer." She poked him on the shoulder with a single finger. "Get back to it."

Jansen killing Jenny's father made sense. It would eliminate the only legitimate claimant to her estate. Few people knew him and his absence would probably never even be noticed. In fact, I had no idea where he lived, except I always assumed it was somewhere in Mason Valley because Bolton must have known him. Jenny's husband had paid her father forty silver dollars as a supposed bride price, and Jenny hated her father for selling her like a piece of livestock. On second thought, I bet she hated him long before he cut his deal with John Bolton.

The news about Richard's killing startled me, however. His death had brought me to Nevada and I assumed that Jenny had been behind the murder of my friend. I would need to deal with Jansen after Jenny finished with him.

When Jansen signed the documents, he looked up pleadingly at Jenny. She picked up the sheaf of papers just as I started to retreat in the direction of the door. There was nothing for us to do at the moment.

She interrupted my exit. "Wait. You can be useful, for once. Read these papers and tell me if they're in order."

I sat down and read them while Sharp and McAllen hovered impatiently. The legal papers basically gave Jennifer Bolton full control over the trust. Claude Jansen had been removed as executor.

"I would have a lawyer read them," I said, "but they appear to give you complete control."

"Can I go?" Jansen asked.

He seemed too eager, so I asked, "Did you embezzle funds from the trust?"

"No. Hell, no! I had complete control, why would I steal from myself?"

"Because you're a cagey bastard and you just might squirrel away some cash in case this day ever came."

"No! No! I didn't do anything of the sort. Let me out of here."

I knew he was lying. "Where did you—"

Jenny suddenly thrust a stiletto into his chest and twisted it twice before pulling it out. Jansen yelped and looked down at his shirtfront. His expression was one of disbelief.

"You said I could go," he whined.

"You can . . . straight to hell."

He looked at his shirtfront again. Now a blood-stain not much bigger than a dime soiled the shirt.

"Shit," he whimpered before collapsing to the floor.

I started to go to him, but Jenny stopped me with an outreached hand. "He's dead."

"Jenny, he was lying. He embezzled money from the trust. Now, you'll never find it."

"I don't care. I'll make more in a month than he stole. I saw the journals and there's plenty left. I didn't want him to stall his punishment with his little secret. I'm back in control. That's all that matters."

"Are you?" I asked. "You could be joining me in court."

She leaned over and pulled his coat front over his chest to hide the bloodstain. Then she opened the office door and let an undertaker into the room.

Pointing at Jansen, she said, "He had a heart attack."

The undertaker signaled with his fingers and two downtrodden men scurried into the office. As they lifted the body, Jansen's jacket fell open. The undertaker pulled the suit coat together and buttoned it closed.

As he left, he said, "We'll take care of everything, Mrs. Bolton. You've been enormously generous in covering the cost of his funeral. I'll make it elegant, as befitting his station."

"It's the least I can do for someone who took such good care of my interests. Thank you."

McAllen took my elbow and nodded toward the door, indicating he thought the three of us should leave.

I agreed. Just before we closed the door, Jenny spoke one more time.

"After the trial, get out of *my* state . . . and don't come back."

Chapter 49

That woman's colder than day-old embers on a frosty morn," McAllen said.

We walked three abreast down the middle of the street with buggies, wagons, and horse riders jigging around us. No one shouted, but several men threw angry looks to show displeasure at our presumption of right of way. Angry men no longer held menace for us; not after we had witnessed a woman put an enemy six foot under without mussing her hair, and having orchestrated the deed so no one would ever be the wiser. Her efficiency was frightening.

"I *want* to get out of *her* state," I said. "Nevada has been nothing but trouble, and Jenny's a puzzle I'll leave unsolved."

"Ya gotta admire her grit though," Sharp said. "She appeared snared, trapped, and hogtied, yet she managed to get her damn empire back and took a good measure of revenge to boot." Sharp laughed. "Yep, Jenny's one of a kind."

"Thank God," McAllen said, under his breath.

Marshal Wilson stepped into the street to stop our progress.

"Good afternoon, Matt," McAllen said. "Problem?"

"Other than you men clogging traffic? No. In fact, I came to tell Mr. Dancy and Mr. Sharp, they are free to go. I suggest you get out of Nevada as soon as possible. Far too many corpses in your wake."

"Seems we've been gettin' that advice a lot lately," Sharp said. "Steve, what do ya say?"

"I say Durango's pleasant this time of year."

"Agreed," McAllen said. "Back to Denver, collect our gear and horses, then off to Durango."

McAllen turned back to the marshal. "Doug and Sam?"

"My deputies have suddenly found employment in another city," Wilson answered.

"Good," McAllen said. "For your information, we've cleaned our house as well. Copley has been fired, and he'll be leaving town as soon as the dentist finishes with him. Seems he lost a few teeth. Miss Channing will assume his responsibilities as soon as she returns from Mason Valley."

"That woman with Mrs. Baker? She's a Pinkerton?"

"One of the best. She'll be our first female lead agent."

"Our? Have you rejoined the Pinkertons?"

"No, slip of the tongue, but they still listen to me. She'll do a good job."

"The practice is mostly political," Wilson said, unconvinced.

"I doubt she'll have trouble gettin' appointments with government officials."

Wilson smiled and shook his head. "Good point."

I wanted to return to the previous subject. "What happened? Why are we free to go?"

"Myers met with the judge to show him his depositions. They all said the other men provoked the fight. Jenny recanted her deposition, so there's no case. Myers did a good job in arguing for dismissal. As for the Capitol Lawn Gunfight, lots of witnesses said you won a fair duel you didn't instigate. Judge dropped all charges. That includes clearing Mr. McAllen for killing Matting."

"Yet you advise us to get out of the state?" McAllen said with a trace of irritation.

Wilson turned a steady eye on me. "I don't know why, but you're trouble. Whether it's Pickhandle Gulch, Virginia City, Mason Valley, or here. You attract bad elements."

"Perhaps instead of attractin' bad men, Steve just don't tolerate their badness," Sharp said.

"Perhaps," Wilson said. "In truth, I can't even order you out of Carson City, but I'd consider it a personal favor if you rode clear of the state. I don't get paid enough to clean up the messes you leave behind."

I smiled. "Then I shall endeavor to bring tranquility back to your fair valley by getting the hell out of Nevada."

"Great . . . but get out of the street first. People have places to go and you're in the way." He started to lead by example, but turned back for a final rejoinder. "By the way, for your information, you'd have to drag Jenny Bolton along with you to bring tranquility to our fair valley."

I threw up both hands, palms out. "Whoa! That's asking too much, marshal. Jenny's born and bred in Nevada. She's yours. You keep her."

"I'm afraid you have that backward; she means to be our keeper. That gal has this state tied up in a pretty pink bow." He appeared genuinely sympathetic when he added, "Sorry to ask you to leave, but when you and Jenny are together, you cause too damn much trouble."

Then the marshal did the unexpected; he extended his hand to me.

We shook.

"It was a pleasure meeting you, Mr. Dancy. Now . . . git."

Chapter 50

McAllen and Sharp stopped for a beer, so I went upstairs alone to look for the women. I found them in my mother's suite sitting on the settees with Congressman Morris. Nobody looked happy, so I blurted out the good news.

"We're free. Everything's taken care of and we can go."

"That's great, Uncle Steve," Maggie said. "When can we leave for Durango?"

I hesitated, not knowing if this was the right time to inform my mother we would not return with her. Besides, Maggie had put me off balance by calling me uncle.

Before I could formulate a response, my mother exclaimed, "Everything's not taken care of!"

"What are you talking about?" I asked.

"That young Jenny girl. Senator Fair is at his wit's end. She has her own candidate to run against him next year. Besides her financial backing, she controls the biggest newspaper and the others are frightened to write articles critical of her under-takings. Beyond controlling key commercial enter-prises, she may soon hold unprecedented political power in Nevada. The governor is worried."

"Not our business," I objected.

"It *is* our business," my mother said. "Family business. The congressman needs the senator's support and he wants you to dissuade Jenny from ruining the senator's career."

I looked at Virginia, and she gave me a slight negative shake of the head. She didn't need to worry, I had no intention of seeing Jenny again for any purpose. We were out clean, and I saw no reason to jump back into the den of a lioness, especially not for a politician. If Senator Fair was not reelected, Morris would find another ally in the opposing chamber. After all, politicians were fungible.

Knowing that with my mother the less said, the better, I simply answered, "No."

"Son, I need your help," Morris interjected.

"Not your son, not even your nephew-in-law yet. You're a politician. These are the kind of problems you fix . . . or maneuver around."

"I can't explain, but I need Fair. I need him in the senate, and the only way he'll remain in office is if Jenny allows him to remain in office."

"Then why doesn't he go see her and pledge fidelity," I said. "He keeps his job and saves her the money and trouble of running a candidate against him."

"The governor and other parties have objected to that solution," Morris said.

"Well, I'm glad it wasn't ethics that stayed his hand."

"Stephen, don't be snide. Here's a chance for you to do something for the family. It will start your union with Virginia off right."

I saw Virginia start to rise from her chair and held her back with an uplifted hand.

"Start the union off right?" I said. "First off, this is not a business union, it's a marriage. And that's your idea of a good start to a marriage. I just left Jenny." I shook my head at the image of her emotionally detached murder of Claude Jansen. "She ordered me out of her state. *Her* state. Ignore whether it's really hers or not, but you have to admit that her royal dismissal doesn't bode well for me changing her mind. She wants me out of her life, not mucking with it. If you think I'm your best chance, then the senator better look for new employment."

"We can do it together," my mother offered.

"What? Do you—"

"We became close in the last week," my mother insisted. "I can help."

"Mother, I won't—"

"Yes, Steve. We'll do it together," Virginia said. "All four of us. Maggie stays, but the congressman and your mother go with us because they'll never believe you unless they see it with their own eyes."

Virginia was right. If I refused, my mother and Morris would always believe that I might have made a difference, but if they witnessed

Jenny's dismissal, this little incident would be over and it wouldn't ruin relationships in the families.

"The three of you go," Morris said. "I can't be connected with any of this."

"Uncle Bill, you are connected with this, and we all know you'll take the credit if we succeed. Either you accompany us to see Steve make an honest try, or we're relieved of any responsibility to haul water for you."

"Virginia, dear—"

"Don't *Virginia, dear* me. Are you coming or do we forget the whole thing?"

After trying an intimidating look, Morris withered under the steady gaze of Virginia. He stood and bid us forward with an outstretched palm.

Evidently, I would reenter the den of the lioness.

Chapter 51

Claude Jansen's office was unlocked and vacant. The room looked neat and tidy, so none of my companions suspected anything untoward had ever happened in the immaculate space. To my knowledge, Jenny Bolton didn't have an office in Carson City, so I wondered where she went after the undertaker cleaned up the remains of her latest errand. We stepped out onto the boardwalk and a passerby said she had headed in the direction of the marshal's office.

When we approached the marshal's office, Jenny came out looking furious as she banged shut the marshal's door. Whatever her business inside, it had not gone satisfactorily.

"Dear, what could possibly be the problem?" my mother asked.

At the sound, she wheeled on us. "What the hell are you doing here?" she asked looking directly at me.

"We need to speak to you," my mother answered.

"No. Go away. All of you."

"Dear, this is in your interest, as much as ours. We only need—"

"You *dear* me again and I'll scratch your eyes out."

I grabbed my mother's shoulders with both hands and gently turned her back toward the hotel. Surely, this demonstration was enough to convince her and the congressman that Jenny could not be sweet-talked. She resisted my pressure with surprising strength and shrugged my hands off of her shoulders.

"Let's step indoors, shall we? This discussion is private." Then she quickly added, "But not the marshal's office."

I could see Jenny waver. She wanted nothing more to do with me, but she wondered what my mother and the congressman wanted. Then her eyes settled on Virginia. I expected to see hate, but instead I saw curiosity. Finally, she suggested Jansen's office. As we headed back in that direction, it occurred to me that his office should be sufficiently private now.

Once we entered the office, we remained standing and my mother spoke without preamble.

"Mrs. Bolton, we came to see what would be required for you to withdraw your candidate for the senate."

I expected an outburst, but instead Jenny appeared contemplative. Finally, she said, "You get the senate seat, I get the governorship."

"Done," my mother said.

"No, it's not *done,*" Jenny said. "I want the governor to resign. You get him to do that right now, and I'll pull my opposition to Senator Fair."

Now it was my mother's turn to appear contemplative. After a fair bit, she said, "I can try, but I'm not sure I can get Bradshaw to quit."

"Then I'll take the senate now and the governorship in two years." She looked at each of us. "Are we done here?"

"What if I made another proposal?" my mother asked.

"There's nothing else I want."

"But there's something else you need."

"I don't need anything you can offer," Jenny said, dismissively.

"Jansen never would have taken advantage of me," my mother said.

Until now, the conversation had been fairly polite, but Jenny instantly tensed. Her eyes flashed and her mouth closed to become so straight it appeared she had no lips whatsoever. I expected a flashing palm to strike my mother, then I remembered the stiletto and started to move between them, but my mother's next calm words soothed Jenny's anger.

"If you'll let me, I can teach you. You'll never again be taken by a lawyer or any other fast talker with a fountain pen. You know how to handle men with guns, but you need to learn how to do the legal part so your accomplishments can never be unraveled. Come with me back to New York. Finish your education."

"New York? I'll never leave Nevada. I have too much at stake to go someplace else to get deburred. This is my place in the world and I'll make it all mine."

"Getting great wealth and keeping it are two different things. Quite frankly, you almost lost it all for a stupid blunder." My mother seemed to examine Jenny. "How old are you?"

"Eighteen," she said.

"You're very young, dear. Your property will hold until you return, and you can rebuild parts that escape as quickly as you gathered them up in the first place. If you don't go now, you'll never go and eventually this will all end badly for you. Come with me and you'll not be limited by this barren state. You can build an empire far beyond what you imagine."

"You have no idea what I imagine," Jenny said.

"Oh, I do. I had the same dreams."

"Do you always try to do good deeds like your son?"

"No, I'm like you."

The two women stood silent, assessing each other. The three other people in the room were excluded from the discussion.

Finally, Jenny asked, "What's in it for you?"

"When my son marries this fine woman, my family's power will extend from New York to Washington, D.C. I traveled here to insure that would happen, but I didn't find the wilderness I expected. I found wealth. This nation will move west, just as Horace Greeley suggested. Controlling the eastern seaboard will not be sufficient." She waved her arm to encompass all of her surroundings. "This land is huge and raw and it will make many rich. I cannot ignore it."

"It will be decades before the West becomes dominant. You must have another reason."

"No, I don't. That's one of the lessons I'll teach you. Fortunes that last, survive through generations. Empires plan for the future. Speaking of which, you'll also need a husband that brings something valuable to the table. I'll help you find a proper one: One that can help you in your endeavors, but won't steal your wealth. I'll even show you how to protect yourself if that becomes his intent. Then you need children because children provide you with a ticket to the future."

"I don't want a husband," Jenny said.

"I know. But trust me, you need one."

"Why should I give you access to my West?" Jenny asked.

"You'll give me nothing. We'll deal, but only after you learn all there is to learn from me. Then we'll make some arrangements and you'll return to Nevada and conquer all."

My mother's smile looked devilish. Damn, they were alike. That gave me pause because I thought I hated my mother, yet I was smitten by Jenny from the moment I first saw her. I glanced at Virginia. She looked repulsed by the conniving she witnessed. Good, I hadn't become engaged to a thirty year younger version of my mother.

Shortly, Virginia and I found ourselves alone in Jansen's office. Jenny had agreed to come east as my mother's protégé, and Morris scurried out to take credit for saving the senator's seat.

Virginia looked wholly dejected. "What do we do now?"

Jenny and my mother were two of a kind. Strong, smart, and iron-willed women, but these strengths were offset by personality flaws that made them self-absorbed and ruthless. They possessed absolute confidence in their judgment and damned any who stood in their way. They and their kind assembled empires. It took a single-mindedness to shove obstacles aside and build something that would last for generations. But I didn't come west to build anything. I came to experience an untamed wilderness before some-one like Jenny put their brand on it. In truth, I came to the frontier for a second chance— a new life unscripted by anyone else. A place where all my mistakes were not merely forgiven, but unknown. The freedom that comes from being released from the constraints that push in one direction and pull in another direction. I wanted to leave family and obligations back in so-called civilization so I could personally engineer a fresh life.

"Steve?"

Virginia had become frustrated with my prolonged musings.

I sighed. "What will we do now? Hell, I say we forget those two and head for Durango. I believe we have a marriage ceremony planned."

Her apprehension vanished in a heartbeat. She hooked her hand through my arm, and we strolled outdoors into the bright and endless sky of the West.

God bless the West.

Center Point Large Print
600 Brooks Road / PO Box 1
Thorndike, ME 04986-0001 USA

(207) 568-3717

US & Canada:
1 800 929-9108
www.centerpointlargeprint.com